FIERCE POISON

FIERCE POISON

WILL THOMAS

MINOTAUR BOOKS
NEW YORK

First published in the United States by Minotaur Books, an imprint of St. Martin's Publishing Group

www.minotaurbooks.com

Library of Congress Cataloging-in-Publication Data

Names: Thomas, Will, 1958– author.
Title: Fierce poison / Will Thomas.
Description: First edition. | New York : Minotaur Books, 2022. |
    Series: A Barker & Llewelyn novel ; 13
Identifiers: LCCN 2021051075 | ISBN 9781250624796 (hardcover) |
    ISBN 9781250624802 (ebook)
Classification: LCC PS3620.H644 F54 2022 | DDC 813/.6—dc23
LC record available at https://lccn.loc.gov/2021051075

Our books may be purchased in bulk for promotional, educational, or business use. Please contact your local bookseller or the Macmillan Corporate and Premium Sales Department at 1-800-221-7945, extension 5442, or by email at MacmillanSpecialMarkets@macmillan.com.

First Edition: 2022

10 9 8 7 6 5 4 3 2 1

FIERCE POISON

CHAPTER 1

S cotland Yard is of the opinion that we at the Barker and Llewelyn Agency are barking mad. They've said it in private, and they've said it to my face, but I notice they've never said it in front of my associate, Cyrus Barker. I'll agree we have our share of work that might drive a man barmy, and once or twice I've wondered about my own sanity, but only because I continue working with the singular monolith that is the Guv. Sometimes I wonder if I stay because I cannot wait to see the next catastrophe enter through our chamber doors.

One would think at some point I would say "Enough! I have now seen everything," but generally I am disproven within a day or two. The problem with our occupation is that a shoemaker has for the most part seen everything in his profession and has watched the same problem cross his door frame a thousand times, whereas I've rarely seen two cases with similar features, which means one cannot carry experience from one case to another. Everything is new, all the time.

That morning a man had walked in off the street with no appointment. He was approaching forty; not a bad-looking chap, a bit sturdy, perhaps. The fellow was clean-shaven and parted his dark hair down the middle, revealing a small red birthmark on his right temple. He was capable looking. I thought he might have been head boy in his school once. He voted Liberal in each election and had stood for the bar. Later, I found out I'd got it all in one. There's more than porridge in the old Llewelyn noggin.

He'd come through the door and stumbled a step in front of Jeremy Jenkins's desk. I blamed the rug at first. It was early, just after nine.

"I have to see Mr. Barker," he said, his voice rough.

"Come in, sir!" the Guv called. "We are not currently occupied. Won't you have a seat?"

He came in and sat. I've described him physically, but not the man's condition. He didn't look well. In fact, he appeared to be in some distress.

"Might I have some water?" he asked, clearing his throat.

There is a table behind Barker's desk containing a pitcher of water and a bottle of brandy alongside a pair of tumblers. Barker is a Baptist. Water is what one drinks when one is well. Brandy is what one drinks when one is ill.

I'd have given him the brandy, but the choice was our visitor's. I went around one side of my partner's desk and poured the water while he went 'round the other to see to the gentleman, who had become quite unwell. I hurried back with the glass while my partner held our visitor's elbow. The man was trying unsuccessfully to speak. He grabbed at Barker's lapels and pulled him close so that they were face-to-face. His eyes were starting from his head, and the veins stood out on his forehead. He raised an arm to his throat and crushed the celluloid collar he wore, ripping it off in one movement, while making a hacking sound in the back of this throat.

"Help me," he cried in a small, constricted voice, barely more than a whisper. "Please!"

"We need an ambulance, Jeremy!" Barker called.

I pressed the tumbler into the man's hand, but he wouldn't take it. He fell heavily to his knees, wobbled there for a few seconds as if considering something, and then collapsed.

The Guv and I rolled him onto his back. His chest spasmed, straining so hard I thought his heart would burst. Then he slowly relaxed, the air emptying from his lungs as if from a balloon.

Barker seized the man's shirt with its twisted collar and ripped it open with a spray of buttons. He put an ear to the man's chest and then grunted.

"I'll not have it," he growled.

Then he put a hand upon the man's chest, a little toward the left, where, according to my rudimentary knowledge of anatomy, the heart could be found. Of course, I had no idea what Barker would do, and thought I was ready for anything, but not this. He raised his right hand high and brought it down like a hammer again on his left hand in the middle of the man's rib cage. Again and again. I supposed he believed that this would start the man's heart again, though I had never heard of such a thing, but then Barker was raised in China, the son of Scottish missionaries, and they do things differently there.

"Careful!" I warned. "You'll crack his rib cage."

"Another minute," he growled.

"I fear he is gone, sir," I protested.

He continued compressing the poor man's bared chest. We didn't know his name or what he did, or why he had darkened our door. He had entered the chambers off the street like hundreds before him and then he died. The specter of death had avoided our offices until then. I supposed it was only a matter of time.

"Look through his pockets, lad," Barker ordered. "I want his card."

The Guv's jacket was on the floor beside him and he'd removed his cuff links. The forearms under his rolled sleeves looked like loaves of bread, and there were tattoos on both: a tiger and a dragon.

"I've got it, sir," our clerk murmured from behind us.

We weren't aware Jenkins had entered the room. I snatched the card from the silver tray he carried and glanced at it. Then I looked again. I read it a third time, shook my head, and handed it to Barker.

"My word," I said. "He's the member of Parliament for Shoreditch!"

"Thank you, I can read, Mr. Llewelyn," the Guv said. "Pray let me think for a moment."

I let him think and avoided the urge to cover the body, to smooth the man's shirt and straighten his limbs. I knew the Guv would want the room just as it was in order to satisfy Scotland Yard. They would find this interesting, an MP falling dead after handing us his card. Even I had trouble believing it, and the Yard is not among our more ardent admirers.

"Roland Fitzhugh," the Guv read, as if he expected it would reveal more. "Liberal MP for the district of Shoreditch."

"Indeed," I replied.

"Damn and blast!" Barker said, banging his knuckles on the floor in anger. "We hardly met the man. We know nothing about him, and yet I am duty bound to find his killer."

"Why is that?" I asked.

"Ye heard the man ask for my help." When my partner becomes agitated, the Lowland Scots comes out in his voice.

"He didn't actually hire our services, sir," I argued. "He just didn't want to die. We may never know what he came for."

Jenkins called an ambulance from the telephone on Barker's desk and returned to his own as if he wanted nothing more to do with the business. Meanwhile, Barker pushed himself up to a standing position, looking down at what I presumed was our new client, in spite of what I said. It was unlikely we would send him an invoice. I wondered if he had any kin, then decided charging them would be mercenary.

Barker sighed a bushel's worth of air. "There's nothing for it, Thomas. You must get Scotland Yard."

"I'll call them on the telephone," I said, reaching for the instrument.

"No," he replied, shaking his head. "Go to 'A' Division on foot, voluntarily. It makes us look more innocent."

"Sir," I countered. "We actually are innocent. We didn't kill Mr. Fitzhugh. He merely died. No amount of thumping on his chest would have done any good. People die every day for little or no obvious reason. Perhaps he had a simple heart attack. He's young, but it happens every day."

Barker remained unconvinced. I shrugged my shoulders.

"I'll be off, then," I said.

The streets were busy, as they always are in Whitehall. I left Craig's Court, heading south past the Silver Cross. I greeted a publican just unlocking the door to The Shades public house and accepted a tart from a boy on the corner who was offering samples to passersby. I hurried down Great Scotland Yard Street and through the iron gate to "A" Division. I opened the impressive front doors and stepped into the lobby. Behind the counter stood Sergeant Kirkwood, my favorite policeman in the world.

"His nibs!" he called to me over a man's shoulders. "What brings you here of a September morn?"

"A bad business, I'm afraid," I replied. "There is a dead man in our offices."

"You gents do offer the Met some excitement," he remarked, raising a brow. "Hold a tick. Constable Burrows!"

After a moment a constable came to the desk, his helmet tucked under his arm. He was chewing something.

"Yes, sir?"

"Helmet on, P.C. Burrows," Kirkwood ordered. "And for bloody sake, wipe the crumbs from your mustache! Go find Detective Chief Inspector Poole and tell him Mr. Llewelyn is at the front desk."

"Yes, sir," the constable said, scurrying out.

"Next, we'll be getting them in short trousers," Kirkwood sneered. "Take a bench, Mr. Llewelyn. The detective chief inspector will be along eventually."

I sat. Five minutes later, Terence Poole sauntered into the lobby, his hands in his pockets. He's between forty and fifty, with scanty brown hair and a gingery mustache. He'd been Barker's friend since I knew them, but their friendship had run afoul when Special Branch Chief Inspector Munro had been promoted to commissioner. He exiled Poole to Outer Mongolia, or Wimbledon, which is worse, over a case in which Poole had shared too much information. Munro and Barker eventually patched things up between them, but now Poole had the opposite problem: when someone died on our patch, he was the one called to deal with it. At least Outer Mongolia was restful.

"Thomas," he said, opening his watch. "What mischief have you gotten yourself into? It's not even ten o'clock yet."

"A stranger walked into our offices just now," I explained. "He asked for a glass of water, and then dropped dead right in front of us. He didn't even have time to say anything. I don't believe anyone has ever died in our chambers before."

"The fact that you can't recall whether or not it happened speaks volumes," he replied with a smirk. "Sergeant, send Burrows along with a litter. And tell him not to dawdle."

"Will do, sir."

We left the building and headed in the direction of Whitehall Street again.

"Did he leave his name, this stranger of yours?" Poole asked.

"His name was Roland Fitzhugh," I replied. "He was a member of Parliament. Shoreditch."

"'Struth!" he muttered.

The inspector did not ask any more questions, presumably because it might color his observations when we arrived. We jostled our way through the crowd to get back to Craig's Court. As we entered the office, Poole passed straight through to our chamber.

"Hello, Cyrus," he said, looking at the body and then glancing around the room. "Has anything been moved?"

The Guv was sitting in the visitor's chair from which Fitzhugh had collapsed, as if guarding the body. Possibly he was praying for his soul. I don't suppose the Baptist faith has extreme unction.

"Nothing has been touched," the Guv replied.

Poole nodded. "Where's the card?"

Barker stood and handed it to him. In response, Poole pulled an identical one from his waistcoat pocket.

"Tell me everything, Cyrus," he said.

"There isn't much to tell," I interjected.

"Did I ask you?" Poole demanded, giving me a sideways glance.

Barker explained what had occurred in the most economical number of words possible. Meanwhile, Poole was going through the man's pockets.

The inspector shook his head. "Two shillings and sixpence, nine pounds in notes, a pocket comb, a very small jackknife, a key ring with two keys, presumably house and office, and a pencil stub. Not much to go into the hereafter with."

"Did you hear anything I said, Terry?" Barker asked.

"Every word," Poole said, standing. "He came in, asked for a glass of water, toppled over and died. You know what that means?"

"Poisoning, I should think," the Guv rumbled.

"A man can't ingest poison and then stroll about London looking for you. He must have swallowed it somewhere very near." He cleared his throat. "I know what Fitzhugh wanted. He came into 'A' Division before he came here. I spoke to the man myself not half an hour ago."

"What did he tell you?" Barker asked, leaning forward.

"He suspected someone was trying to poison him."

My partner raised a brow. "Apparently he had good reason to believe so."

"Yes, but you see, not a person in recent memory has come into 'A' Division claiming to be poisoned who wasn't doolally. There is a condition of the mind some have where they believe they're being poisoned. We get two of them in regular every month. It's a sad thing. They end up skin and bone eventually, although this fellow looked well fed. Anyway, he came to see me shortly after eight, while I was yawning over tea, and claimed he was being poisoned. He said he drank coffee at lunch three days ago at a coffee-house in Bermondsey. Mr. Fitzhugh said he went to the counter to get a spoon, and when he returned to the table, he immediately suspected someone had tampered with his coffee. He said it seemed 'off.' This morning he stopped for breakfast at a public house in Paddington called the Dove Inn and he immediately felt ill. Then he walked in my door demanding I do something about it. I told him we'd investigate the two locations. Now he's dead and we have no idea what happened."

"I see. And what is your next step, Terry?" the Guv asked.

"He wore no ring. I've got to tell his parents," Poole replied. "If I can find them, that is. It's not my favorite part of the job."

"Thomas and I will go to the Houses of Parliament and track down the Liberal Party leader," the Guv said. "I assume the news of Fitzhugh's death will have some consequence."

Poole nodded. "I'll search his rooms after that."

"He must have been a barrister before he was an MP," I remarked. "I'll see if he had a partner. Barristers always have someone who hates them. It is a hazard of their profession."

Terence Poole put his hands on his hips. "We are cooperating on this one, aren't we, Cyrus?"

"We are," Barker agreed. "I'll share information if you will."

"Right."

He turned to leave and then pointed at me.

"Stay out of trouble," he said.

Burrows appeared belatedly with the hand litter, another constable at his heels. We watched the two wrestle the corpse on top
of it. When they were gone, I sat in my wooden swivel chair by
the rolltop desk, and watched the Guv behind his outsized one in
his equally outsized green leather chair.

"It's not really a case," I argued. "Fitzhugh didn't ask you to
investigate anything. He didn't actually hire you. He asked for
help. He would have asked anyone."

"We are hired," he stated, as if it were an end to it.

"You know we've talked about this recently," I replied. "We
need clients that are willing and able to pay us. I know you are
rich as Croesus, but this is a business, not a charity. Hansom cabs
are dear in London, you know. The purpose of a business is to
make money."

"We are hired," he repeated.

Apparently, that was an end to it.

CHAPTER 2

I was unsettled. Despite the reputation of enquiry agents as hardened men immune from emotion of any kind, we are living, breathing mortals. Watching a man die is a traumatic experience, even after years spent around bodies and pursuing people who plotted murder. I suppose my time at Oxford studying classics had made me a sensitive soul, but then I hadn't attended university with the intent that I would become a private enquiry agent. Would I ever be cold-blooded enough to watch the candle flame leave a man's eyes without feeling its loss? I don't even step on a cricket if I can help it. I'm a church man, but in matters such as this I inclined toward thoughts of karma and beliefs from the Far East.

"What are you thinking, Thomas?" Barker enquired as we left our offices.

"Being poisoned is a terrible way to die," I answered. "Have you investigated a case like this before?"

"Just once, but it was straightforward enough," he answered, clutching his stick in his hand. "I hope this will prove so again. Does it make much difference if a murderer cuts one's throat with a knife, shoots one with a revolver, or pours poison down one's gullet? The purpose is the same, as is the result."

"It's cruel," I insisted.

"It is efficient," he replied. "Men sometimes recover from a shot or knife wound. Both of us have done so. But poison! Fitzhugh was dead within a minute."

"It is cowardly," I insisted. "One need not face one's victim."

"Thomas," he remarked as we passed the old Banqueting House on Horse Guards Avenue. "You will never give up the notion that things are fair or unfair. Things simply are. Nature is not a gentleman. It is a cold world, but we are fortunate to have one of the few professions that attempts to do something about it."

It was a straight walk down Whitehall Street to the Houses of Parliament. Neither of us spoke, for we were both formulating what our next step might be. In our first case, Barker had counseled that I should learn patience. That was ten years ago but I still found it a trial.

I wondered if I had heard of the Liberal Party leader and decided whoever he was he would be a pompous ass. Granted, I would have found the Conservative leader worse, but I wasn't looking forward to the experience.

Big Ben tolled eleven just as we arrived under it. It was a novel experience. I've passed near it thousands of times but never actually stood under the bell itself. When it peals, the pavement shakes, and one cannot help but clap hands to one's ears.

The clanging stopped as we stepped inside. There was a tall desk nearby and Barker approached it. A man sitting high on his perch looked down at us through a pair of spectacles.

"Sir," Barker rumbled, his voice echoing in the chamber. "I have a question for you."

The man raised a brow. "I will endeavor to answer it."

"Where might I find the leader of the Liberal Party?"

The brow arched even more keenly. "I'm not able to give that information to a stranger, sir. Nor can just anyone roam about the halls at will."

"He might want to know the information we bring," the Guv persisted. My partner pulled a card from his pocket and put it on the edge of the desk. This was Barker at his most professional, giving the man an aspect that said he was almost if not completely equal to every man in the building, like one of them. Likewise, for example, when he walked into Nichol Street, the most dangerous in London, he made it known to all that in spite of his wealthy appearance he had a right to be there and heaven help you if you try to stop him. "Mr. Fitzhugh, the MP for Shoreditch, passed away not an hour ago. The Liberal Party leader must be informed immediately."

The clerk's eyes went to the ceiling in thought. Should he or should he not? The gentleman we wished to speak with might not want to be disturbed, but then the information we possessed was crucial. In other words, the man could get himself into trouble either way.

"That is St Stephen's Hall," the clerk said at last, pointing east. "If one were to stroll casually to the far end to the Members' Library, one might accidentally come upon the esteemed gentleman. He is often there about this time. I cannot guarantee it, you understand, but as I said, you gentlemen are just strolling about."

"Of course," Barker replied. "Thank you."

We passed down the corridor through a large chamber and down another hall to a second, and at last reached an end. A few dozen yards away we found the entrance to the library. There, Barker buttonholed the first fellow he came across.

"Excuse me, sir," he said. "Could you point us in the direction of the Liberal Party leader?"

"Yes, of course," the man answered. "He is there by the fire."

The chamber was nearly empty save for the one fellow. The leader himself sat staring into the fire, one arm resting across the back of the sofa. He looked old from where we stood, wisps of white hair swirling around his reddish cranium. We came around the sofa and stood beside it. I could not help blanching when I saw him.

It was William Gladstone, former prime minister of Britain four times over, and still in charge of his party. I'd have recalled that if politics were my life's blood. Still, politically, no matter who was prime minister, Gladstone was the man of the age.

He turned and regarded us, trying to place who we were. His nose was hawk-like and he had white side-whiskers that hung to his collar. His eyes were a steely gray.

"Sir," the Guv murmured. "My name is Cyrus Barker. I come with ill news, I'm afraid."

"I've had more than my share of that, thank you very much," the old man replied in a high, reedy voice. "Who are you gentlemen?"

Barker bent and offered his card, which was accepted reluctantly. The politician read it and then looked up at us.

"We had a mutual acquaintance, sir," the Guv continued. "I was sparring partner to Handy Andy McClain, once heavyweight bare-knuckle champion of England."

Gladstone's face brightened.

"Andrew!" he exclaimed. "We used to go through the East End rescuing fallen women from their so-called 'protectors.' Not a few women left his mission to become wives and mothers. He is sorely missed."

"He is indeed, sir," the Guv agreed. "Not a week passes that I don't think of him."

Andrew was a boxer turned evangelist and owner of a mission in Mile End Road, serving the lowest of society, the city's castoffs. Barker funded the mission and visited when he could. McClain had been foully murdered as a warning to Cyrus Barker. His mission was passed on to General Booth and the Salvation Army, but the Guv still paid for the upkeep of the building, which I believe he saw as a duty.

While Gladstone had the audacity to go into Whitechapel and other Tower Hamlet districts, actively trying to turn low women from their ways, Andrew would go into public houses and gin palaces preaching on the dangers of strong drink. Both found themselves in trouble with the press, and there were humorous illustrations about them in *Punch*. Neither cared. The work was important, and their missions were frequently successful. People talked openly about the ills of the East End.

"You are Mr. Barker and I assume this young man is Mr. Llewelyn. He looks as Welsh as a corgi." Gladstone frowned. "I suppose the two of you should sit."

He looked at us for a few moments, possibly hoping to deduce what our news might be.

"Very well, Mr. Barker. You're not going away and neither is the East Wind you bring. What is your news?"

"Mr. Fitzhugh of your constituency passed away in our offices not an hour ago," my partner stated. "We've just come from speaking with Scotland Yard. It has not been confirmed, but we suspect he was poisoned."

Gladstone shook his head and I'm blowed if he didn't pull a handkerchief from his pocket and wipe an eye.

"Oh, what a waste!" he exclaimed. "Such a solemn young man, with so much promise. I barely knew him yet. Why, he was elected only six months ago or a year at most. I don't remember precisely."

The fireplace was stifling, but then, old men's bones are always cold.

"How did he come to your door?" he asked before turning to me. "Young man, what are you scribbling?"

I looked over my notebook to find Gladstone staring at me. It felt strange to be scrutinized by a man I had studied in school.

"Shorthand, sir," I answered. "I record notes when I can. Sometimes a case can turn on a single word. We believe Mr. Fitzhugh's arrival at our door was circumstantial. We were chosen because we are the closest agency to Whitehall Street."

"And how do you know this?"

"He visited Scotland Yard before coming to Craig's Court."

The old man stared into the fire again.

"I find it ironic that Mr. Fitzhugh should be poisoned after having spoken to two separate investigative agencies," he said, a trifle tartly. "Did he come to Whitehall because he feared he was being poisoned?"

"He did, Your Lordship," Barker rumbled from his chair. "Chief Inspector Poole of the Metropolitan Police has confirmed it. Do you know if he was working on a project of importance, one that might endanger his life?"

Gladstone frowned, his dark and bushy brows knitting together. There were spots at his temples. He'd been in government a very long time. His chief rival, Benjamin Disraeli, had been dead a dozen years at least.

"Let's see," Gladstone muttered. "There is the Navy Bill. It is intended to fund a new fleet of vessels to defend us against the Germans. But his voice was not particularly important there. We believe it will pass for all our efforts, which endangers my bill for universal health care. Not that it matters. It would never pass the House of Lords."

"Is there anything else?" the Guv asked. "Anything he was actively involved in?"

"Well, Mr. Barker," he said. "I believe there is one, come to think of it. It's a small bill rearranging the country into smaller self-governing districts, called town councils, which will be run locally. It will take a certain amount of doing, but the spanner in the works is that we have added an addendum to the bill that women be allowed to serve on these councils."

You crafty old devil, I said to myself. *You just sneaked suffrage into a dull old bill, hoping to get it passed unnoticed.*

"How was Mr. Fitzhugh involved?" Barker asked.

"The bill was deadlocked when we last put it forth. But we had new blood like Mr. Fitzhugh. We hoped he might be the deciding factor."

"Might someone kill a person to stop this bill?"

"Mr. Barker, who can understand the complexities of the human heart? It seems doubtful to me. He was a good chap, Fitzhugh. Very serious, very earnest. He could have accomplished great things for his constituency. Gentlemen, I've a mind to pay your expenses. Let us see what you can uncover. I'd very much like you to find the man who took poor Roland's life."

"Sir, we already have a client," Barker replied. "Mr. Fitzhugh pleaded with me to help him. Of course, I couldn't do anything at that moment. He was seconds away from dying. But I can avenge his death."

"'Avenge not yourselves, but rather give place unto wrath,'" Gladstone quoted.

Barker came as close to grinning as he could get. "Romans chapter twelve, verse nineteen. 'For it is written, Vengeance is mine. I will repay, saith the Lord.' However, we do not seek to punish. We are but spies in the Land of Canaan. We question, we seek to know."

A corner of Gladstone's jowly cheek raised. "You look as if you could punish rather well if you wished to, Mr. Barker."

I thought of the myriad of times we had punished, and it was true. I feared for anyone who came under Cyrus Barker's scrutiny. I've always thought him the most dangerous man in London.

"I must take your word for it, then," Gladstone said. "I assume you will find this fellow, the two of you and I wish you well. And yet I still insist you give me the invoice when all is said and done. In a way, Mr. Fitzhugh worked for me as well as the British people. I would not add a further burden to his family."

"Sir, would you be willing to give us a note stating that we are working on your behalf?" the Guv asked. "It might open several doors."

"And close others," the old man said. "Let me consider the matter. Will you be discreet? Can you perform your duties with decorum and without violence?"

Well, that brought us up short. At times we were forced to resort to certain measures.

"We shall, sir," Barker replied. "Save that I cannot promise the last clause. We do not know what we shall face. I give you my word we will not instigate any violence. We also will not use the note unless we have no other option."

Their eyes met, or rather, Gladstone stared into the inky blackness of my partner's quartz-lensed spectacles. It went on five seconds, which can seem like an eternity in conversation. Then the former prime minister pulled a memorandum book from his pocket, scribbled a message in it with a small pencil, and ripped the page from the book.

"Mr. Barker," he said, holding it out to my partner. "Do not make me regret this."

"Did Mr. Fitzhugh have a wife, sir?" I asked.

Gladstone nodded. "I believe he was engaged to be married."

"Poor fellow," Barker said. "Or rather, poor young woman."

"Star-crossed lovers," the leader answered, nodding.

"'Whose misadventured piteous overthrows'; *Romeo and Juliet*," I added.

"Heavens," the old man said. "A Bible scholar and a classics professor. I assumed all detectives were ruffians."

"We can be ruffian enough when necessary, sir," I replied. "But only then."

"We'll not take up any more of your time, Your Lordship,"

Barker said, rising to his feet. "You have business to attend to as do we."

Cyrus Barker does not wait to be dismissed. We made our way back through the corridors and the Guv and I stepped outside into the sunlit street again. It made the old building seem a dry and dusty sepulcher.

"*Romeo and Juliet*," he murmured. "A sad little play, as I recall."

"It was indeed."

Barker quickened his pace. "Let us hope this enquiry is not also a tragedy."

CHAPTER 3

Wre returned to our offices and tried to decide what to do
next. Poole had not sent along any information yet, so
we were at loose ends. I have no trouble waiting; I've
always got a book in my desk. In fact, I had not read Mr. Collins's
The Woman in White before and was anxious to begin. One would
think having worked with the Guv for ten years I would know better than to try to read in the office.

"Lad," he said, forgetting he promised to stop calling me that
since I was now thirty. "Did you try Kelly's Directory?"

"I did," I said, nodding. "But Fitzhugh wasn't in this year's
book."

"Try last year."

I retrieved the telephone directory. We had the last eight years
on our shelves, a kind of archive of what businesses had existed
in London and for how long. I began flipping through the pages.

"Here's one," I said. "Lindsay and Fitzhugh, Barristers, 18

Theobald's Road. That's hard by Lincoln's Inn and the law courts, I believe."

I made a long arm for the candlestick telephone on Barker's desk and asked the exchange to put me through to the number.

"Edward Lindsay's office," a man said. He sounded young and East End bred. He was probably a clerk.

"Yes, hello," I replied. "Is Mr. Fitzhugh there?"

"Mr. Fitzhugh is no longer with this firm, my good man," he replied. "He's the member of Parliament for Shoreditch now."

"Oh, my mistake," I said. "How about Mr. Lindsay?"

There was a brief pause. "He's in court. 'Spect him back in an hour or so."

"Thank you." I rang off and looked at the Guv. "Did you hear that?"

"I did," Barker said. "Let us meet Mr. Lindsay there."

I went out into Whitehall and waved at a cab with my stick. The springs creaked when Barker climbed aboard. After we were seated, he lit one of his innumerable bent-stemmed meerschaum pipes. This one was smooth and uncarved, but as the bowl rose it grew from snowy white to a tawny yellow and the lip was charred black from use. The smell of tobacco filled the cab. I'd have objected if I didn't like the blend he had ordered specially from Astley's.

Theobald's Road is between Drury and Chancery Lanes, a mixed neighborhood of townhomes and businesses, the latter including jewelers, architects, import businesses, and of course, law offices. Lindsay's name was splashed across the window, but if one looked carefully, one could see a smudge or two where his partner's name had once been. I wondered if they had parted amicably.

Inside, the rooms were well-appointed. Matching law books filled numerous bookcases, and there were several tables, a desk, and three doors in dark mahogany leading to private offices. A glass panel was set in one door and I assumed it was a meeting room for private conversations with clients.

"Good morning, gentlemen," the clerk greeted as we approached his desk. "What can I do for you?"

It was the specimen I'd spoken with on the telephone, Barnaby Smoot by name. He was twenty or so, with a nest of black hair that caused me to wonder if he owned a comb.

"We'd like to speak to Mr. Lindsay, please," Barker said, offering his card.

"He's not here, sir," the clerk replied. "But I expect him before long. If you'd come back in an hour . . ."

"We'll wait," the Guv said, sitting in a chair, one of a row against the wall. He placed his stick perpendicular to the floor, with both hands on the brass ball atop it. Elephants could not have moved my partner. I sat beside him. My partner stared straight ahead, and if the clerk felt that he was being intimidated, I didn't feel the need to disabuse him of the notion.

Edward Lindsay strolled in ten minutes later. His barrister robes were thrown over his shoulder and he held his powdered wig in his hand. He was a small man, nearing the mid-century mark, with curly graying hair and a pleasant aspect. I could not imagine him hectoring a jury.

"Gents to see you, sir," Smoot told him as he handed Lindsay the card. The man glanced at it and regarded us carefully.

"How may I help you gentlemen?" he asked in a tired voice.

"We would speak with you about a private matter, sir," Barker replied.

Lindsay paused, considering, then waved us to the meeting room. It contained a large table and a dozen chairs. The two of us sat across from the barrister as no doubt a thousand men had before.

"What is this in relation to?" Lindsay asked.

"Cyrus Barker, enquiry agent," the Guv replied. "And this is my partner, Mr. Llewelyn."

Lindsay frowned. "What is the nature of your visit, sir?"

"We bear sad news, I'm afraid," my partner stated. "Roland Fitzhugh passed away this morning."

The barrister's face appeared to register genuine shock.

"What?" he cried. "How? If this is some kind of joke, it is in poor taste."

"I assure you, sir, he fell dead in our very chambers a mere two hours ago," the Guv continued. "Our agency would not make light of such a tragedy."

"But that is impossible," Lindsay protested. "He is not yet forty and in excellent health. He plays tennis at the Queen's Club twice a week and used to trounce me terribly. A heart attack, then?"

"No, sir," Barker replied. "He was poisoned."

The problem with registering surprise is that if there is a greater need for one coming along, one has shot one's bolt. He was struck momentarily dumb, a rare thing for someone in the legal profession, I was certain.

"But it's impossible," Lindsay insisted again. "He had some important work before him in Parliament. He was getting married!"

"I'm afraid he must forgo them both," Barker said, ever the stoic.

"I can't believe it," Edward Lindsay continued, scratching his head. "Poisoned? Roland? He was the very last person to be involved in something sordid. Who could have done such a thing?"

Cyrus Barker gave a cold smile.

"We came here with the hope you could tell us," he said.

"You think it could be due to an old case?" Lindsay asked. "That seems unlikely."

"Perhaps," my partner said. "And yet we must enquire into it fully. With your permission we'll want to start going through his old cases. Does anything come to mind which may have led to threats?"

Lindsay considered the matter. He seemed a very sage-looking fellow. I thought he would make a good judge.

"Nothing particular comes to mind," he said, shaking his head. "Well, one, perhaps, but it was not technically a case."

"Do tell," I said. My notebook was open on my knee, and I was using my Pitman shorthand again. I've used it so often I don't need to look at it. I've even transcribed a conversation with my notebook in my pocket.

"It happened that our clerk was taking money regularly from the safe," Fitzhugh's former partner replied. "It had been happening for years, but we hadn't noticed. The sums were not substantial in themselves, but the amount accumulated over time. It was Roland who first saw the discrepancy. One day he noticed the fellow, Albert Mallock, sporting a gold stickpin. We went over the books and found the system he had used to subtract from the accounts. Then Roland called for a constable. Two, actually, and it required both to restrain him. Albert put up quite a fight, threatening us all the while. He said he'd kill Roland. I heard it myself."

"Is the fellow still at large?"

"He was in Holloway Prison when last I heard. I assume he is still there."

"I see," Barker said, crossing his arms. "Does any other name occur to you?"

"Not offhand, no."

"Tell me, Mr. Lindsay," I asked. "How would you characterize your former partner?"

"Roland was the salt of the earth," Lindsay said, leaning forward. "He was a decent fellow all around. Hardworking, conscientious, serious, civic-minded."

I stifled a cough, thinking it only goes to show the dangers of engaging in such behavior.

"Tell me, was Mr. Fitzhugh actually from Shoreditch?"

"Oh, yes," Edward Lindsay answered. "Born and bred. A true East Ender."

Barker frowned. "Was his election contentious?"

Lindsay leaned back in his seat and looked at the ceiling in thought. "Contentious enough, I suppose. He unseated Henry Mills, who had held the position for a dozen years and expected to keep it for a dozen more at least. However, the controversy was confined to the newspapers and innuendoes. I don't believe their feud, if I may call it that, would manifest itself through poison. My god!"

The barrister raised his hands and seized his own iron-gray hair in his hands. "I cannot believe it! He and I were partners for years. He was one of my closest friends."

"When did you last speak to him?" the Guv asked.

"A month ago, I think," he replied. "We played a tennis match, then I took him to lunch."

"Before he died Mr. Fitzhugh told Scotland Yard that he thought someone had attempted to poison him quite recently."

The color drained from the barrister's face. "He should have come to me if he was in trouble. He was among new friends, you see, and did not rely upon me as he once did. He was young when we began our partnership and often relied upon me for advice during our years together. I wonder whom he relied upon recently."

"Were you surprised to see him go?" the Guv asked.

"Well, of course, but I encouraged him to run for office. He was young but sober. He was just the thing his party needed."

"His party?" I asked. "Not this agency?"

The barrister gave me a steely look. "You gentlemen seem determined to suggest something untoward here."

"We're merely testing the knots," the Guv replied. "We question everyone thoroughly. For example, can you inform us of your whereabouts this morning?"

Lindsay's features darkened.

"Oh, come. You are a professional, sir," the Guv said. "Surely you are accustomed to cross-examination."

Lindsay gave a rueful look. "You are correct, gentlemen. I have not been interrogated myself since university. You might have made a passable barrister yourself, Mr. Barker."

The two stared at each other for a moment, not speaking, then Lindsay continued.

"This morning I arose at six-thirty, walked my dog Reg through Finchley Park, and broke my fast at the George and Vulture in Cornhill."

"Can anyone verify your story?" the Guv asked.

"I am known at the G and V. They will verify my visit."

"You've been very helpful, Mr. Lindsay," Barker said. "I know you are a busy man. I thank you for seeing us without notice."

"Not at all," he replied, standing. "You are welcome to look through Roland's files if you wish. This is such a tragedy. I can barely believe it. Has anyone informed his fiancée?"

"I cannot answer that question, sir," Barker said. "Scotland Yard was going to notify his parents, but no mention was made of a fiancée."

"Good heavens!" Lindsay exclaimed. "Gwendolyn may not have heard! I suppose I must break the terrible news myself. Once and for all, gentlemen, assure me this is not some sort of horrible prank!"

"I fear every word is true, sir," the Guv replied. "Tell me, do you have Fitzhugh's address?"

Lindsay led us into the outer chamber and set down the address on a slip of paper.

"Find the man who murdered Roland, gentlemen," he ordered. "I intend to prosecute the case myself, if I have to wrestle every barrister in London for the opportunity."

"Is his chamber now empty?"

"It is not. I believe his files were of little use in his new life. He was a very busy man." He led us to a door and opened it. "Here you are, gentlemen. I suppose if Roland had any secrets, he is beyond them now."

We stepped inside. It was a Spartan office even by Barker's

standards. There was a wall of legal tomes, a desk, a serviceable chair, and a cracking tall filing cabinet of stout oak. I heaved a sigh at the sight of it.

"I suppose we'll have to search through that file by file," I muttered.

Barker nodded. "It's got to be done, Thomas."

I looked through Fitzhugh's desk. There were a few notebooks full of legal records, but nothing resembling a diary.

Barker opened the wooden cabinet and peered inside. "It is in alphabetical order, I'm afraid. Not chronological."

"Of course it is," I answered. "Why make it easy for us?"

CHAPTER 4

After a cursory examination of Fitzhugh's files, we took ourselves off to his flat in Fournier Street, Spitalfields. As we arrived, we found a row of old but respectable three-story houses with mansard roofs and window boxes full of blooming plants. It was as if someone had moved a street from the West End to the East, respectability and all, but then, the East End is like that. When one assumes the district is downtrodden and crime-filled, one turns in to an out-of-the-way lane and discovers a refined oasis such as this. I was thinking of Fitzhugh when a door opened and two blades came out, their silk hats set at a jaunty angle, joking with each other. Then I got it. These were bachelor apartments, an East End attempt at the Albany flats where promising young men stayed until they found brides and moved into more familial accommodations.

Barker opened the door and we stepped inside. The paint was

fresh, the carpet not new, but fine enough, and there was even a concierge of sorts in an alcove as one entered.

"May I help you gentlemen?" the man said with a slight air of displeasure.

The fellow was approaching forty, and with one glance I believed I understood him. He was a combination of doorman, chucker-out, disapproving uncle, and factotum. He was both captain of his ship and crew. I supposed such a fellow must be proud and possessive of his land-locked vessel. There was a ledger book open on his desk. Barker lay his card atop the book.

"We are private enquiry agents, working with Scotland Yard," the Guv said. "We are here to examine Mr. Fitzhugh's flat."

He reached forward and put a finger in the book over the entry that read "Inspector Poole, Scotland Yard," which was the final entry in the book. We were behind our friend, but only just.

"You are Mr. Barker?" the Cerebos asked.

"As the card says," Barker rumbled.

"Please keep your voice down, sir. The gentleman from Scotland Yard left a note saying if you arrived, I was to give you entry." He turned to me. "What is your name, sir?"

"Thomas Llewelyn."

"Your name is not in the note," he said in a disdainful tone. "You may not enter the late Mr. Fitzhugh's rooms."

"The devil you say," I told him. "Mr. Barker is my partner."

"Be that as it may, I cannot let you in."

I raised a brow. "More likely, sir, you cannot *not* let me in."

"Out!"

When I didn't move, he moved 'round the desk and came for me.

"A murder?" I asked in a very loud voice, stepping back. "Right here? And you didn't tell anyone? I'm astonished all your tenants haven't moved out *en masse* by now!"

The fellow had fire in his eyes. He reached out a hand toward my neck. However, I'm not as innocent as I look. I seized his thumb and twisted it palm upward. A thumb can do many things, but it is not designed to touch one's forearm. The man began struggling and tried to free his hand. Feeling a little sorry for his loss of dignity, I let go, and he jumped behind his desk again, shaking his wrist.

"I believe that settles the matter," Barker stated. "If you are dissatisfied with your treatment, please feel free to summon a constable. I'm certain Inspector Poole would be delighted to go to the bother of coming here from Scotland Yard again to add my partner's name to your ledger."

"Very well," the concierge conceded. "Mr. Fitzhugh's flat is number twelve at the top. Pray keep your voices low and do not move furniture about. This is a respectable establishment."

The Guv and I climbed the stair. The third floor was as presentable as the ground floor, though there was a faintly musty odor, the kind one finds in old hotels. Barker unlocked the door and we stepped inside.

We found ourselves in a remarkable room. A row of tall slanting windows graced the front, offering an unparalleled view of the entire district. The room was wide and well lit, so that one had the feeling one was in a glass house. It was furnished with antiques and there were low bookshelves stuffed full beside a pair of comfortable leather chairs and a stool for a side table. If they had allowed wives on the premises, I'd have signed the lease there and then.

"This is one of the old Huguenot houses," I remarked. "The French refugees in the 1600s wove silk up here and required light for their looms. My word, what a view!"

Barker nodded. If anyone could appreciate a good attic room it was he. He stood in the center of the space and looked about, arms akimbo, as if he were going to fight me for possession of it.

I began looking through desk drawers. Fitzhugh was an uncommonly tidy man, unless there was a manservant who came to clean the rooms. I doubted Poole and his lads had anything to do with it. I stepped over and perused a shelf of books, all Greek and Roman classics. An odd chap Fitzhugh was, reading the latest broadsheets from 100 B.C.

In the bedroom, a dresser held only clothing and the wardrobe was filled with coats, hats, and shoes. Fitzhugh was in no way a dandy, avoiding colorful ties and fashionable collars. I found his choice of dress too staid for my taste.

"Have you found anything useful, Thomas?" the Guv asked.

"Not much," I admitted. "I wonder what Poole carted away with him."

Barker came forward, carrying a small picture in a frame. "This was behind the mantel clock. Could it be his fiancée?"

"She's pretty," I remarked, studying the young woman in the photograph. "But the dress is out of fashion. This looks as if it were taken a decade ago."

"Good observation, lad," he replied.

"Why keep a photograph in a frame on the mantelpiece to display and then hide it behind a clock?" I mused. "Do you suppose a constable moved it there while the Yard was tossing the room? Or put it there at Poole's orders?"

"Terry knew we were coming," Barker said. "He would not intentionally move things about to fool us. It would change the game."

Game, I wondered? Had that been what this was for the last ten years, a gentleman's game to keep the Guv occupied? No, that seemed to be a simple answer about a complicated man.

"I'm looking through the books," I said. "Perhaps one is full of banknotes."

"I shall inspect his pockets in the wardrobe."

A few minutes later, I shrugged.

"Nothing here," I said.

"And I found nothing in his coats or his evening kit."

I shook my head. "I do not trust tidy men, sir. They are generally up to something."

"Then no one could ever accuse you of being up to something,"

Barker replied. "Sometimes I think you married Mrs. Llewelyn because you needed a maid."

"Ours is a love for the ages," I replied. I looked about the room. "Do you suppose there are any secret compartments?"

After scouring the room thoroughly, we found nothing, not so much as a loose floorboard.

"Could you sketch the face of the woman in the photograph?" Barker asked. "We might need it for future reference."

I pulled my notebook from my pocket and copied the image before me. I can create a reasonable likeness. The skill was taught at my school in Wales and Barker has made use of my ability on more than one occasion. The young woman in the photograph was very demure, and something about the face reminded me of someone, but I couldn't recall who.

"Done," I said, tucking the notebook into my pocket.

"Let us go, then," he answered.

We lingered for a moment, taking in the beautiful windows and the view, loath to leave the comfortable rooms. In the lobby, the Guv stopped once again in front of the concierge, who stepped back as we approached, eyeing me warily.

"Excuse me, sir," Barker said. "Would you happen to know who was responsible for cleaning Mr. Fitzhugh's flat?"

"I don't know," he answered. "How would I know?"

"Oh, come now, sir," the Guv insisted. "I know the sort of fellow you are. This establishment is your life, and it is obvious that you are proud of it. You would be well acquainted with the servants in your building when they came and went."

"His name is Ogilvy," the man conceded. "You might find him at the Pump Handle. It's—"

"We know where it is," I interrupted.

"Let's go, Thomas."

Back in the street, I pulled up my collar and dared put my hands in my pockets as a light drizzle began to fall. Aside from knowing all the streets in London, an enquiry agent needs to be familiar with every public house. People meet there, take their meals, and sometimes get out of the rain. And so, on occasion, must we.

There were no cabs to be found. It was a ten-minute walk to the Pump Handle and a few more to find Ogilvy inside. We finally located him in a chair by the fireplace, his table already littered with glasses. To me, he looked like a music hall version of a Scot: bald on top, with a fringe of ginger hair coming up over his ears and descending to form side-whiskers. All he needed was a kilt and bonnet to complete the semblance.

"Mr. Ogilvy," the Guv said, as we approached. "My name is Cyrus Barker. My partner and I are investigating the death of your employer."

The man lifted his glass. "Can't you let a man drink in peace?"

"I'll do more than that, sir," Barker replied. "I'll buy that ale and another just like it."

The man's eyes brightened. "That'll do, I suppose. Where are ye from?"

"Perth," the Guv answered. "And you?"

"Fort William," Ogilvy said, sloshing his drink as he set it on the table.

"It's a bad business, this," the Guv continued, shaking his head.

"Who are you gentlemen offering to buy me a drink when we don't know each other?" the servant asked, narrowing his eyes suspiciously.

Barker gave him our card. "Your employer dropped stone dead in our offices this morning while we were talking to him just as we're speaking to you now. The only comfort I can offer is that he did not suffer long. One second my partner, Mr. Llewelyn, was pouring him a glass of water, and the next he was gone. It was that swift."

"Poor Mr. Fitzhugh," Ogilvy said. "He was always an easygoing master. It's a crime what happened to him."

"It is," I agreed, sitting down next to him. "That's why we're here. How long did you work for him?"

"Going on seven years it was," Ogilvy murmured. "I reckoned he'd be good for another twenty years, at least. Now I'll be looking for work at the agencies like I was a second footman or something."

"That must be a blow," my employer said, taking a stool beside him. "How is the market for servants these days?"

Ogilvy wiped his mouth with the back of his sleeve. "Oh, I'll find work, but it will never be as easy as with Mr. Fitzhugh, bless him. The man was a true gentleman. Never asked for much, willing to change his plans if something happened in my family. A generous employer, too. I never had reason to consider myself ill-used."

It had started, I thought, the deification of the victim. He was a saint, a friend to all. Never had a bad word to say about anyone, gave to charities, and was even-tempered. It made me wonder what people had thought of him the day before he died.

"No doubt," Barker rumbled, trying to sound sympathetic.

"Why do you suppose he was killed?" I asked. "Who had it in for him? Did it have to do with his work as an MP, do you suppose?"

"Nothing to do with that," Ogilvy stated. "He'd barely started at the House of Commons. Perhaps when he was a barrister someone didn't get what he wanted. He was very successful before he went into politics."

The Guv nodded. "Was there any particular case that he was concerned about over this past year?"

"Oh, bless me, sir," Ogilvy declared. "He didna discuss his work with the likes of me. I just tended his clothes and grilled his cutlets for him."

"There were no important votes, then," Barker pursued, "the sort that appear in *The Times*?"

"He was not the type of fellow who liked to be in the newspapers, sir," Ogilvy asserted. "He was a retiring sort of man, not after fame and such. A humble person, and if you don't believe me, ask Father Michaels at Whitechapel. He knew him as well as anyone."

I nodded, adding the name in my notebook.

"Was he always that way?" Barker asked. "Was he never ambitious even when he started as a barrister?"

The Scotsman finished his drink and the Guv immediately motioned for another.

"I don't know, sir," he replied. "That was before my time. I do know he wanted to make a name for himself in his chosen profession. I hear he wanted to make his wife proud."

"Hear?" I repeated. "From whom?"

"Mrs. Pomeroy, his former servant."

Barker and I looked at each other.

"He was married?" I asked. "I thought he was betrothed."

"He married the prettiest little woman about a dozen years ago," Ogilvy said. "A prize she was, from a good family with a proper dowry."

"She was better off than he, then?" I asked.

He belched, and set his glass on the table, which rattled the tumblers around us.

"She was," he agreed. "But rumor has it she was ill, gents. I'm sure it was difficult, studying at night for a case, prosecuting the next morning, and seeing to a sick wife. Then it's back to studying again."

"What happened to her?" I asked.

"Well, she died, didn't she, and he had one of those attacks of the nerves. Went into one of them sanitoriums in Europe. He stayed for a good six months and came back a far different man from the way he left. I was hired after he came back to London."

"Was that her picture on the mantel?" Barker asked.

"Indeed, it was, sir."

"Why was it behind the clock?" my partner pursued.

Ogilvy sniffed. "I suppose Mr. Fitzhugh put it behind the clock before he entertained his future bride."

"How well do you know this Mrs. Pomeroy?" Barker asked, furrowing his brow.

"She was the one who watched Mrs. Fitzhugh when her husband was gone," Ogilvy said. "The woman didn't think it proper to continue with Mr. Fitzhugh after the woman's death, it being a bachelor establishment then, you know. She stayed just long enough to show me how he liked things. Afterward, he moved us here to Spitalfields, to erase the terrible memory."

"Do you remember Mrs. Pomeroy's Christian name?" I pressed.

"Mabel, her name was," he said. "Mabel Pomeroy. But she's dead now or must be. She was nearly seventy then."

We sat silent for a minute or two, taking the story in.

Ogilvy shrugged. "Anyway, it was a long time ago now and has no connection to what happened to Mr. Fitzhugh."

"Perhaps," the Guv muttered.

Ogilvy rose unsteadily. "Thank you for the ale, gents. I haven't been treated to a pint in years. By god, I needed it. Who'd have thought this morning I'd be out of work and my employer dead?"

"Come, Thomas," Barker said, rising from his seat. "We should see if any new information has come in at our chambers."

We walked to the door and then I turned back.

"What was her name?" I called to the manservant. "Fitzhugh's wife?"

"Alice," Ogilvy replied. "Her name was Alice."

We left the Pump Handle, and I raised my stick for a cab.

CHAPTER 5

In Barker's Asian boxing and bar-jutsu classes, there is an exercise we practice from time to time. One man stands in the middle of the mat, encircled by the rest of us. He is blindfolded and one at a time, at random, an opponent steps in to attack. The objective of those around him is merely to get close enough to tap him on the shoulder or arm. His objective is to point to the attacker before being tapped. One learns stealth and develops heightened senses.

Working at 7 Craig's Court is like that. We are blindfolded in that we have an improper view from the bow window into Whitehall Street and one cannot man it all day long. Therefore, anyone can enter at any time. Famous men and dignitaries have arrived unbidden as well as criminals of the worst sort. Men have entered with pistols drawn. Scotland Yard has arrived with darbies and leg-irons. We've also received officials summoning us to Buckingham Palace, though not necessarily to give us a medal or a pat on the back. When I hear the slight squeak of the hinge and the sound of traffic outside, I push back the casters of my chair and put a hand within easy reach of my Webley revolver just in case.

A man arrived late that afternoon after Jenkins had gone for the day. He approached the desk so that he stood in profile from where I sat. Removing his top hat, he looked about the room. His dark hair was gray at the temples in that way other men envy, but it receded at the temple on either side. He was well if soberly dressed in a frock coat and black kid gloves, his shoes glossy. I recognized him at once, though he'd never darkened our door in Whitehall before.

"Dr. Applegate!" I called.

"Thomas," he said, bowing. "It's good to see you. Hello, Cyrus."

"Doctor," he said, rising to his feet. "Welcome to our chambers. This is a surprise."

"Yes, well, I didn't expect to visit myself," Applegate replied. "I've just come from Scotland Yard. Dr. Vandeleur tells me that a patient of mine passed away here this very morning."

"You're Johnny-on-the-spot," I remarked.

Our physician nodded. "I received a telephone call not an hour ago from another patient, who'd been told the news in the House of Commons. What has happened? Vandy suspects it is cyanide."

I tried not to smirk at the desecration of Vandeleur's distinguished name.

"Aye," Barker said. "Have a seat, please."

"Death and I are well acquainted," Applegate said as he settled into the chair. "I'd like to hear precisely what happened if I may. I cannot believe Roland is gone, the poor fellow. To think, I outlived him."

Dr. Applegate had patched us like an old coat a dozen times. He'd set my arm twice, dug bullets out of my partner's hide, and stitched us both on a number of occasions. Though he had a grand office in Harley Street, he lived not far from us in

Newington and came at a moment's notice in the middle of the night when required. I suppose we were a far cry from the imagined illnesses and gout of his wealthy clients, but I liked to think we were friends, as well.

Barker told him the story as taciturnly as possible, and then I embellished in my usual way. Meanwhile, the doctor stared clinically at the carpet in front of him with a brow raised, as if imagining it all. His chin rested on his knuckle as it had a dozen times before while I explained how I'd managed to break a finger or sprain an ankle.

"It could not have been suicide, then," he remarked when we were finished. "Else why consult the two of you? But he could not have swallowed the poison far from here or he would never have reached your door. Cyanide doesn't play about. It sets in quite quickly. What an unfortunate situation."

We concurred.

"And it was going so well for him," the good doctor continued. "The election. His promising engagement."

"Promising?" I asked. "How so?"

"He was betrothed to Halton's daughter. You know, the lozenge king. I've never been introduced to her but I've seen her at gatherings. A beautiful woman, though rather young. Bad luck for them both."

"Aye," Barker rumbled.

"So," Applegate said, counting off on his gloved fingers. "You say he entered in mild distress and asked for a glass of water. Thomas, you got the water while Cyrus came around to check on him. He ripped open his collar, seized Cyrus, and fell over onto the floor. Then he spasmed and died."

"Correct," I said, and Barker nodded.

"And it all occurred in under a minute?"

"Not much longer than that, certainly."

He nodded decisively. I've seen him do it a dozen times.

"Cyanide without a doubt, though I'll wait for Dr. Vandeleur's postmortem results. I've asked to sign the death certificate. The fellow was my patient for years." Dr. Applegate stood. "I won't take up any more of your time. You've got a culprit to find and I a patient or two waiting. Thank you, gentlemen."

He leaned across the desk and shook Barker's hand. Generally, Barker prefers not to shake hands. It immobilizes a limb he might need. Applegate shook mine afterward and quitted our chambers.

"You don't think it was Gladstone himself who called him, do you?" I asked the Guv when he had gone.

"It would not surprise me," Barker replied. "He was the physician I was recommended to the first time I was shot. Not many general practitioners have such a fine reputation."

"Only in our profession can one say, 'the first time I was shot,'" I observed.

Barker gave me a grim smile. Jenkins had left his post an hour earlier for his perch at the Rising Sun, and we locked up the offices and took ourselves off. We hadn't gone five feet before we were accosted again. A constable called our names and came up to us.

"Excuse me, sir," he said. "Are you Mr. Barker?"

"I am," the Guv replied.

"I was sent along to find if you were closed for the day," he continued. "Dr. Vandeleur is finished with his postmortem."

Barker waved him on. "Lead the way, then, Constable."

We followed him back to Scotland Yard and all too soon I was smelling the reek of carbolic and looking at Vandeleur's ascetic features again.

"Gentlemen," he said when we arrived. "You've come. I thought I'd missed you. Look at this."

The coroner set down a glass tray with some sort of malodorous lump resting in a dingy liquid.

"What is it?" I asked, standing well back.

"It's Roland Fitzhugh's stomach contents," the coroner said.

"And right here, this is what killed him. As I suspected, he was poisoned with cyanide."

He pointed to a small purple mass.

"What is it?" I asked.

"It's a bite of pie or tart. Raspberry. That's what killed him."

"I need to sit down," I said. "Now. Someone get a chair before I fall down."

Vandeleur and Barker looked at me curiously. The coroner crossed to a far corner of the lab where shelves contained jars full of grotesque specimens. At that moment I didn't want to think about them. Good Old Vandy brought me a chair.

"There was a boy giving away samples today on the corner here," I said, putting my face in my hands. "He was a friendly boy but persistent. He wouldn't surrender until I took a morsel of his raspberry tart."

"Description?" Barker asked sharply.

"Perhaps ten," I muttered. "He came up to my stickpin, I'd say. Towheaded, pale. He didn't wear a jacket and held a tray in front of him with a strap tied about his neck. The box was only a third full. The tarts were quartered, each on a square of paper."

"I assume only Mr. Fitzhugh's sample was poisoned, or the area would be littered with corpses, yours among them," the doctor said.

"Get that away or I'll give you another sample," I said, pointing to the glass tray with the offending stomach remains.

Vandeleur moved the jar. "He should not have been able to walk all the way to your door from Whitehall and Great Scotland Yard. He must have carried it and ate it just before reaching your offices."

"I can image that," my partner said. "He was pestered by the boy into taking the tart. When he arrived at our offices, he had no wish to come inside with the unwanted tart in his hand, so he popped it in his mouth at the last moment."

Vandeleur pointed at him.

"That is precisely what happened," he said. "There were crumbs and a smudge of what looked like jam on his handkerchief."

"Do you suppose it was random?" Barker asked, more to himself than to either of us.

"You mean someone giving out samples, with only one of them poisoned?" the doctor asked.

"If so, no one was intending to murder Fitzhugh," I replied. "It would have been mere chance that he took a poisoned tart."

"That is possible," Barker said. "But until we have proof that it was mere chance, we must assume, based on Fitzhugh's history, that he was the intended victim and continue to search for a motive."

"It was a walloping dose, by the way," the doctor informed us. "It would have brought down a dray horse."

"Apparently our murderer wanted to make certain his quarry would not survive," Barker replied.

"Gentlemen, I hate to shoo you along," Vandeleur said. "But I have dinner and concert tickets waiting."

I stood, wobbly on my feet, and we said our adieus. I wondered about Vandeleur and his evening plans. Was his wife awaiting him, or his mother, or a nubile demimondaine? I'd never thought of him outside of his Body Room before. I didn't know they let him out.

Outside, we headed toward Whitehall Street to find a cab.

"You don't think it was some kind of prank, boys not realizing how lethal cyanide can be?" I asked.

"Where would they get it?" Barker rejoined.

"For that matter, where would they get raspberry tarts?" I argued. "The bite I had was top drawer, too expensive for a tatterdemalion like that boy. And why give it away? If I were the child, I'd have gobbled down the tarts and been done with it."

We found a cab and clambered inside.

"Have you found your sea legs again, lad?" the Guv asked.

I nodded. "I wasn't ill, merely shocked. Suppose I had taken the wrong tart? Rebecca would be without a husband and you without a partner."

"One never knows how many times one is facing death, even on a daily basis," the Guv observed. "Perhaps that is for the best."

That evening, I was upstairs with my wife beginning the first chapter of Mr. Collins's novel, trying not to dwell on what my partner had said. Rebecca was staring into our back garden.

"What is wrong with Mr. Barker?" she asked.

I was trying to concentrate on the page, but looked up at her, ingesting the question.

"Nothing that I know of," I replied. "He was perfectly normal all day. Normal for him, anyway. Why? What is he doing?"

Reluctantly I put down the book and came to the window. The Guv was in the garden late at night, exercising. They were Chinese exercises, which generally involve moving from one dangerous pose to another. It often took half an hour or more.

"He's exercising," I said, shrugging. "He does it all the time."

"Mr. Barker exercises in the morning before you wake up," she continued. "This week he's been exercising twice a day."

"That is not especially unusual."

"And this evening, he took a half portion of his coq au vin and roasted potatoes," she added.

"Perhaps he's attempting to lose some weight," I reasoned. "He's put on a good stone since last year when he injured his knee. You'll have to do better than that to convince me. So far this is weak tea."

"This morning, he was speaking to Etienne when I entered the kitchen and they both stopped immediately when I came into the room."

I didn't think it odd that Barker and our chef, Etienne Dummolard, would have some things to discuss in private. I put my arms around my wife and looked over her shoulder into the garden at the eternal enigma that is Cyrus Barker.

"Perhaps the subject was indelicate," I said. "You know how proper he can be."

"Perhaps," she acknowledged. "Were you aware he has called someone every night this week after we came upstairs? You know my ears are sensitive. It was Philippa, which of course, I would not listen to. Then he spoke to Ho in Mandarin. Tonight, he spoke to Etienne in French."

"You speak French," I said. "Did you catch any meaningful remarks?"

Rebecca put her hands on her hips, not a good sign in any wife.

"It was a private conversation. I didn't listen."

"Of course not," I replied.

She crossed her arms and cocked her head. "I did overhear one thing."

"Ah," I said, returning to my chair.

"Mr. Barker asked if everything was ready."

I lifted my book. "They could have been discussing dinner."

"Honestly!" she chided. "And you call yourself an enquiry agent. You know Mr. Barker has no interest in what he eats and Etienne wouldn't consult him in any case. You must learn to think more subtly."

"Like a woman, I suppose," I said.

She nodded. "Women are very subtle."

"So was the serpent in the Garden of Eden."

I ducked when she threw a pillow at me.

"Very well," I agreed. "I concede that women are subtle, and I admit that Barker is altering his routine, or appears to. If you provide more evidence, I will believe you, but so far a Scottish court would consider your conclusion Not Proven."

She wagged a finger at me. "I'll prove it, then."

"Do so," I said. "I have every confidence in you, Inspector Llewelyn."

"Inspector Rebecca Llewelyn."

I gave a hint of a smile. "As you say."

CHAPTER 6

A knock sounded on the front door in the dead of night. I raised myself on an elbow and reached for a match with nerveless fingers, then popped open my watch. It was half past three. What sort of person has the brass to wake a fellow at half past three in the morning?

I donned my robe and slippers while downstairs I heard the murmur of voices. Mac had answered the door. I'd have let him handle whatever it was, but I knew the visitor would be looking for the Guv or me. No one calls in the middle of the night to ask a butler how he keeps dust off the stairs. I shuffled down the steps. It was a constable. His oilskin cape was dripping on the parquet and by a distant lamppost I saw that Newington was blanketed in a thick fog.

"What's going on?" I asked.

The officer tugged on the brim of his helmet.

"Are you Mr. Barker?" he asked.

"No, I'm the other one."

"Beg your pardon, sir, for knocking you up but Chief Inspector Poole requests your attendance."

"Invite Chief Inspector Poole to jump up his own nose," I replied.

The constable brushed his mustache with his hand to hide a smile. That remark would make the rounds at "A" Division.

"Inspector Poole says it is part of a case you are working on together. He made me promise not to say what happened, only to tell you that you won't see anything like it. He says, 'Tell Mr. Llewelyn it is 'tray-oo-tray.'"

It took a moment to decipher that. *Très outré.* I was intrigued.

"Very well," I told the constable. "We'll dress and be along. What is the address?"

"Number 42 The Highway."

"Inform your superior we shall be there shortly."

The constable tugged his brim again and faded into the night. Three-thirty. I knew what that meant. No cabman would be up and about at half past three, which meant I'd have to go and hitch my horse Juno to Barker's private cab. I turned to climb the stair and found the Guv standing at the bottom fully dressed.

"Who was it?" he asked.

"A constable," I answered with a yawn. "Poole wants us in the East End, something concerning the case."

"You'll have to put Juno in her traces," he remarked.

"I didn't want to walk there."

Barker stretched his arms. His hair was unkempt from sleep.

"Thomas, it is too early for your cheek."

I dressed and put on my waterproof and bowler hat. Then I plunged into the sopping night. It wasn't raining, and yet one felt as if one were swimming. The fog clutched at me, encircled me, hovered about my head. I could not see a dozen yards ahead, which meant I'd have to be on my toes not to spill us into the Thames when we reached it.

Juno was no more enthusiastic about trading a warm stall for a wet night, but Poole did not care for the opinions of a horse, or for that matter, a private enquiry agent. I buckled her in, climbed up on the perch of the private hansom, and eased out the door of the stable and down the ramp into the street.

A half hour later we reached 42 The Highway. I slowed to the curb and let Barker out and then found a post with a ring to tie one's horse to. There were signs that the neighborhood was older and more respectable than the flats we were to visit. The building I glanced at was not a warren but would be in another ten years, I thought. All the windows on the ground floor were open. For some reason, I felt down in the mouth. Whatever we were brought here for, I didn't want to see it. There was a sour odor lingering in the air.

Poole suddenly filled the doorway, resting an elbow on each side. "Are you gentlemen going to stand about all night, or will you come inside?"

As we approached, he raised a brow. "Jump up my nose, eh?"

"Who was murdered?" I asked, to change the subject.

"The question is, Mr. Llewelyn, who bloody wasn't?"

We stepped inside and looked about. The flat appeared to belong to a working-class but respectable family. There was a souvenir plaster model of the Royal Pavilion that said, "Welcome to Brighton." The front room was clean and there was an antimacassar on the back of a chair. The sofa was tired but serviceable. Somewhere there was a woman living here who was doing her best. Then I noticed a wooden toy in a corner. She wasn't alone. She had a family. I followed Barker down the hall and we stepped into the kitchen. The woman of the house was lying on the floor. She had a careworn face even in death, as if she spent her entire life worrying. Worrying if they'd have the rent, if her husband would have steady work. And now this. All that work and worrying she'd done, and it all had come to naught.

"How long ago did it happen, do you think?" the Guv asked.

"The neighbors called two hours ago," Poole replied.

"And found her here?"

"And found them all here," the inspector answered. "The complete Burke family: Clarence and Judy, sons Peter and Tommy, and the baby, Bridget. All dead save for the tot. Judy's here. Clarence is outside in the back. Peter is in the stairwell and little Tommy is upstairs in bed. He'd been sick something awful."

"What killed him?" the Guv asked.

"You'll like this," he said. "A big, walloping raspberry pie. They ate all of it and probably licked the pan clean. I'll bet they hadn't had such a treat in months."

"Raspberry pie," I echoed.

"A prize for giving away all the tarts," Barker stated. "Or at least that must have been how Tommy Burke saw it."

I muttered a word I wouldn't say in front of the ladies. Barker let that one pass.

"May we see the pan?" he asked.

"It's on the kitchen table," Poole said.

To get there we had to step over Mrs. Burke's body. I told myself not to look, which of course, I did. Her face was pale and waxen, eyes half-closed, hair unkempt. Yes, even in death she looked as if she was worrying. I looked away and walked over to the table.

The pan that had contained the pie was nothing special. It was a tin made in Bournemouth where the company probably stamped them by the thousands.

"See?" Poole asked. "Clean as a whistle."

"What poison was used this time?" Barker asked. "If it were cyanide, they'd have died here around the table."

"We ruled out cyanide, yes," Terry Poole replied. "It might be arsenic, might not. I'll leave Vandeleur to work out what it was with his beakers and pipettes. I just want to know why. Why did he use a second type of poison? The first worked well enough, as we all can witness. I think this poisoner we're hunting for is a lunatic. He didn't get any benefit out of switching poisons, unless it was for the pleasure of watching the poor family die slower and in even more agony. This is a new low, Cyrus, even for London. I'm going to find this monster if it's the last thing I do."

"Don't take the case personally, Terence," Barker exhorted. "You know what Mignon would say."

Mignon was Poole's wife, a French woman I'd met once. She was too good for him, but I suspect he'd be the first to admit it. I was acquainted with the feeling.

"I suppose you should see the rest of them," Poole replied. "Come along."

The eldest son, Peter, was sprawled at the top of the stair. He was perhaps fourteen. He'd lost most of what he had eaten but had ingested enough to kill him. There was a red stain on his shirt. Raspberry.

Detective Chief Inspector Poole led us out the back door to a small derelict yard. There were some flowers in pots. That was Mrs. Burke again, doing her best to make something out of nothing in this cold and brutish world. Mr. Burke was lying in the yard alone. I wondered if he was the last to die. He had no jacket and his braces hung about his knees, running from room to room in a blind panic, until he burst out here. Despair killed him as surely as any poison. I noted he was large, but when I looked carefully, I saw he wasn't much older than I.

"Profession?" I asked.

"Cat's meat salesman," Poole answered. "He'd have been out bright and early this morning at the knackers. It's not proper work for a family man. That's the difference between the West End and the East End. Here, the work chooses you."

"Are his tools here?" Barker asked.

Poole nodded. "Yes, a few knives wrapped in an apron."

"And the youngest boy?"

"He's this way," Poole answered. "Follow me."

We climbed the stair again, avoiding Peter's body. Poole is a bit of a showman. We could have seen the younger child after the elder, but the inspector wanted us to see the boys in order of their death. I was not only an enquiry agent here. I was also a witness.

Tommy was abed, propped on a couple of pillows, including his brother's. He was tucked in and there was a glass of water on a table by the bed. That was Mrs. Burke's doing, I was certain. He'd been sick on the floor beside the bed.

The boy was ten years old at most. Blond hair, gray eyes. A diligent looking lad. The cap he'd been wearing when I saw him the day before lay on top of his shoes at the foot of the bed. I'll bet Mum gave Tommy the lion's share of the pie for bringing home such a treat.

"Well?" Poole asked.

"It's him," I murmured. "There's no doubt. Where's the baby?"

As I spoke, a constable passed through the hall with a small child perched on his hip. The girl was just over a year old, her dark ringlets curling about her face. She reached for me as if I were her da, and began to cry when they carried her away.

Poole sighed, turning away. "Bridget Burke," he said. "There's an orphanage who comes to take children until relatives can be found."

"Do they have relatives?" I asked.

"I haven't looked, Mr. Llewelyn," the inspector said. "I've been rather busy. It's the ruddy middle of the night, in case you hadn't noticed."

Poole had taken to calling me Mr. Llewelyn when he was displeased with me, just as Barker did, but I didn't care. There was a baby alone, her family slaughtered. It was unconscionable.

"Why didn't the poisoner kill the baby?" I asked. "How would he know she wouldn't waken and start crying in time to save the family?"

"She was doped to the gills," Poole answered. "Pupils big as marbles. Laudanum. Could have been the killer, or it could have been the Burkes, helping her sleep. Helping them all sleep. As I said, Clarence Burke sold cat's meat and had to be up and about early."

"They'd give their own child laudanum, even while nursing?" I asked, aghast.

"Needs as must," Poole replied. "It's a common practice in the East End."

"Terry," the Guv said. "Let us wander about for a few minutes and then we'll come down and compare notes."

We looked about, searching for any clue that might have been overlooked. We knew all the places one should search. Unfortunately, so did Scotland Yard. When we came downstairs a few minutes later, we were empty-handed.

"How was your visit to the Palace of Westminster," Poole asked with a trace of sarcasm.

"Mr. Gladstone was distressed," Barker answered. "He thought Fitzhugh might have been a deciding factor in a few bills on the House Floor. I suspected he liked his newest member, if only to present him to the public."

"He hired us," I added.

"Old Gladstone hired you, eh?" Poole asked. "I thought you already had a client."

"We did, but this one insists on paying us," the Guv answered. "I couldn't convince him otherwise."

Poole smiled.

"That is an enviable position," he remarked. "Where else did you go today?"

"We went to Mr. Fitzhugh's flat," Barker said.

"Ah." Poole nodded his head. "Snug little rooms. Nice view."

There was a flash outside and the sharp tang of magnesium smoke came in through the open window. Someone had taken our photograph, or at least a photograph of the building. I stepped to the window and leaned out. The darkened street was full of reporters. Everyone reacted, calling to me, shouting questions, requesting an interview. I stepped back and was jeered at by the crowd.

"I suspect all the neighbors in the rooms nearby are speaking to the press," Poole said. "Where else did you go?"

"Edward Lindsay, Barrister," I replied. "Formerly 'Lindsay and Fitzhugh.'"

We stepped aside as one of the corpses was brought out on a stretcher. As it was carried out the door, I heard people calling out and saw more puffs of smoke. I believed it was Mrs. Burke's body. For some reason, I felt protective of her, though I couldn't say why. She was past caring, I told myself. In a better place I hoped, where she'd never have to worry again.

"How do they always know?" Poole asked, looking out the doorway as the last constables stepped through with their burden.

"They have informants," Barker replied. "Some of them are policemen, as I'm sure you know. But we were discussing Mr. Lindsay."

"Oh, yes. How was Fitzhugh considered by his peers?"

"He was competent, sober, perhaps a bit dull," I replied. "Despite his conviction rate, I don't believe the prisons are full of people crying for his head."

Poole rested an elbow on a cracked and peeling wooden mantelpiece.

"But there are some," he said.

"One," Barker agreed. "A former clerk at the law offices. Fitzhugh caught him embezzling. He spent several months to consider his actions. We don't know his situation."

Poole reached into his pocket for his notebook, as did I.

"Name?"

"Albert Mallock," I supplied from my notes.

"Is that it?" Poole asked.

"The clerk is the most obvious suspect so far," my partner replied. "But I haven't studied Fitzhugh's law cases yet. The chances are excellent that our poisoner's name is in his files somewhere."

"Files," Poole said, looking none too pleased.

"We located Fitzhugh's manservant," my partner continued.

"Ogilvy?" Poole asked. "We've been looking for him. Where did he go to ground?"

"He was diving to the bottom of a pint of stout at the Pump Handle," I told the inspector. "He found himself suddenly unemployed and was feeling sorry for his lot in life."

"The Pump Handle," Poole said, jotting in his own notebook. "Anything else?"

I yawned and it spread like an infection. The next body was carried out, little Tommy Burke. I thought of him the last time I'd seen him, so alive, so industrious, hoping to bring home a treat, like a great walloping pie.

"I'll have a list of suspects for you by tomorrow," Poole stated. "Keep me informed of your progress."

We walked out of the house and Inspector Poole locked the door behind us, ignoring the press. The best way to handle reporters is to treat them as if they were misbehaving dogs. Ignore them completely as if they aren't there, because if you don't, they'll bite you where it hurts the most, on page one of a scandal rag. Barker climbed aboard the hansom. I untied Juno and climbed up behind the cab.

"I notice you didn't tell him about Mrs. Pomeroy," I called through the hatch as we turned in to the next street.

"We are working together," he called back. "But I am not obliged to tell the Metropolitan Police everything, Mr. Llewelyn."

CHAPTER 7

Cyrus Barker can be stringent at times but he is not a martinet when cases wake us in the middle of the night. We arrived back in Newington a little after five in the morning and he told Mac to send word to Jenkins that we would arrive shortly before nine. It was a bit strange to crawl into bed as the sun is rising but I gave it my best effort. Rebecca was planning to spend the day with her family and was buzzing about the room like a bee, lighting here for a pair of gloves, there for a parasol. Meanwhile, I had a pillow over my head and was in that state that was neither sleep nor wakefulness. With a kiss on the top of the head she was gone, and I found myself in the Land of Nod, wherever that is, for the next three hours.

A half hour after I woke, we were in a cab headed toward Whitehall. I was feeling somber, my mind dwelling on that house, that scene, that poor family. It dwelt, too, on the baby, Bridget Burke. What sort of family would take her in? Would they be better parents than the Burkes? I thought, too, about my own life. Rebecca and I were eager to have a child of our own someday, so far without any success. I hoped the child would be given to a family who wanted a child as much as we did.

When we opened the door to our chambers, we were treated to a rare sight. Our clerk, Jenkins, was wide awake. His coat was off, there was a cup of tea in front of him, and a cigarette dangled from his fingers. The newspapers—our newspapers—were spread across his desk, the one on top open in front of him. Generally, his eyes were half-glazed until after lunch, but now he was perched on the edge of his seat. I didn't even know his chair had an edge.

"Jeremy?" I asked.

Jenkins jumped up and quickly folded the newspaper again.

"Sorry, Mr. B., Mr. L. Didn't know for certain if you'd come when you said, and I saw the story here." He gathered the newspapers and handed them to me. "If you'll excuse me, I'll be back in a few minutes."

He passed us and disappeared out the door, looking keen. Jeremy Jenkins? Keen?

"What's happened to him?" I asked, looking at the Guv.

"I don't know," he replied. "But I'm sure we shall learn soon enough. I'll have *The Times*."

"I'll try *The Courier*, I think."

We took our morning news to separate desks and began to read. I found the article I was looking for at once. It began as follows:

Entire Family Poisoned

Mr. Frank Trease and his wife Florence of The Highway were awakened around midnight by the sound of a baby crying in the flat of the tenants next door, Mr. and Mrs. Clarence Burke. When the crying continued for more than fifteen minutes, Mrs. Trease convinced her husband to knock at their door and ask them to quiet the baby. Mr. Trease was unsuccessful in bringing anyone around so he stepped into the street and summoned a constable. Believing the child was in danger, the two men kicked in the door. They were unprepared for the scene inside. Clarence and his wife were found dead on the ground floor. Their elder son Peter was found on the stair and the younger son Tommy in his bed. Only baby Bridget survived the massacre.

"Ratcliffe Highway Murders, gents!" Jenkins called from the other room as he entered. "Only they was poisoned, not beaten to death. Baked in a pie, it said. Very Sweeney Todd!"

He carried another armful of newspapers and waved one of his lurid journals in the air. He spent half his days elbow deep in the things. In fact, he kept large ledger books with yellowed articles pasted in them, going back ten years or more. I've seen him purchase two copies of an edition in order to paste both sides when one was printed on the back of the first.

"The Ratcliffe Highway Murders," I echoed. "I read about that at university in an essay by Thomas De Quincey. Two families murdered a couple of weeks apart."

"Yes, sir. The Marrs and the Williamsons." Jeremy looked pleased at the chance to discuss his morbid hobby. "The Marrs got it first. Seventh of December 1811. Husband, wife, baby son and apprentice, all battered to death. The halls were bathed in gore. The weapon was left behind, a seaman's maul. It's in the Black Museum at Scotland Yard now."

"Then twelve days later," he continued, "in the same street a second attack occurred at the King's Arms, a respectable inn. The publican, his wife, and their maid were viciously attacked, but their granddaughter Catherine was untouched and slept through the entire thing."

"What was the killer's name?" I asked.

Jenkins frowned at me. He'd hoped to drag out the story a little longer.

"It was a sailor, John Williams, an old acquaintance of Timothy Marr," he continued. "He was arrested for the crimes but hung himself with his own scarf before he could confess or tell why he committed the crime. After he died, his body was placed in a carriage and there was a procession through the East End. One hundred and eighty thousand people attended."

"My word," I exclaimed, which mollified our clerk somewhat.

"This is only the second case I have looked into concerning a poisoner," Barker said. "Are you familiar with poisoning, Jeremy?"

"Lord love you, Mr. B.," he exclaimed. "I know every detail of every poisoning in this century. Most from the last as well. You might call it a specialty of mine."

The Guv and I looked at each other. We were so used to being with Jenkins every day and watching him read his popular rags that it never occurred to us to think there might be actual information therein. For the first time I realized that his being our clerk, Barker's clerk originally, might have been because Jenkins wanted to work with a man who concerned himself with murders. He also got satisfaction cutting out and pasting those articles that appeared concerning my partner, though Barker always did his best to keep his name from the press.

"I know who died from what, where the killer got the stuff, and how he gave it to 'em," Jenkins concluded. "Take arsenic, sir. You can buy it at a chemist's. In most of the cases the murderer said he or she wanted to kill rats or put down a sick dog."

"She?" I asked.

"Sure, Mr. L.," our clerk said, nodding. "Didn't you know? Poisoning is a woman's weapon. They put it in their husband's stew, some for insurance money, some to punish him for taking a mistress, but more than one done it because he was thumping 'em hard."

"You're a fount of information this morning, Jeremy," Barker remarked.

That pleased him, I thought. It had never occurred to me to ask him anything before.

"Where was I?" he asked, glancing at the ceiling and then

pointing a finger at me. "Right. You have to sign a ledger at a chemist to buy arsenic, and that's how most women got caught. However, others realized you could boil flypaper, which you can buy anywhere for a few pence. Mind you, Mr. B., you'd have to have a walloping dose to kill somebody in just a few hours. Most poisoners give their victims small doses over time. People just think someone is sickly. An invalid. Even a doctor won't notice it if he's not looking for it."

"Fascinating," I murmured, scribbling as fast as I could.

"There are two different methods of poisoning in this case, though," he said. "That's one for the books. Why change poisons?"

"If one of the family died on the spot from cyanide the others would not eat the pie," Barker answered.

"But why?" I asked. "Why kill everyone and not just the boy?"

"Presumably because the boy, Tommy Burke, had met his killer face-to-face and if he lived, could give a description of the killer. If he alone were poisoned, they might have taken him to a hospital in time to save his life. Therefore, all of them had to die."

"The Mad Pie Man," Jenkins said, savoring the words. "That's what they'll call him and soon it will be on the front page of the *Policeman's News*."

Our clerk looked supremely satisfied.

"The Pie Man," Barker grumbled, giving a look of distaste.

Jenkins held up a finger.

"The Mad Pie Man, sir," he corrected. "Mark my words."

The Guv shook his head. "We have reached an age where men boast of their killings and court monikers such as this."

"Why not Pie Woman?" I asked.

Our clerk rolled his eyes.

"Simple Simon didn't meet a Pie Woman, did he?" he asked, as if that settled the matter.

"Of course," I replied. "I don't know what I was thinking."

"Let me look at that, Jeremy," Barker said, indicating the journal.

Jenkins gave it over as if he was afraid Barker would tear it to pieces. I thought it likely myself. Instead, my partner stuffed one of his larger pipes with tobacco, sat in his chair, lit his pipe, and began to read. Jeremy and I glanced at each other. Then we all began to read.

Detective Chief Inspector Terence Poole had his name in *The Courier*, assuring the citizens that whoever killed the family would be apprehended.

"Why is there no mention of Fitzhugh?" I asked, looking up.

Barker grunted from behind his newspaper. "I suspect Poole's keeping it out of the limelight as long as he can."

I opened a window before my suit became saturated with smoke. Jenkins was actually humming to himself. The world was in danger of running mad. I stopped when I saw mention of the Burkes' surviving child in *The Courier*: "The infant, Bridget, was taken into custody where Inspector Poole assures the public she will be safe until a living relative can be found."

What if there were no living relatives, I wondered? Or what if there is but he or she is not able to care for a child? What if he's a bully or she a slattern? It was troubling to contemplate. I'd seen the look in Rebecca's eye when a perambulator went by or a little girl skipped past in a pinafore. I'd felt that tug myself once or twice. My brothers and sisters were raising flocks of children and here we were. Barren. Such a harsh and soul-crushing word.

There was a low slap as Cyrus Barker dropped *The News* onto the glass top of his desk. He leaned back and I watched as his hand rose to his collar, as if adjusting his tie. I heard the subtle rasp of his nails across the follicles of his newly shaven throat. That is always a good sign. The Guv was thinking. I looked at Jenkins and we both smiled. A full fifteen minutes later, Barker spoke.

"Jeremy, will you come here, please?"

Our clerk came out from behind his desk and stood in front of his employer's looking curious. "Yes, sir?"

"Sit."

Barker gestured toward the visitor's chair. I could see the cogs turning in Jenkins's mind. What was happening? He never sat in it before. He wouldn't dare.

"Sir, I—"

"I didn't ask."

Jenkins sat, flustered. Barker bent forward, knitted his fingers together in front of him on the glass top and glared at him like a judge about to pass condemnation.

"Jeremy, these stories are often lurid and hackneyed, but sometimes there is the ring of truth in them. The way the information is presented reminds me of court records."

"They are, sir," our clerk said, nodding. "That's often where reporters get their information."

"You are familiar with court records, then, I assume."

"'Course I am," he said, smiling. "Even forged a few."

Jeremy Jenkins was the son of a famous forger and no mean artist in his own right. We had used his skills to our own advantage more than once in the past.

"I suspect the solution to the case involving the late Mr. Fitzhugh is moldering in a legal file somewhere," the Guv continued. "I can feel it in my bones. Nearly all of his life was spent in court and he's had too little time as an MP to make someone seek to take his life."

Jenkins nodded. "Yes, sir."

"I want you to examine the court records of every case Roland Fitzhugh prosecuted. You will begin with the records at the offices of Mr. Lindsay, the barrister. If Lindsay cuts up rough about this, I shall persuade him. As I recall, his clerk is garrulous. I suggest you take him to lunch. Have no more than two ales."

"Yes, sir, Mr. B."

"I expect you to keep office hours: seven-thirty to five-thirty," Barker continued. "Mr. Llewelyn will give you an allowance for cab fare plus expenses. Purchase some new shirts and ties. You are representing the agency, after all. Be as professional as possible with Mr. Lindsay but be casual with the clerk. Do you understand?"

"Yes, sir," he replied. "But who will watch the front desk?"

"I'm afraid we must do without at the moment," Barker said. "It's a matter of all hands on deck. Your work may be vital to the case. We are fortunate to have you."

Jenkins blinked. Compliments are rare in our office, as we both well knew.

"Thank you, sir."

"Is this agreeable to you?" the Guv asked.

"It is, sir," Jenkins said, looking from Barker to me and back again. "Of course. You can count on me."

"We do," the Guv said. "Take the rest of the day off. Get a shave and a haircut. Have your shoes polished. Buy a proper notebook and some pencils."

"Should I report each day?" he asked.

"No, every other day will be fine."

"Detective First Class Jeremy Jenkins," I remarked.

Jenkins grinned. "Cor."

"It will be necessary for him to purchase newspapers every morning to keep abreast of the case," I said. "I suggest he purchase one of those cases in which solicitors carry their briefs. Not a new one. The more worn the better. He should be able to find one in Petticoat Lane."

"That's good thinking, Thomas," Barker said. "Could you provide him the necessary funds?"

"Of course, sir."

I pulled the agency's wallet from my pocket and gave Jenkins twenty pounds. He stared at me as if I were handing him the crown jewels.

"One last thing, Jeremy," the Guv added. "And this is important. Be very careful what you eat or drink. If someone pulls a pint for you, watch it being poured. Be vigilant. Do you understand? You watched a man die in this chamber yesterday. I don't want you to be next."

"Thank you, sir," he said, his voice sounding strained. I wasn't certain if it were emotion or pride. "I'll be off then."

When he was gone, I drummed my fingers on my desk.

"I hope that was a wise decision," I remarked. "There's the chance that he might break under the strain."

"A little responsibility will be good for him, lad," the Guv argued. "What did you call him? Detective First Class?"

"Yes, sir."

"I'd make him one if he comes back with the information we need."

CHAPTER 8

Scotland Yard had tracked down the first suspect in Fitzhugh's murder, Albert Mallock, the former clerk. The man had been released from prison after two years and was presently working on the docks as a stevedore. That was quite a change, to go from working in an office to carrying trade goods onto and off ships in the Docklands. He was currently unloading a vessel from Virginia, and he frowned as we approached. Barker and I can afford a better tailor than your average inspector, and yet this fellow worked out who we were almost immediately.

"Back again, eh?" he asked. "I said all I have to say!"

Mallock was nearing five and thirty, unless he was younger and his time in prison had aged him. A halo of gray surrounded his dark hair. He was of average build, but he was lifting bags of heavy tobacco with relative ease.

"Mr. Mallock, we are not policemen," Barker replied, handing him one of our cards. "You need not speak to us."

Mallock turned away, hefting the heavy sack onto his shoulder. "Sod off, then."

Barker inhaled and then exhaled, trying to be patient, I assumed.

"You heard the man, Mr. Llewelyn," my partner said. "Let's leave him to his work."

I nodded and we began to walk away.

"That may be the shortest interview ever recorded," I said.

"Wait," the Guv murmured.

"I read the newspapers!" Mallock called after us. "He died in your offices, didn't he?"

We stopped and turned.

"He did," Barker answered.

"Poisoned."

The Guv made no response.

"Can't say I dislike the idea, but I didn't do it, as I told Scotland Yard."

"And they didn't believe you?" I asked.

Mallock grinned. "Amazing, isn't it? Look, I don't want no trouble from Scotland Yard or anyone else. I can account for the morning in question and the night before. Besides, I wouldn't poison him. If I cared about him anymore, I'd have held him down and beaten the tar out of him. I'd want to see his face."

He hefted the sack off his shoulder and onto a pile. It was backbreaking work, an entire ship's cargo carried out by a few men. Inside the hold it was stifling, but it was warm out in the sun.

"Mind you," Mallock continued, heading toward the hold again. "I can't really put the blame on Fitzhugh. He was just doing things by the book. I did this to myself. I knew it then."

"You said some dangerous things," Barker growled. "You made threats."

"Of course I did," the man replied. "My blood was up. I was hoping he'd back down. I wanted to intimidate him into letting me go."

"Did you—"

"Look, Mr. Barker," Mallock interrupted. "I don't got time for words. I don't get paid unless this ship here is unloaded."

"We'll help you with the cargo if you will answer our questions," the Guv said, removing his jacket. "How will that be?"

Mallock looked at us, and then at the men in charge. When he asked his boss, the man shrugged. He didn't care who did it as long as the job was done. I removed my coat as well. Barker wore a shoulder rig, while I had a revolver in the waistband of my trousers. We attracted a good deal of attention, but when we started toting sacks, they let us alone.

"How did you hear about Mr. Fitzhugh's death?" the Guv enquired.

"Scotland Yard Johnny came down and rousted me yesterday. 'Where you been the last few days?' 'Where do you think? Breaking my neck on this blasted dock.'"

"How did you feel when you heard the news?" I asked.

"Felt worse, I'll say that," he replied. "The beggar put me in stir. I mean, I done it. I took the money. I was young and stupid, and I liked to gamble. You like a flutter now and again when you're young. I wasn't married. Parents were dead. Brother off in India. So, I made a few mistakes and then a few more to cover the first. It worked for a while. That's good, right? No, you done it once, you'll do it again, right, fellows? I was an idiot."

I unhooked my cuff links and rolled up my sleeves, lifting a sack that must have weighed three stone. There were easier ways to question a suspect, I thought.

The conversation had become communal. All of the stevedores were listening to us and some nodded. A few squinted their eyes at us in warning: don't mess with the stevedores' union.

"Took money from the till once," Mallock continued. "Nobody noticed. Took it again, gambled, did all right, so I put it back and pocketed my winnings. Should have stopped then, but I didn't. Eventually Mr. Fitzhugh realized that money was missing. And who did it? It wasn't as if half of Whitechapel was parading in front of the safe all day. He asked, I copped to it, and he called 'H' Division. It was over before you could say 'knife.' He didn't yell at me or kick me out into the street. No. He just made sure I did time for it. I thought he might prosecute me himself, but there are rules against it. What are you smiling at?"

The latter remark was addressed to me. I expect I was musing.

"Eight months in Oxford Prison," I said, holding up my hand. "Theft."

He gave me a grim look. "We're a bleedin' fraternity!"

I heard the men chuckle behind me.

"Oy!" his boss called.

We hefted the sacks again and descended into the hold.

"What's happened since?" Barker asked.

"I changed my ways," he replied. "I don't drink, don't gamble, don't steal. Don't do nothing. I keep myself to myself. Still, I get knocked up by the police and when they don't like my answers, they put me in a cell. Once a felon, always a felon."

"How long did you work for Messrs. Fitzhugh and Lindsay?" the Guv asked.

"Five years," Mallock said. "Since the very beginning, really. I was Fitzhugh's first clerk."

"Was he a fair employer?"

Mallock gave a sharp laugh, then hefted another sack. "I thought of topping myself once or twice while I was working for him. He's the sort of fellow that makes you want to do it. Sanctimonious prig."

Barker grunted. "What was your opinion of Mr. Lindsay?"

"He was a decent sort," Mallock said. "Lindsay would have brought me in, raked me over the coals, changed the lock on the safe, then let me be. Lesson learned. Or he might have sacked me, but he wouldn't have called the police. I wish it were he that caught me. On the other hand, it would have been difficult to look the man in the eye after what I had done."

"It smells good in here," I remarked, indicating the hold.

"Strange, that," Mallock replied. "Tobacco smells terrible when it's growing, I hear, but it smells good after it's dried. Then you light it and it stinks again."

I'd been stuffed into enough smoking cars with the Guv traveling around the country. Barker's blend is one of the best I've been around, but I didn't care to make a dinner of it.

I was growing tired. Each trip from the hold to the dock seemed farther away, but then it would be, since we were working our way deeper into the hold. I wished my partner would run out of questions soon. If I had any thought of quitting enquiry work, it wouldn't be to become a stevedore.

"Are you aware of anyone who might have hated Fitzhugh enough to poison him?" the Guv asked.

"Nary a one," the man said. "Unless someone didn't like his politics. I mean, yeah, there were some like me that he put in prison, but I've never known him to fear for his life. In the years I was there, we never had the police for his personal safety. Until me, that is."

This brought another chuckle from his compatriots.

"Did Mr. Fitzhugh and Mr. Lindsay ever row?"

Mallock chuckled. "No. You couldn't make Mr. Lindsay angry if you slapped him. He'd apologize for putting his face in the way. A very genial man. I reckon he'll have a partner again soon."

"Mr. Mallock, you knew Fitzhugh," Barker said. "We only met him once and for a few seconds. What do you recall about him?"

Albert Mallock stopped and put his hands on his hips. "He was a quiet sort of fellow. He was harsh, though. Everything by the book. No mistakes forgiven. It seemed as if he always hoped to find one. It's hard to like a man who thinks that way. I got out of Holloway last year and found out he was to be an MP. It stands to reason. He gets the step up and I get the boot. Still, like I said, I did it to myself and have regretted it ever since."

We were setting a few sacks on the pile on the dock and Mallock ran an arm across his forehead. Out of nowhere, two assailants seized him by the knees. They were both about five years of age, sallow little girls with dark hair and bows on their heads. I couldn't tell if they were twins or sisters a year apart. They climbed up on his shoes and he began to walk around with them clinging to him and giggling.

Their mother came up behind them and watched. Life had not been any kinder to her than to Judy Burke. Her face was lined, her clothes probably handmade or purchased secondhand. She carried a basket under her arm. Her hat didn't come from a haberdashers in the West End. However, she had her babies, which I surmised were not Mallock's, and she had her fellow, which was more than many a woman could boast in the East End. They were a family cobbled together, but a family, nonetheless. They were poor and yet they looked as content as anyone has a right to be in this town.

"Gentlemen, it is noon and I have an hour to myself," Mallock stated. "Have you any further questions?"

Barker lifted his hat to the woman and bowed and I did the same. I wished I had thought to do it first.

"None, Mr. Mallock." He turned to the man's wife. "Ma'am, what lovely children you have. We'll leave you now. Enjoy your meal."

The woman gave a wan smile as we left them in peace.

"Impressions, Mr. Llewelyn?" the Guv asked when we had left the docks and were approaching Emmett Street.

"If he is trying to look innocent, he's made a very elaborate play. The common-law wife, the children, the basket. Pork pies and ginger beer, no doubt."

"Common law?" Barker enquired.

"She wore no ring."

Barker gave a rare, satisfied smile.

"Good observation," he said.

It had grown blustery. A breeze had come in from up north. It was a number of streets to Commercial Road, but there were few days more comfortable for a good walk.

"Still," I murmured. "We should not cross him off the list, merely move him lower. He could be a good liar."

Barker looked to the left and when I followed his gaze, I recognized the area.

"We're going to Ho's, aren't we?"

"I'm hungry," he replied. "Aren't you?"

"I'm a bit peckish, I suppose."

He let that bit of slang alone. We found Narrow Street at the north end of Limehouse Reach and were soon nearing Ho's tearoom.

Ho was an ill-favored Chinaman who had once been the first mate on Cyrus Barker's boat, the *Osprey*, while they were plying the South China Sea. I found it extremely difficult to believe he had once been a Buddhist monk, but Barker claimed it is so. Ho is sullen on his best days. He owned a tearoom in a vile alley that one could reach only through a tunnel under the Thames. The room was of dark wood and festooned with red Chinese hanging lanterns that gave it a hellish look at times. The chairs were old and scarred. Scotland Yard kept an eye on the premises. Things were planned here, few of them legal.

"Ratcliffe Highway," Ho said to my partner. "Yes, I read about it. Arsenic. You haven't dealt with poison since *her*, have you, Shi Shi Ji?"

Shi Shi Ji had been Barker's name in China. It means Stone Lion. He had knocked around Southern China for most of his life getting into and out of one scrape after another.

"No, I haven't," he replied.

"Nice family," Ho remarked, meaning the Burkes. "Parents and two boys? Bad joss."

Barker nodded. "Yes. And another man, a barrister poisoned right at my door."

"Bad luck, old chap," the Chinaman replied, switching to upper-class English.

"Thank you," the Guv replied acidly.

"You have been exercising?" Ho asked. He stuffed a thimbleful of tobacco into a metal pipe, an Asian contraption that looked like a watering can.

"Every day."

"You are not as fat as you were." Ho grunted. "But you still fat. You practice, you walk, you beat the heavy bag?"

"All those things."

"Work harder," Ho said. He hooked a thumb in my direction. "How is this one coming along?"

"Well enough," Barker said. "He took down a fellow quite handily yesterday."

"Him?" Ho laughed. "Impossible."

A waiter brought us lunch, though we had not ordered any. The plate set in front of me held garlic poulet and fried soybeans in a saffron gravy. It was my favorite. Barker's was some sort of boiled monster. Monkfish, perhaps.

"You have become a lazy Westerner or a Mandarin," Ho continued. "You will never fit into the sort of clothes you wore when you first arrived here."

"Nor will you," Barker replied. "You look like a woman ready to give birth."

Ho slapped his bulging stomach. "Hard as a stone. Strong as iron."

"Let me eat in peace," the Guv said. "Haven't you something to do?"

Ho stood. "I have messages to read. Then I can count my money. Business has been good. It's a shame. You! Stupid boy!"

I realized he was addressing me.

"Yes?"

"You use those sticks like oars," Ho said. "It's a wonder you get any food in your belly at all."

I watched as he left, knowing I used my chopsticks as well as any European. He was merely looking for something to complain about.

My mind raced furiously. If I had my notebook ready, I would have written myself a few notes. Barker was in training, but what for? Ho was keeping him to task, the way an instructor speaks to a student in China. Who was the woman they referred to, and how did it concern poison? And whatever they were doing, Ho was a part of it.

"Thomas, what are you thinking?" Barker asked.

I put down my bowl and speared a prawn from a dish nearby.

"The case, obviously," I answered. "Who would kill an entire family merely to drag a red herring across our path? I doubt the boy could have even given a good description of the poisoner. He was only nine or ten."

My partner lifted a thousand-year-old egg with his chopsticks and bit it in half. I leaned away. No mummified eggs for me, thank you very much. I swallowed the thimbleful of tea in one sip. I can tolerate Earl Grey, but this tasted like bilge water. Barker swallowed his and immediately poured another. Eventually, he put down his bowl and lay his sticks across the rim.

"Are you ready, Thomas?" he asked.

"Yes, sir," I said, doing the same.

CHAPTER 9

W here shall we go next?" I asked as we stepped out of Ho's and back into the bright sunlight of Limehouse Reach.

"Let us try the public house Fitzhugh visited yesterday morning," the Guv rumbled. "And the coffee shop he went to four days ago."

I flipped through my notes. "That would be the Dove Inn in Paddington and the Old Vienna in Bermondsey."

"Excellent," Barker pronounced.

"I have trouble believing someone would dare poison a pitcher of water in the middle of a public inn," I ventured.

Cyrus Barker shrugged his wide shoulders. "Roland Fitzhugh said he thought he'd been poisoned. Were I going to deliberately poison a man, it wouldn't matter to me if other people died from drinking out of the same pitcher. I'd have already surrendered my humanity."

"Right," I answered. "Just as the Burkes were killed in order to silence Tommy."

"And the boy himself was killed because he could identify the poisoner."

"This killer has no conscience," I stated.

"Aye," Cyrus Barker agreed, flagging a cab. "Either that or he hated Fitzhugh so much he would stop at nothing to see him dead."

A hackney coach pulled over to the curb and we boarded. Barker is known about town as a generous tipper.

"Bishop's Road, Paddington," I told the jarvey, and we were off.

The Dove was a classic inn with tables stained with rings and surrounded by chairs that had lost their mates over the decades. Barker ordered a Scotch ale, and I a Nut Brown, before we sat. I'd seen better establishments and worse, but it would do.

The Guv leaned his head to one side an inch. I took a sip of ale, looked away for a second or two, and then casually glanced over my shoulder as if I'd heard a sound. It is standard procedure for enquiry agents. One doesn't want to be obvious. At the end of the bar there was a tall glass pitcher with a few tumblers beside it, upside down. We drank for a minute. Two. Then my partner stood with a casual air, crossed the room, filled a tumbler with water and drank, then made a face.

"Barkeeper," he said.

"I'm the publican here," said a man behind the counter. He had an impressive set of muttonchops attached to his mustache.

"Better yet," the Guv answered. "Is this water fresh? It tastes off."

"Off?" the man demanded, his cheeks flushing. He poured another tumbler and drained it.

"Tastes all right to me," he said with a shrug.

Barker lifted the pitcher and examined the water through the glass. "An acquaintance of mine was in your establishment yesterday and the water made him ill. Does it sit here all day?"

"Yes," the man admitted. "I've had a pitcher there for fifteen years or more and no one's complained until now."

"Were there others who became ill?" Barker pursued.

"Two or three," the publican admitted. "Never happened before. Not even close. We thought maybe something was in the water we washed the pitcher in."

I came to the bar while they talked and raised a brow. "Perhaps someone deliberately put something in the water."

The man crossed his arms. "What are you saying, Mister?"

"My acquaintance went to Scotland Yard after visiting your establishment fearing that someone was trying to poison him," Barker explained. "A half hour later, he was dead of cyanide poisoning."

The man leaned over the counter. "Lower your voice, sir, or you and me will have words. Who was this man?"

"His name was Roland Fitzhugh," Barker replied.

"The MP?" the proprietor exclaimed. "He's been in here before several times. Drank only water, but he had a proper breakfast so I didn't complain."

"And you say others become ill as well?" the Guv persisted.

"Yes, two, including a barmaid, but only mildly," the publican said. "She recovered quickly and returned to work. I mean, no one else keeled over and died. You think someone has done it again?"

"I do, but there is no reason to alarm anyone," the Guv answered. "This gentleman and I are enquiry agents working with Scotland Yard. If you will wash this pitcher in hot soapy water, and provide the public with fresh tumblers, I believe there's no need to mention it again."

The owner looked relieved.

"Done," he said.

"Where do you get this water?"

"From a pump down the street."

"It might be best if you ceased leaving the pitcher on the counter for public use," Barker said. "Have water brought to a customer upon request instead. For your own sake, I mean."

"That seems easy enough," the man replied. "So, this water is safe to drink?"

Barker poured another glass and drank it. Then he set the tumbler down on the bar.

"Refreshing," he stated. "Pay the man, Thomas, and let's be off."

I looked at my Nut Brown Ale, half full and inviting. I hated to waste it. I thought of my days at university when a pint was dear. With a sigh I tossed some coins on the table and didn't even count them. They were considered an enquiry expense. I took a final pull from the mug and trotted after the Guv. He wasn't the sort to wait while I finished the dregs of my beer.

We crossed London Bridge to Bermondsey next, on the Surrey side of the river. The district had tried to distance itself from its larger, louder neighbor, Lambeth, by attempting to invigorate itself and show some civic pride. Tabard Street was tidy and the buildings looked recently painted. There was a marble drinking fountain on the corner. The Old Vienna had probably been built for a completely different purpose, but now approximated an Austrian *kaffehaus* with rows of small windows and a facade of brown beams and tan plaster. The scents of coffee and cinnamon wafted to my nose as I opened the door. It seemed promising as we stepped inside.

The coffeehouse was neat as a pin. The floor gleamed as if Mac himself had been at it for hours. The coffee aroma was heady and a glass case held small decorated pastries. In fact, the entire building resembled a decorated pastry. I promised myself I'd bring Rebecca to sample the wares. She'd love it. Meanwhile, the Guv stood in the center of the room looking outsized and menacing, as he soaked in every nuance of the place.

"No common pitcher here," he murmured in my ear, which meant only half of the patrons heard him.

We ordered coffee and looked about. Most of the chairs were full. The place must have been bustling throughout the day. The clientele looked intellectual, even cosmopolitan. Someone looked in imminent danger of reading a book. I recognized a few of my wife's acquaintances, and the man at the next table was either a French artist or a German anarchist. The coffee was so good I began doubting I was still on English soil.

"There are two women behind the counter," I remarked. "I'd say the man standing between them is the husband of one and the father of the other. It is a family business."

"This does not seem the place for a meal," my partner murmured. "A cup of coffee and a bun, a moment's conversation, then on your way. One customer arrives as another departs, like the figures on a Tyrolean clock."

We sat and sipped our coffee, watching as the younger waitress brought a tray with two glasses of water to some customers. I turned my head toward the bar and found we were the object of scrutiny by the proprietor, a thin, bald-headed fellow. He frowned when our eyes met. Then he wiped his hands on his apron and came out from behind the counter.

"Gentlemen," he said in a low voice. "Will you please to step outside with me?"

Cyrus Barker would not refuse such a well-mannered request. I followed him. I wouldn't be fooled twice, though, and downed the last of my coffee before I joined them.

In the street, the proprietor looked agitated.

"You are Scotland Yard?" he asked.

"No, we are not," the Guv assured him. "But we are working with them on the same case."

The man looked from Barker to me and back again, curious.

"How clean are your cups, sir?" I asked.

"Everything is washed daily in very hot water," he stated forcefully. "And I drink the water every day, not to mention serving it in my coffee."

"No doubt," my partner said, stuffing one of his traveling pipes with tobacco. He lit a vesta against the side of the building to the owner's indignation. Then he cupped the match over the bowl and lit it. "It probably wasn't water this time, Thomas. More likely, something was put in his coffee."

"We do not poison our coffee here, sir!" the proprietor exclaimed, crossing his arms.

"No, but perhaps someone else did," Barker said. "We have an acquaintance who became ill after drinking your coffee. He might have gone to the counter and someone was brazen enough to drop something into his cup while it was unattended. The tables and chairs are so close together, a man need only reach out to drop something in another patron's cup."

"Wouldn't the gentleman have recognized the perpetrator, sir?" I asked the Guv in a low voice. "Presumably they knew one another."

"Thomas, look in the window there," the Guv ordered. "What do you see?"

I peered through the small window beside me. It was dim. The light came from outside.

"Black coats and hats, for the most part," I answered. "Everyone is anonymous."

"Precisely. If one went to the trouble to lower one's hat one might not be recognized."

"This is too much, gentlemen," the proprietor growled. "Large burly men such as yourself don't often come here. You are frightening the customers. You assume a man was poisoned here because he had visited our establishment? Where was he before? Where did he go after? He was not poisoned in the Old Vienna Coffeehouse, I assure you. Not by my coffee!"

"Did any of your patrons show signs of distress four days ago?" the Guv asked.

"Not to my knowledge," the man answered. "Nothing was reported to me."

Barker cocked his head. "Did anyone act suspiciously?"

The man frowned. "No, they did not. I do not allow misbehavior in my coffeehouse."

"But that day, it must have been crowded and most men are dressed in similar attire. Our client specifically told Scotland Yard he came here and became ill afterward."

"We do not fault your coffee, sir," I interjected. "It is marvelous. We believe one man entered your establishment with the intent of assaulting another. He hid his motives well. You could not have known."

"I don't want Scotland Yard gadflies in my establishment."

Barker puffed his pipe and nodded. "I'll be certain to tell them the next time I see them."

The man smiled as if certain he had driven us off successfully, then stepped inside again. The Guv turned, put his hands behind his back, and emitted a cloud of smoke. Then the proprietor jumped out at us again like a Jack-in-the-box.

"Wait," he called. "I just thought of something."

"Well?" the Guv demanded eagerly.

"I don't generally watch my customers, but I might notice a particular man if I have reason to. However, if two men came in together, I cannot watch them both. As it happens two men did come in together four days ago, and one of them was very distinctive, so that I didn't notice the other one. It could have been he."

"How was the first man distinctive, sir?" my partner asked.

"He was a priest," the man replied. "Young, with a dark beard."

"Excellent," Barker replied. "Thank you. You've been most helpful. Here is my card. If any more Yard men come in, give it to them and send them away with a flea in their ear. Come along, Thomas."

Barker turned and walked off, filling the air around us with smoke. I quickened my step to keep up with him.

"Interesting," he said as we walked along Tabard Street.

"What is interesting, sir?" I asked.

"Why did the third poisoning kill Fitzhugh when the first two did not?"

I shrugged. "I don't know."

"It wasn't rhetorical, man," he said, quickening his pace. "Think!"

"The first two attempts could have been warnings, I suppose," I reasoned. "Or the poison might have been too weak."

"Perhaps it might not have been poison, after all," Barker stated. "It could have been a drop or two of ipecac, enough to give one a stomachache or cramp, or to make one retch."

"To what end?" I asked.

"To herd him toward Scotland Yard and an unknown appointment with a small boy and a large tray."

"That's a lot of trouble," I answered. "Why not just poison him outright?"

"I can think of several reasons why," he rumbled. "Perhaps he hoped to see Fitzhugh choke and die in the gutter. Perhaps he wanted to establish an alibi. Or perhaps he enjoyed tormenting the poor fellow. It wasn't enough that Fitzhugh die. He wanted to be there to witness it. If so he must have been frustrated when our client stepped inside our chambers."

We walked along the pavement, passing a glove maker's, a boot shop, and a milliner.

"He knew his killer," I said, looking up at the Guv.

"Most certainly."

"And the man hated Fitzhugh enough to kill him."

"Or she did."

We turned the corner and the wind snatched away the smoke that encircled my partner's head. The dottle in the bowl looked like coal from a railway engine's firebox.

"You still believe it could be a woman?" I asked. "She'd be very conspicuous in a public inn."

"True," he replied. "But if it were a woman, she did not

approach him, she just put something into the pitcher or at least that is what I believe the poisoner did."

"And the coffee shop?" I asked.

Cyrus Barker stopped and turned on me so quickly I nearly walked into him.

"You see?" he chided. "He planned this meticulously. He followed him about without Fitzhugh even noticing. He hired the boy hours, perhaps days before Fitzhugh's inevitable death. He was sitting a few yards away at the Dove. He may have been at his very elbow at the Old Vienna. I believe the poisoner was standing across the street at Scotland Yard when Fitzhugh took the tart, then followed him all the way to our door in time to see him swallow it. Then Fitzhugh walked into our offices. That would have been disastrous for him and I still intend that it shall be."

"Do you suspect he was standing outside the Burkes' house when they died, as well?"

I tried to imagine it, but it was a grim thought.

Barker sniffed. "I think it possible, if not likely."

"He followed Fitzhugh before he killed him," I noted.

"Aye."

"Then he followed Tommy Burke to his home."

"Which means . . ."

I raised a brow. "Which means he might think Fitzhugh told us something before he died. Or even if he didn't, you might get enough information to take the case."

Cyrus Barker knocked the ash from his pipe. "Which means . . ."

"Which means he could be following us this very minute."

The Guv's mustache bowed in appreciation. "Very good, Thomas."

I turned and looked about. A man was delivering crates of produce to a restaurant. Another with a boutonniere passed us in a fashionable lounge suit that made me think of Oscar Wilde. A washerwoman collected laundry from a house across the street.

"I don't see anyone," I said.

Barker shook his head. "The poisoner knew we would be coming here today or perhaps tomorrow."

"He's ahead of us," I stated.

"He is, lad."

"How do we change that, sir?"

A cruel smile spread across his thin lips.

"Now there's an interesting question," he purred.

I was suddenly fully awake, fully alert, and it wasn't due to the coffee. I was waiting for someone to appear, a menacing figure. In a chef's hat? No, of course not. The Mad Pie Man was a myth created by the *Pall Mall Gazette* and others. In a cape like Mephistopheles, or a cloak and top hat like Jack the Ripper? Hardly. More likely he was the fellow delivering vegetables, or the woman with her washing.

Just then a storm began to rumble. It wasn't an ominous one, merely the late-summer kind that whips leaves into the air like a man tossing cards. Fat droplets of rain began to fall. My first instinct was to run under an awning, but just then a hansom cab rolled into my line of sight and without thinking, I sprinted to stop it. Cabs vanish like cubes of sugar in the rain, and I wasn't going to let this one pass. I was foolhardy enough to step into the path of the horses. I'll admit that sometimes my zeal gets ahead of my common sense. Obligingly the cabman strained at the reins and pulled the brake so that the cab was literally dragged the last few feet along the slick limestone setts of Tabard Street. He gave me a few choice words and I apologized, but to tell the truth I didn't much care about the opinions of an anonymous cabman when it was raining so hard. Barker climbed aboard and so did I.

A memory came unbidden then. Years before, on my first case, a cabman named Racket had tried to kill me. This cab today had appeared out of nowhere, as well. I had no reason to say with any certainty that this foulmouthed driver was following us with the intent to add us to his list of victims. More likely he wanted to find a cabman's shelter and wait for the storm to pass.

My partner did not sense anything untoward about the man, but he saw the tension of my body, which had much the same result. He pulled a pistol from his pocket and raised it so that when the cabman lifted the hatch to ask us where we were going, he found himself contemplating the barrel of a gun. The man jumped and began to curse again.

"The City," Barker growled, filling his coat pocket as readily as he had emptied it. "Twice the fare if you don't dawdle. And mind your mouth or I'll mind it for you."

A destination, a juicy fare, and a warning all in the span of two seconds. For once, the man had no rejoinder. I could see his mind turn over and it was the thought of the double fare that first floated to the surface.

"Right!" he shouted. I heard the whip crack overhead.

I fell back in the leather seat as the cab lurched into motion. "You really believe the killer is out there somewhere, watching us, perhaps following us?"

"Would you not in his shoes?" the Guv asked. "We are the closest to unmasking him."

I wagged a finger at him. "Now, now," I said. "Terry Poole might very well be ahead of us. He's got a dozen men at his call."

"Bright fellows one and all," my partner agreed.

"The best of Scotland Yard," I added. "So, tell me, what's in the City?"

"We're going to Whitechapel. If I'd said so he'd have cut up rough."

"He did cut up rough," I argued. "Very well, what's in White-chapel?"

"The White Chapel itself."

"The priest!" I cried. "Father, Father, Father . . ." I began flipping through my notes. "Father Michaels! That's the fellow. The clerk, Smoot, said he and Fitzhugh were mates."

"Aye, and who better to know a man than his best friend?"

I nodded. "And father confessor."

"Let us hope."

When one passes through Whitechapel from any direction or travels down Commercial Road, the chapel is so omnipresent that one might be forgiven for believing there were half a dozen of them. There's just the one, however, St Mary, built in the thirteenth century, not especially beautiful or grand, but sturdy and reliable when her congregation needed her.

Once there it took us over ten minutes to track down the priest. He had been in the vestry after a funeral had been hurried along by the storm. He was young but serious looking, with dark hair and eyes and a short beard. Tall, thin, almost cadaverous, in fact. He looked a prophet-in-training.

"What can I do for you, gentlemen?" he asked, hooking an old and faded stole around a very modern-looking hanger.

"We are working with Scotland Yard," the Guv said. "A Mr. Barnaby Smoot told us that you were well acquainted with the late Mr. Fitzhugh."

"Roland," he said with a pained expression. "Smoot is—was—his clerk. Yes, you could say I was well acquainted with Roland."

"I am Cyrus Barker, and this gentleman is my partner, Thomas Llewelyn. We are enquiry agents. Mr. Fitzhugh passed away in our offices."

"In Mr. Barker's arms, to be precise," I added.

"We need to know what sort of person he was," Barker continued. "It is germane to our investigation and may aid us in apprehending his murderer."

"He was the salt of the earth. A good man," Father Michaels said. "He was a member of the Temperance Society and the Men's Morality League. He spoke occasionally at rallies to encourage the younger generation."

"Were you aware that he married a decade ago?" the Guv asked, raising a brow.

"I was," the clergyman replied. "However, I'm afraid it was not a happy union. Apparently, his wife Alice had mental issues before they were married and they manifested themselves not long after the wedding, from what he's told me. He took her to the Continent to Baden-Baden, hoping to get her treatment, and when it failed, he was forced to put her in an asylum. From time to time, when she was lucid, he would bring her home, but he was always forced to take her back again."

"Poor fellow," I murmured.

Barker nodded. "Indeed," he said in his gravelly voice.

"She seemed to be getting better," Father Michaels said. "At one point, he thought it was safe enough to bring her home for Christmas. He wanted to mend the relationship, so he bought a fancy French wine and had a fine meal prepared to give her a treat. He was standing by the fire, trying to uncork the champagne, when she said, 'I've already got my drink, Roland.' She held out a goblet full of some sort of brownish liquid. Then, she toasts him, and pours the contents down her throat. And what do you think it was?"

We looked at him in wonder.

"Prussic acid, gentlemen," Father Michaels pronounced. "She drank the whole draught off in one. Killed her standing, it did."

"My word," I exclaimed.

The Guv and I looked at each other, thinking the same thing. Albert Mallock had said that Fitzhugh was the sort to make one want to top himself. I thought it was a rhetorical remark, but now I wondered.

"What happened afterward?" Barker asked.

"He came to the church to see me," the father replied. "It was how we met. He was in a bad way, but I helped him through a dark period of self-loathing. Eventually, he recovered from the trauma and as a successful barrister, was introduced to polite society. To my knowledge, he avoided any further entanglement with the fair sex. That is, until he met Gwendolyn Halton last year. It's my understanding that she encouraged him to run for office. I have not met her, but I hear she is a headstrong young woman."

"I believe you had coffee with him four days ago where he became ill," my partner continued. "Did Fitzhugh tell you he thought he was being poisoned?"

Father Michaels was sitting in a pew with his hands clasped between his knees as if he was cold. With his dark hair and beard, he reminded me of a rook.

"Good heavens, no!" he exclaimed. "I know he felt ill at the coffeehouse, but you're suggesting there were other attempts on his life?"

"I am," Barker concurred. "How was his health?"

"He complained of a stomach ailment, but he didn't claim he had been poisoned."

"Was he in good spirits?"

The father nodded. "Roland was in great spirits despite his indigestion. He was to be married in a fortnight and he was very much enjoying being the newest and youngest member of Parliament, where he felt he could do good for Shoreditch."

"You would say he was at the pinnacle of his life," my partner stated.

"Yes, I would," Father Michaels said, nodding. "He came through a terrible time, but he was focused on doing good for his community."

"Thank you, sir," Barker said. "It was a pleasure to meet you. We thank you for your time."

We had left the building and were a street away when he flagged a cab and called out "Chelsea," to the driver.

We climbed aboard and I furrowed my brow.

"Who is in Chelsea?"

"We are, lad, in about a quarter hour."

CHAPTER 10

"Where are we going, precisely?" I asked.

"The Chelsea Physic Garden," the Guv replied.

"We're visiting gardens now, in the middle of an investigation?" I grumbled.

"Poole gave me a list of suspects. We're going to see one now."

I'd heard of the garden before, or seen the sign in passing, but I couldn't tell you what the place was about.

"What is a physic garden, exactly?"

"It is a garden for growing medicinal plants," the Guv replied.

I don't know what makes people gardeners, though I've heard it said we are a nation of them. It was inexplicable to me. Gardeners toil in the hot sun all spring and summer, and then watch everything die in the fall before they begin again the following spring. Having been associated for the last ten years with a well-known garden, albeit a private one, I now saw the importance of creating such beauty, but I would never be induced to grow anything on my own. I had become a city man. Vegetables come from France and one purchases them at booths in Covent Garden. Why should one toil in the hot sun? Let the French do it.

We reached a street of brick walls and nondescript buildings along the Embankment. Most bore no indication of what their purpose was. A sign, which had once been claret red but had now faded into a rusty pink, hung over a doorway bearing the name Chelsea Physic Garden. We stepped inside the building, where plaques and bas-reliefs of famous gardeners lined the walls. The building was deserted and dusty. A set of open doors lit the lobby on one side and the light pouring in was so bright it hurt the eyes. When Barker and I stepped out into the sunlight, we raised our hands to block the sun.

The garden was far larger than I had anticipated, four acres in comparison to Barker's one half. Three men were working that I could see, but the garden looked overrun. Plants spilled over the banks of low brick walls built to keep them tidy. Flies and bees buzzed about while the gardeners perspired, loading barrows with an inexhaustible supply of flora. Cats lay about everywhere.

"We're closed, gentlemen!" one of the men called. He was sixty at least, with a short white beard, dark brows, and a misshapen Irish tweed cap. The man was as brown as a chestnut. He wore no jacket, and his sleeves were rolled to his elbows.

"Are you the curator?" Barker asked.

"Sorry," the man said, wiping the sweat from his brow. "The curator died five years ago, and they haven't got 'round to hiring a new one."

The Guv nodded. "Times are hard."

"What do you gentlemen want?" the man asked.

He held a hoe, trying to look menacing.

Barker cleared his throat. "I'm a patron of your garden, sir. I've sent several specimens here from my garden over the years."

The gardener snapped his fingers, remembering something.

"Orchids," he said. "*Galieris spectabilis*. You're Cyrus Barker."

"Yes, and the *Polystachya vulcanica*."

"Bless my soul, sir," he said. "I'd like to shake your hand. My name is Alf Chumley. I'm the caretaker."

"What has become of the place?" my partner asked. "The garden was flourishing when I visited ten years ago."

"People stopped caring about medicinal plants, I suppose," Chumley answered. "Mr. Thomas Moore, the last curator, became ill and people stopped contributing. He dropped dead right over yonder one day. I watched him fall. The place has been like this ever since."

"Such a pity," Barker replied. "Thomas, remind me to write a cheque when we return home."

The gardener looked a trifle skeptical. I'm certain he'd heard those words before.

"In fact," the Guv continued, "what is the largest note you carry?"

That was a new one to me. He'd never asked for anything that large before. I pulled the wallet out of my jacket pocket and extracted the note at the far end. It took a good bit of unfolding to see what denomination it was.

"A hundred pounds sterling, sir," I answered.

"Give it to Mr. Chumley," Barker said. "I'm certain he needs it more than we."

I handed it over and the gardener held it, blinking. A sudden breeze tore it from his hand and he chased after it, capturing it again a dozen yards away. He shoved it into his dirty trousers.

"Thank you, Mr. Barker," he said, twitching with wonder. "You don't know what this means to us. We can do good work with this money. Patronage is low. Everyone is going to Kew these days."

I cannot describe the amount of venom he put into the name of that famous institution.

"But you haven't come to give me money," he continued. "What can I do for you gentlemen?"

"I understand you have a small garden here," Cyrus Barker replied. "A specialized one."

"You must mean the Poison Garden, sir."

"I do."

"Come this way," he said, waving us along. "You've more than earned a tour."

We followed Chumley down a path. He was short, gnomelike, and walked with a limp. At the far end of the garden, I could hear the Thames lapping on the other side of the wall. The old man stopped and pointed proudly at a plot of land. More plants, I saw, looking much like all the others I'd just passed.

"What have we got here?" Barker asked. He leaned over, entranced. In fact, he was very nearly excited.

"Let's see," Chumley said. "We've got *Atropa belladonna*, *Brugmansia*, and laburnum. There's *Ricinus communis* and hemlock, right there, and this is *Strychnos nux-vomica*."

"There is foxglove on this side," the Guv continued. "Larkspur, oleander, and the humble poppy, *Papaver somniferum*, the scourge of the East. You have quite a collection here, Mr. Chumley. Who asked you to create such a garden?"

"Nobody did, Mr. Barker. I did it myself. Read about it in an old gardening book in the library. Sixteenth century, I mean. Thought I'd give it a try. Maybe people would come and see what I created, but you know, most of the plants are either in a regular garden or look like any other plant. Didn't draw anyone in, really, except for Scotland Yard."

"Were they here?" I asked, my ears pricking up.

One of an enquiry agent's tools is playing innocent and sympathetic. It draws out the speaker. Stating that you already knew something makes them go sullen and silent.

"They were," Chumley replied. "I think they'd have liked to clap darbies on us and shut down the whole garden. They asked if I ever was in jail and who I was working for, and why I work here for only a pittance. I just thought it was interesting work, and no one cares what we do here anymore."

"Did you provide an alibi for the time in question?"

"I did, sir. The constables took it down."

"Tell me," the Guv said. "Are you familiar with the name Roland Fitzhugh?"

The head gardener nodded vigorously. "Of course we knew him, Mr. Barker. He's the monster that put us out of business. Our late founder, Mr. Moore, intended to donate his fortune for the upkeep of the garden in perpetuity, but his sons and daughters saw differently. They hired Mr. Fitzhugh and who could we get? Ned's cousin is a lawyer of sorts. I say 'of sorts,' 'cause we didn't get a brass farthing. That was that. We're just limping along on subscription now. I expect we'll have to lock up the place permanently one of these days. Such a shame. It would have been such a nice garden when we're done."

"Could you use a half dozen more gardeners here?" Barker asked. "I have some that manage my own. They could come here at my request for a few days."

"Bless you, sir."

"Would it matter to you that they are Chinese?"

The man laughed, showing a few missing teeth. "Mr. Barker, they could be moon-people and I'd accept them."

"What would happen to you gentlemen if the Physic Garden shuts its doors?"

"Oh, we'd do all right. People need experienced gardeners. But it wouldn't be the same. This here is a labor of love. Isn't it, lads?" he asked, turning to his two fellows who were listening nearby. They were both as old as he. "A labor of love?"

They all agreed. They wore patched orange corduroy trousers in danger of falling apart and sprung boots to toil in their much-loved garden. For all that, they looked happy. They had the plants and the bees and the cats all to themselves. They had their feet in the mud and their hands in the soil. I'd have been happy for about a minute and a half in their shoes.

Barker had gone down on one knee looking at the plants, each of which had a stone carved with its Latin name to identify it.

"Do you lock the building at night?" he asked.

"Of course," Chumley said. "Had some boys tearing up the plants once. I open at six-thirty in the morning and close at six-thirty at night."

"Have you seen anyone lurking on the grounds or by the entrance?"

"Haven't," he said, shaking his head. "We don't get much traffic 'round here."

"What about lunch?" I asked. "Do you gentlemen eat together?"

"Sure, we go down to the Railway Arms around twelve," Chumley admitted.

"Do you lock the doors then?" the Guv asked.

"I don't see why we should. If we can't draw them in on a Saturday afternoon, we won't get them at one o'clock on a Monday. Anyway, why would someone break in and steal something if he can find it in any garden?"

"Perhaps for the satisfaction of knowing where it came from."

Chumley sat down by a yew tree and regarded us.

"Has someone else been poisoned?" he asked. "Was it that fellow Scotland Yard was after that killed that family? I hope they get that beggar proper, but if they're trying to arrest a harmless gardener, what good are they?"

The Guv stood. "Thank you for allowing us to view your fine gardens."

"Bless you, Mr. Barker," Alf Chumley said. "You are a proper gentleman, and we shall use the money wisely."

"Poor fellow," I said when we were back in the cab. "Working in a crumbling old building, practically alone, wishing a visitor would come along."

"Twelve hours of uninterrupted gardening every day?" my partner rumbled. "It sounds like paradise."

"Yes, sir," I said, smothering a sigh.

We had a visitor waiting when we arrived in our chambers. Gwendolyn Halton was in residence, the daughter of Sir Robert Halton and the former fiancée of the late Roland Fitzhugh. She wore a small bowler hat and a black coat with a collar of sable.

Barker entered our office and bowed to the young woman. She in turn put out her hand as if it were to be kissed. I was surprised when the Guv felt duty bound to take it. He squeezed it lightly and stepped back. It was an awkward exchange.

"Is this where he died?" she asked, surveying the room.

"It is, Miss Halton," the Guv replied. He pulled out the second visitor's chair and offered it to her and then went about the desk to his chair. She stared at the Persian carpet as if it were stained with Fitzhugh's blood.

"Tell me what happened," she ordered.

Barker gave her an abbreviated version of the truth, leaving out the part where he was beating on her fiancé's chest.

"I demand to know who killed Roland and why," she said, gripping her reticule in her gloved fingers.

"Mr. Llewelyn and I would like to know that as well," Cyrus Barker intoned. "We have been retained to find the perpetrator."

"May I offer you an incentive to work faster, or allow you to hire more men to work with you?"

The Guv gave a frosty smile. "Thank you. I require no extra incentive, nor do I require any help."

She raised a brow. "Then why haven't you caught whoever murdered my fiancé?"

"Because the man who committed this crime is one of four million people in this City and will do all he can to remain free. However, we are experienced man hunters. We are in the business of finding men who do not wish to be found. I believe we shall soon discover who killed your fiancé."

There was a furrow between Miss Halton's pretty blue eyes. She was having trouble trying to understand what the Guv was about. I wished her luck. I'd been trying for ten years so far and had made little headway.

Gwendolyn Halton was of the blond ringlets school. She looked every inch the coddled daughter. I found myself wondering what she saw in a middle-aged barrister, MP though he was.

"May I ask you a few questions, if it will help us find Mr. Fitzhugh's murderer?" Cyrus Barker asked, leaning back in his chair and tenting his fingers.

She looked at him suspiciously, then intrigued. "What sort of questions?"

"Did he ever speak about his past?" the Guv asked from the interior of his green leather chair.

"Not a good deal, no," she replied. "I know he was married once, but he didn't like to talk about it. The subject was painful to him. I gather the girl was ill. Mentally, I mean."

"Do you have any idea why he was poisoned or who was trying to poison him? Had he made enemies among his constituents or acquaintances?"

"Of course not," she snapped. "Roland had a sterling character. You should speak to Father Michaels at St Mary. He will vouch for him entirely. No one who knew him could ever hate him or wish him ill."

"Were you aware Mr. Fitzhugh believed he had been poisoned recently?" the Guv asked.

"Poisoned?" she exclaimed. "Do you mean he believed he had been poisoned before yesterday? He did tell me he was ill a few days ago, but I thought it was indigestion."

"It was more than indigestion, I assure you."

"I'm certain you are wrong. I believe you are an inferior fellow,

Mr. Barker," she said with a cold look. "I don't know why anyone hired you."

Ah, I thought. The kitten has claws.

"That is your right, Miss," he answered, not taking offense.

"I think I'll speak to Mr. Lindsay about what sort of ruffians he hires," she continued. "You are really most unsuitable."

"You are not the first to believe so, Miss Halton, and I'm certain you shall not be the last," Barker said. "And yet our ruffianly business prospers. However, you should know that Mr. Lindsay did not hire us. Your fiancé did. His last words were 'Help me.'"

"I knew it!" she said, as if she had tricked us into walking into a trap. "You are trying to worm your way into a false investigation, which will no doubt come with an exorbitant bill. I've heard of schemes like this."

She leaned forward and glared at the Guv, attempting to bend him to her will. She was the kind of girl who rarely hears the word "no."

"Anyway, I believe you have invented this odious plot," Gwendolyn Halton hissed.

The Guv shrugged his beefy shoulders. "I cannot help what you believe, Miss."

A pale pink spot appeared on each of her cheeks. He was vexing her. I enjoyed watching him do it. In fact, I thought it time I might try it myself. After all, she was insulting my agency as much as his.

"Wait," I said, as if it just occurred to me. "Are you the daughter of Sir Charles Halton?"

Barker looked at me. I gazed at the girl, who broke out in a full flush and turned to the Guv again.

"Halton's Throat Drops," I said. "Mint or lemon."

The girl frowned. I had uncovered her secret: she was a tradesman's daughter. He was an incredibly wealthy tradesman, who had become a lord and exported his goods throughout the empire, but a tradesman nonetheless. I imagined most of her friends were higher born than she and it rankled, though her father could have purchased their estates with the stroke of a pen. London society is a cutthroat business.

"I've used your father's drops," I continued. "I find them very soothing when my throat is sore. You must be proud of your father. He's a great man, and a benefactor to us all."

She jumped to her feet. "I—I've said all I will say in this matter. You shall hear from Gerald, my brother. He is a solicitor. I will instruct him to box your nose."

I looked at the Guv, and he at me.

"Which one of us?" I asked, all innocence.

"The choice is yours."

"Mr. Llewelyn," Barker spoke up, no doubt seeing an argument about to commence. "Be a gentleman and see Miss Halton to a cab. We'll be in touch, Miss Halton."

"Of course, sir," I said, standing. "Miss Halton, thank you for sharing your concerns with us. I assure you we'll take them to heart."

She made no comment and sailed out the door into Whitehall Street, jumping when I whistled for the cab. She wouldn't accept my hand to help her up into the hansom when it slowed. When she left, I returned to the office. I'd have wiggled my brows at Jeremy Jenkins, but he was already off at the Guv's bidding.

CHAPTER 11

We had a late lunch at the Clarence public house, good beef off the joint between slices of crusty bread. I took a drink of my ale and watched as the Guv devoured the pickled onions of which he was so fond. We were hungry after the long morning and did justice to the meal.

"Who is next on the list that Terence Poole gave us?" I asked, pushing back my chair, and wished I had time to sit and digest my meal.

"An herbalist," Barker replied. "Mrs. Zinnia Elder. Five years ago she did a stint in Holloway for murder."

"What happened?" I asked.

"She was responsible for a woman's death," he explained. "She made a sort of tisane, pennyroyal tea, which is, in effect, a sort of poison. Abortionists use pennyroyal oil for unwanted pregnancies. It's sometimes effective, but it is a very dangerous and painful treatment. I could imagine a delicate woman succumbing to it quickly."

"I suppose Fitzhugh was the prosecuting attorney," I postulated. "Or her name wouldn't be on the list."

"Very good, Mr. Llewelyn," the Guv said. "The woman lives in Peckham."

"Deep south, then. Barely London at all, really."

"I did not expect an herbalist to live in Threadneedle Street," he replied. "Let us go pay a visit."

The Underground is comprised of a half dozen railway companies competing for right-of-way. The lines had grown to the extent that they could take a man or a woman anywhere in London, even to the wild frontiers of Peckham.

When we arrived, we spoke to a ticket seller who pointed us in the direction of Fordham Street, a distance of a mile or more in the hot afternoon sun. There were no cabs here, only shoe leather. Unfortunately, an enquiry agent cannot pick and choose his suspects.

We passed by a cluster of shops and houses that I assumed was the core of the village. Then we came upon Fordham Street, which consisted of houses with outbuildings and stables. As we approached Mrs. Elder's address, I could see a couple of makeshift buildings cobbled together from scrap materials and odd window frames, which had been painted green for a harmonious effect. A yew hedge surrounded the property with shrubbery and trees inside it. Somewhere I heard wind chimes and then a rooster. This was rural, indeed.

When we reached the gate a lazy tom sitting in a basket chair on the porch began to bawl, as if announcing our presence. An attractive woman came out of the house drying her hands on a tea towel. She wore a floral apron over a blue dress and had a cloth tied over her blond hair. She watched us cautiously. I'm certain she wondered why two men in black suits and bowler hats should come out here afoot. I wondered the same, myself.

"Can I help you gentlemen?" she asked, eyeing us.

"Mrs. Elder, I am Cyrus Barker," the Guv said. "And this is

my partner, Thomas Llewelyn. We are private enquiry agents aiding Scotland Yard in a case."

"They were here yesterday making accusations," she replied archly. "Trying to blacken my name, as if it could be blackened any further."

"We're here to ask a few questions. That's all," I said. "The quicker we can cross your name from the Yard's list of suspects, the quicker we can find the person who poisoned Mr. Roland Fitzhugh. Are you familiar with the name?"

"You know I am, or you would not be here," the woman answered. She turned to the cat. "Solomon, shut it!"

The cat stopped mewling, turned away and went to sleep, having earned his keep for the day.

Mrs. Elder turned back to us. "I've seen your names. He died in your offices, didn't he?"

"He did," Barker said.

"Cyanide," she said. "At least it's quick. He would have had to take it shortly before he reached your offices."

"The poison was found in a sample of food he was given in the street by a vendor."

"Won't you gents come inside?" she said. "It's cool and I have the kettle on."

We followed her into the house. It was a jumble of furniture covered in shawls and there were tables littered with bric-a-brac. Plants of all sizes and types hung upside down from the ceiling, drying. I saw the Guv stiffen then continue on. What made him pause, I wondered? Then I saw it myself. There was a large black book on the table with the title *Grand Grimoire* and a candle half melted next to a small figure made out of straw. Just then the cat jumped on the top of the chair beside me and stared at us. He was black and his eyes were a harvest orange. Oh, my word, I thought. We were in the home of a witch. The woman caught my eye and smiled.

"Have a seat, gentlemen," she said. "I'll pour the tea."

I sat in a chair across from the Guv and looked about. At my elbow was an Egyptian scarab next to a glazed clay ankh. While I shifted uncomfortably in my seat, the woman poured boiling water into a blue teapot. It looked completely safe, but of course, one never knows.

Mrs. Elder looked me directly as she gave me the porcelain cup. "It's rosehip. I grow it myself."

I prefer my tea made in the Far East and blended by Mr. Thomas Twining. I certainly would not care to drink any concoction made by this woman.

Barker took the proffered cup and downed it in one gulp as I had seen him do at home. It was scalding, but he seemed to take no notice.

"Well, well, Mr. Barker," she chuckled. "You are a brave man to swallow my offering so cavalierly."

"Not at all, madam," he replied. "If I fall over dead, Mr. Llewelyn is instructed to take matters in hand."

The cup still sat in front of me. I stared inside it doubtfully.

"You strike me as a pious man, Mr. Barker," she observed. "Mr. Llewelyn appears more worldly."

"Aye, madam," he said, holding his cup out for more. "But we have high hopes for him."

Zinnia Elder refilled his cup, then sat down and folded her hands in her lap. They were a farm woman's hands. "You have questions for me, I believe."

"Most refreshing," the Guv said after he had downed his second cup. "As I said, we want to find the identity of the person who killed Roland Fitzhugh. You may be able to shed light on the matter."

"How do I know you won't abuse the privilege, sir?" she asked. "You have no reason to be lenient with the likes of me."

"I give you my word, madam," Barker answered. "We are only after the truth. If you did not kill Roland Fitzhugh, you have no reason to be concerned."

"I have plenty of concerns, Mr. Barker," she answered. "Very well. What questions do you have for me?"

"Were you acquainted with Mr. Fitzhugh?"

"I was not," she stated. "Not until I faced him in court."

As he questioned her, I watched the expressions on her face change. Her eyes were green and there was a spray of freckles on her cheeks. She was perhaps five and thirty. I was faintly disappointed. I didn't expect a pagan to look so normal. Still, I was just taking impressions.

"Do you travel into London often?" the Guv continued.

The woman rose and took down a jar. She removed the lid and arranged some biscuits on a plate, gingerbread figures in the shape of children.

"You are enjoying this at my expense, madam," I said.

She smiled and looked at my partner. "Every Saturday I have a stall in Covent Garden. I also deliver my teas and crafts to a few shops in the area. I must have several occupations in order to keep the wolf from my door."

"Including abortionist?" Barker asked.

I thought he expected a reaction from her, but she merely sipped her tea.

"I don't midwife anymore," she replied after a moment, setting down her cup. "I lost three years of my life that way. But you should know I am visited every month by women begging me to help them. Men can't understand. They only moralize."

"What was the name of the woman who died?" the Guv asked.

"Ellie Flanders," she answered. "A dear young thing. She was married, you know, and already with child. She would dearly have loved to have it but she had a weak heart. Her doctor said there was no hope of her carrying it to term. In his opinion, she was done for. If she were lucky, the baby would survive, but she wouldn't have had a chance. I told her the pennyroyal tea would as soon kill her as give her the results she wanted, but she said she was going to die either way, so what did it matter?" Mrs. Elder shook her head.

"The choice was hers. As it turned out, she was right, but the punishment fell to me."

Barker sighed.

"What say you to that?" she challenged.

"I am not your judge, Mrs. Elder," he said. "But a person does not do evil because they think it is evil. They do so because they believe it is good."

She gave him a searching look. "You are a philosopher, Mr. Barker."

"Have you any poisons here?" I asked.

"Arsenic is hanging right over your head, sir," she replied.

I looked up and saw flypaper strips swaying in the breeze like ribbons.

"Do you think that boiling a strip of flypaper would kill a man?" I asked.

"One strip?" she replied. "That's hard to say. If it were reduced over a stove, most definitely."

She poured Barker the last of the tea. I had not touched mine.

Barker leaned forward in his chair. "What about arsenic?"

"Oh, you're talking about that poor family," she said, shaking her head. "That's why my name is on the Yard's list. Them I did know. That boy, little Tommy? A beautiful child. I was his midwife. Do you have any more questions? I need to get back to my work."

"Just one," I spoke up. "Do you bake little Hansels and Gretels just to frighten visitors?"

Zinnia Elder threw back her head and laughed. "Very well, Mr. Llewelyn. I confess. I do like to watch people's faces when they see them. Try one. They won't poison you. I grow my own ginger."

I declined the offer.

"No?" she said. "Very well, suit yourself. Mr. Barker?"

He lifted one of the biscuits from the tray and bit the tyke's head off.

"I don't generally enjoy sweets," he remarked, "but I must admit I am fond of an occasional bit of gingerbread. It's obvious the ginger is fresh."

"It's nice to have my work appreciated," she said. "And to have company. You're ever so much more polite than the peelers."

"I am pleased to hear it," Barker replied. "Though I can outstrip them if I am crossed."

He finished the final sip of his tea and stood.

"You see, I have been honest," she said, "as I believe have you. I poisoned that girl, but at her insistence after a strong warning and I did not intend for her to die. She was a sweet thing in a terrible bind. She left behind a heartbroken young husband. I haven't seen Fitzhugh since my sentencing. I don't know who poisoned him, but I am sure there are many who wanted to."

The Guv raised his hat. "Come, Thomas. This woman should be getting back to her business."

We walked through the gate and out into the chalky road. When we were a few hundred yards away I began to increase my pace.

"A witch," I said. "We saw a real witch! You know, I think I saw a broom standing in a corner."

"Spare me, Mr. Llewelyn."

"I never expected this when we arrived. An herbalist-midwife-witch! Those are occupations out of the seventeenth century."

"I'll take your word for it," he said with a patient air.

"I expected you to come down on her head with blood and thunder, but you were very polite."

"I came to question her, not to put her in the dunking chair. Civility is its own reward."

"I suppose it is."

"She seems a canny woman, which she has to be to do what she does. She is better educated than I expected. I noticed a good-sized bookcase. Some titles were unsavory reading, but I believe I saw philosophy and even a Bible."

"A witch with a Bible?" I asked.

"All the same, she bears watching. I'm not going to believe she stopped being a midwife based on her assertions. Mr. Chumley might be able to grow oleander, but only Mrs. Elder knows how to turn it into a tisane."

"I thought you were going to fall over dead from all the tea you drank," I remarked.

"If I had, I knew you would arrest her. I also knew you wouldn't touch the tea. You only drink coffee."

"Do you really think she's a witch? I mean, does she practice and study it? Is she part of a coven? Is witchcraft even real?"

"It's fortunate that you became an enquiry agent, Mr. Llewe-lyn," the Guv said. "You ask more questions per hour than any man I've met."

CHAPTER 12

The telephone was ringing in our offices when we returned. All my muscles tightened. Such calls rarely bring good news to the offices of private enquiry agents. At best they are from prospective clients seeking help. At worst? Let us merely say that each of us had received very ill news from that slender stalk of painted brass, even Jenkins. I had stood beside him when London Hospital broke the news to him that his beloved father had died.

As the set jangled, Barker and I glanced at each other. I lifted the receiver to my ear and cleared my throat.

"Barker and Llewelyn Agency," I said.

"Hello, darling!" Rebecca chirped into the telephone, sounding as happy and energetic as always. I instantly felt better. The sun broke through the dark clouds, so to speak, and began to shine.

"Rebecca!" I exclaimed. "How is your day so far?"

"Oh, well enough," she answered. "My sister and I are at our parents. I suspect I'll be a little late."

"Of course," I replied.

When we ended the call, I put the receiver back in its cradle and looked at Barker a trifle sheepishly. I could have chatted for ten minutes and given her an expurgated version of my day if the Guv were not five feet away, glowering at me. I'd have flirted with her as well, but one does not do so beside a man whose Chinese name means Stone Lion. The Guv was aptly named. Canny people, the Chinese.

"Mrs. Llewelyn is stopping at her parents' house," I stated for his benefit.

"Ah," he said, and no more.

At five-thirty Jenkins took himself off to the Rising Sun Public House. He'd had a stimulating day with a new lurid murder printed on the cover of his crime journals. He worked in an enquiry office and yet murder was still something he read about in the press. I noticed he hung back when Roland Fitzhugh choked out the last few seconds of his life. Perhaps a death on the premises had been all too real.

"Cab or Underground, sir?" I asked the Guv.

"The day is still fine," he answered. "The Underground will do."

I locked the door behind us and we headed north toward Charing Cross Station. There were advantages and disadvantages to the Underground. We avoided being caught in Whitehall traffic at six o'clock, when it was often at a veritable standstill, but we were crammed into passenger carriages where seats were hard to come by and one was often shaken about from one turnout to the next. Hansom cabs were a misery when it was raining, but on the other hand, it was several streets from the Elephant and Castle Station to our home. There was no clear advantage. Quite often I wished we had chosen the other.

When we reached Lion Street, I was ready to sit down with a good book. I thought I might raid the larder for one of Etienne's bacon tarts and take it upstairs to pick up where I left off with my Wilkie Collins. It was reminiscent of my bachelor days.

As I entered the house, something brought me up short. A body lay prone on the tile floor of the hall. I made a strangled cry in my throat.

"Mac!" I shouted, as I realized who it was.

I ran to him, Barker at my heels. Jacob was lying facedown on the runner, motionless, possibly even dead. There was no blood on the floor and no obvious sign of a struggle. Gently, Barker and I rolled him over. The Guv pulled his watch from his pocket and seized Mac's wrist.

"I can't get a steady beat," he growled after half a minute. "See if Dr. Applegate is at home, and then call the Priory for an ambulance."

That was our recourse when one of us was severely injured, which happened more often than I would like to admit.

The Priory of St John was another charity indebted to Barker, and there was always a bed there for him should he be injured. It is not a hospital open to the public, but it did have an ambulance service, the first in London. I called the number and delivered the message.

"They're coming," I told the Guv. "The evening traffic might slow the ambulance a bit, I think."

Jacob's face was pale and waxen. His lips were blue and drawn together. His suit was rumpled, and it was startling to see him in such a disheveled state. I knew he would hate to be seen looking anything but elegant.

Mac and I had not always gotten along. At first, we did not warm to each other, but now we were like brothers of a sort. We'd played pranks on each other, made caustic remarks at the other's expense, and did whatever we could to embarrass the other in front of Barker. However, we pulled together when there was an emergency. Dr. Applegate arrived first. Like most surgeons, he can be a bit brusque.

"What was his pulse when you found him?" he demanded, dropping to one knee next to Mac's unconscious form.

"It's been erratic," Barker replied.

Applegate opened one of Mac's eyes and then smelled his breath. Our visitor pulled a scalpel from the bag and in one smooth movement cut Mac's clothing from chin to waist. He sliced through his collar, his Liberty tie, his Savile Row waistcoat of green and silver as well as his shirt. I shuddered when I saw it. Most of Mac's salary went toward clothing, although I knew he supported his parents, as well. When he woke he would be scandalized and angry at being shriven of his waistcoat and his dignity. Then I wondered if he would wake up at all.

"His heart is racing," Applegate muttered. "It could give out at any moment. Is he prone to suicide? Was he currently taking any medication?"

He received a negative reply for both.

"Mr. Barker, it appears your servant has ingested something dangerous, a poison or a drug." He stood and turned squarely toward us. "I cannot be certain which. He is gravely ill. He may not survive the evening. Whether it is an attempted murder or an accident, Scotland Yard must be called."

The ambulance arrived ten minutes later. Applegate gave the driver instructions and then took his leave. Two men brought the stretcher out to the vehicle and lifted Jacob into the back. Then the driver made a clicking sound with his tongue and a pair of horses pulled the ambulance away slowly on its rubber tires.

Barker and I returned to the house, and I locked the door behind us. We went into the front room and sat. Suddenly he turned and looked about. "Where's Harm?"

We rushed into the library where the dog's bed had been made up on the floor. Harm opened his jet-colored eyes to look at us and his tail twitched slightly. Then he closed them again.

"He's been drugged," I said.

Barker knelt by his beloved Pekingese, holding his palm over the top of his head as if checking for a fever.

"I need a cab at once," he declared. "I'm taking him to Bok Fu Ying and then I will meet you at the Priory."

Fu Ying was Barker's ward until her marriage. She regularly took Harm for her former guardian to groom and care for him. If anyone could help the poor fellow now, it was she.

I nodded and called a cab for my partner. When it arrived, he left carrying Harm in a blanket. The first year I had known him, he was fond of sinking his teeth into the bare flesh of my ankles, but over time, we had developed a truce, he and I. Before I married Rebecca, I often found him at the foot of my bed at night. I didn't want the poor beast to suffer.

I was still standing in front of the house when Rebecca arrived. I helped her from the cab.

"Darling, we just sent Mac to the hospital. We found him collapsed on the floor."

Her hand went to her throat. "What happened? Was he shot?"

"We believe he was poisoned."

The color drained from her face. "We have to go to him."

I stopped the cab before it had gone ten feet and we alighted again. Once inside, she clutched my arm. "I'm frightened, Thomas. I don't want Jacob to die. I've known him since we were children. It's unthinkable! Is this because of a case?"

I don't always tell Rebecca about every client or situation. Some are dull and others too distressing to share. Still others are private, or we are restricted from telling anyone because it is a state secret. But now that tragedy had followed us home, she had to know. I informed her about what had happened since Mr. Fitzhugh had walked into our offices. Well, almost everything.

"You really think Jacob was poisoned?" she asked.

"Something happened to him," I said. "Applegate says to prepare for the worst."

My wife raised a gloved hand to her face.

"As bad as that?" she asked. "No, that would be too cruel."

I wanted to tell her that in my opinion there was nothing too cruel in London, but it would only distress her to see me so nihilistic.

Rebecca suddenly jumped in her seat. "Sarah! We didn't tell Sarah!"

Sarah Fletcher was a so-called "lady detective," having only female clients apart from the times we hired her services ourselves. Her offices were above ours and she let it from the Guv. Miss Fletcher and Mac had become close over the past year. I wasn't certain if there was an understanding between them. They were both private people, so I gave them their privacy.

"And what of his parents?" she continued. "You must take me to the Priory and then go and get his parents and Sarah as well."

Delivering bad news was the last thing I wanted to do that evening, but it had to be done. I left her at the door of the Priory and went to the City where Mac's parents lived. They were a lovely old couple, a matched set, Mr. Maccabee with a small, pointed mustache and Mrs. Maccabee with spectacles clipped to her nose. They were devastated by the news. Jacob's father said they would go to the Priory in their own vehicle, leaving me to find Miss Fletcher. Half an hour later, I was knocking at the door at Number 5, beside our offices.

After a few moments, an electric light was switched on above my head and Miss Fletcher came down the stair.

"You must come at once!" I called through the glass pane. "Jacob is in hospital. He has been poisoned!"

She opened the door immediately. Sarah Fletcher is a plain, no-nonsense sort of girl, but it was clear the news alarmed her.

"Poisoned!" she repeated. "How? Where is he? Tell me he is alive!"

"He is, but only just," I replied. "He was collapsed in the hall when we arrived home. We called a surgeon to attend him and put him into an ambulance wagon. They took him to St John's Priory. Rebecca said I must bring you at once."

Miss Fletcher paused, took in all that I had said, and nodded. "Give me a minute to get my shawl."

With that, she turned and mounted the stair. I returned to the cab and she joined me a few minutes later, in her customary boater hat and shawl, clutching a small reticule. She climbed into the vehicle beside me.

"Now, Mr. Thomas Llewelyn," she ordered. "You must tell me everything you know about how and why Jacob is in hospital, and I promise you, if you leave one thing out because it is a secret or to spare my feelings, you will not live to regret it."

I'd have laughed if I didn't completely believe her threat to be real.

"Very well, Miss Fletcher, but I will not offer you any conclusions. Those you must supply for yourself."

She looked at me with those small, fierce eyes of hers.

"Done," she said.

CHAPTER 13

When we entered the Priory, Miss Fletcher and Rebecca promptly stuck to each other like a pair of magnets. I slid into one of the wooden chairs next to Barker. He was leaning forward with his feet splayed and his elbows on his knees.

"Has there been any change?" I asked.

"Not so far," he answered, "but Applegate has determined what Mac was given. It was digitalis."

"Digitalis?" I asked. "I thought that was medicine."

"It is, but as Lucretius said, 'What is food to one man may be fierce poison to others.'"

"Poor Mac," I said, shaking my head. "I wonder how it happened."

"I don't know," the Guv admitted. "But this was no accident, Thomas. Fitzhugh came to our office and was poisoned, then the Burke family was attacked the following morning because

Tommy Burke could identify the killer, and now Mac. It is not coincidental. Someone means us mischief."

A half hour later, a young doctor came down the hall and gestured for Barker and I to follow him. Miss Fletcher gave us a sour look. We were led to a private room with granite walls that I suspected had once been a monk's cell, to find Mac lying in an iron bed. He wore a frayed nightshirt that he would never knowingly don, and he was still unconscious.

"I'm Dr. Peterson," he said. "I'm afraid your friend is gravely ill. His heartbeat is erratic. It may take days for the digitalis to leach from his system and I cannot assure you that the heart will return to its regular rhythm afterward. It is possible that Mr. Maccabee will be an invalid from now on and unable to fulfill his duties."

That was an unexpected blow. Even Barker appeared shaken.

"What can we do?" the Guv asked.

"This is not a convalescent hospital," the doctor replied. "I suggest you move him to a sanitarium down south in a few days. A view of the sea and fresh air is sometimes invigorating. I could recommend one or two I've used in the past. Eastbourne has several."

"Thank you, Doctor," Barker said, without emotion. I knew he had them, but he guards them carefully.

The doctor turned and left. Barker did not move for a full minute, as solid and silent as a statue. I held my breath. Finally, he spoke.

"Mr. Llewelyn, let us say you are besieging a castle," he said, turning to me. "What would be your first move?"

I hated it when he posed questions like that, as if he were a schoolmaster and I the troublesome student caught out again.

"Catapults?" I ventured.

"Very well," he said, nodding. "Directed at whom?"

"The guards, I suppose."

"Why would you do so?" he persisted.

"So they could not alert the castle, and to render them unable to fight back," I said. "A siege nearly always succeeds."

"Very good, Thomas," the Guv replied. "Our poisoner has felled our guards, Mac and even Harm, who has been drugged. It could have happened an hour ago, or even five. If it is the latter, there is no telling what he may have done to the house. Our castle is vulnerable. We are all in danger."

"You mean he would have dared enter the house? What shall we do, sir?" I asked.

"We cannot return to Lion Street tonight, Thomas," he replied. "We shall spend the night in Mrs. Ashleigh's town house in Holland Park."

"Is that necessary, sir?"

"You understand the gravity of the situation, don't you?" Barker continued. "The killer, whoever he or she is, wanted Mr. Fitzhugh dead and to cover their tracks, to the point that an entire family was murdered in the most horrible way. We are a loose end, and someone holds the scissors. This person does not care about Mac's involvement in this any more than he thought about Tommy Burke's family. The purpose is to stop the investigation. Do you understand?"

"I do."

"No, Thomas," he argued, pacing in front of me. "I don't think you do. Our poisoner could have been in our home for hours. Everything inside is forfeit. If the assailant has access to more poisons, there is no telling what is in our residence right now. We cannot go back. Our entire home has been compromised."

"You don't believe you are exaggerating the danger, sir?" I asked. "I mean, goodness knows how Mac ingested the digitalis but it has not killed him. It is a stretch of the imagination to think that the Pie Man, or whatever you choose to call him, has decided to kill us all. Who is to say he has even heard of us?"

"I wish that it were merely coincidence, Thomas, but Harm was clearly drugged. Laudanum, I'd say. His pupils were dilated.

As for digitalis, it is extracted from foxglove. Its medicinal purpose is to regulate the heart, but an overdose can be fatal. There
is no other way Mac would have come in contact with it save by a
deliberate attack. I think it likely it was put into his tea. I had the
misfortune once to mistake his cup for my own. The amount of
cream and sugar he puts into his cup would choke an elephant.
It is an insult to the leaves themselves. They were picked on a
mountainside and went through a dozen processes merely to be
drowned in a saccharine sludge."

"But what are we to do?" I asked him, turning over the question in my mind.

Barker considered the matter as well, crossing his arms and
looking at himself in the mirrored gloss of his shoe.

"I will not let go of this matter until I find the man who killed
Roland Fitzhugh. I promised to help him, and I shall. I will not
lay down my client's request until I find his killer, no matter how
long it takes, no matter what obstacle is thrown in my path, and if
I die, I expect you to take this case with as much seriousness as I."

"I will, sir," I stated. "You need have no concern on that score."

"He has invaded my house," the Guv continued. "And he will
pay for it."

"What shall we do, then?" I asked. "Must we go through the
rooms one by one?"

"There seems no other way, I'm afraid, but there's a man I
know who specializes in that sort of thing. I'll send him a message tonight."

"What about Etienne?" I asked.

It occurred to me that our cook was coming the following
morning. He would be in a towering rage if someone had touched
his pristine kitchen.

"Aye, I've been worried about the same thing," the Guv replied. "I'll get a message to him, as well. In this case, I don't believe there is any way to stop the tempest but to batten the hatches
and endure."

"He'll have apoplexy, but then, he hasn't had a good tantrum in months," I said. "So, tell me about this fellow you mentioned."

"You'll meet him yourself tomorrow, Thomas," Barker replied. "At the moment, you need to tell Mrs. Llewelyn we will spend the night at Lady Ashleigh's London home. I'm not certain the house on Camomile Street is safe, either. Be vigilant. For all we know, we may be in danger in these very halls."

I nodded and returned to the waiting room to see my wife.

"Let's go to the café on the corner," I said, offering my arm. "We need a few minutes to ourselves."

I looked up and found Miss Fletcher staring at me. She did not frown, however, and a moment later looked away. A brother of the Order of St John came by then and she jumped to her feet and followed him. I knew she wouldn't stop until she had seen Mac for herself.

Rebecca and I walked under an ancient arch onto Camberwell Road and went inside a nearby tearoom. There were few patrons, and we found a table in a quiet corner.

"What's happening, Thomas?" she finally asked after we had been seated.

"Mr. Barker believes the house in Lion Street is too dangerous for us to stay there," I said.

"Does he?" she asked.

I nodded. "He thinks the poisoner has been in the house. Mac was poisoned somehow. And while he generally keeps the front door locked, the back door isn't because Harm goes in and out all day."

Her large brown eyes grew wide. "You mean he simply strolled in the back door and poisoned Mac?"

"That's right."

Rebecca looked troubled. "He could have gone into our rooms, as well?"

I nodded. "I'm afraid so. We don't keep them locked during the day."

"Someone could go through our drawers and wardrobes?" she persisted.

"This person is not a voyeur," I answered. "He's a murderer."

She frowned again. "He could have put poison in our rooms, then? But, how?"

I shrugged my shoulders. "I don't know. I certainly wouldn't eat anything from the kitchen again. I wouldn't trust your perfume or lotions, either."

"Why not?" she asked. "I won't be drinking them."

"He's already used at least three poisons so far. Some poisons are externally toxic. Remember last year when poison ivy sprung up in your rose garden? Your hands were so swollen, you couldn't hold anything for days."

"But how will we know when the house is safe again?" she said, clearly agitated.

"Barker's bringing in a fellow tomorrow," I said. "Some kind of expert who will go through the house from stem to stern."

She folded her arms and arched a brow. "More men going through my private things. Surely this monster is not coming after me. I've done nothing to deserve his wrath."

"Neither did the Burke family," I reminded her. "And neither did Mac. I believe that whoever poisoned the tea—if that's what Mac ingested—did it because he was trying to kill Barker. You could as easily have drunk it in his place. This poisoner is not discriminating. In fact, I suspect he enjoys the mayhem he causes."

"Even Mr. Barker hasn't done anything beyond looking about and asking a few questions," she said, throwing down a spoon in anger.

She was upset. If we had been at home and not in a public place, she would have stood and begun to pace about the room.

"Why?" she asked, shaking her head. "Why do you go out and deliberately hunt down the worst sort of people? No sooner do you bring one to Scotland Yard than another arrives on our doorstep. Quite literally, in this case! What was that quip you made the other day?"

"'A policeman's wife is not a happy one.'"

"Precisely!" she said. "But even a policeman doesn't have to worry about his tea in the morning. Mr. Barker seeks out these fellows. He thrives on the danger, I think."

"He's got a knack for it," I said.

"I think it more a curse," she replied. "His eagerness to hunt after the most sensational cases verges on obsession. Thomas, I promised I would not insist you find other work. I know what working for Mr. Barker has meant to you, and I must say he pays well. I'm also not saying you can't be a detective—"

"Private enquiry agent," I said.

She stopped and pinched the bridge of her nose. "I'm saying you could find work at Scotland Yard as a CID man. I imagine Commissioner Munro would hire you in a trice and be glad to have you."

That made me smile.

"You don't know the commissioner," I said.

"Very well," she answered, heaving a great sigh. "Be obstinate. But if I keel over one morning between the cream and the sugar, you have only yourself to blame."

"You want us to move to the City permanently and live in Camomile Street," I stated. "That's what you mean."

"It isn't that far away," she said. "And with the Underground you can be at the Elephant and Castle in ten minutes. We have a telephone. It's not as if 'the Guv' would have to send a messenger. You'd still be with him ten and a half hours a day at the very least. That's more time than you spend with your wife! Naturally, you could go out with him late if some sort of event occurs. I just don't want you to reach the point where you crave the kind of stimulation your partner does."

"I don't," I replied. "But Barker relies on me."

"Yes," she said, nodding. "A little too heavily."

I must have pulled a face, because she smiled.

"You're not a carefree bachelor anymore like your partner," she said. "You have responsibilities. You could be a father one of these days."

"Could I?" I asked.

"Perhaps not yet, but someday," she answered. "Someday soon if I get my wish. A child can't live in Lion Street, Thomas. I would forbid that."

I looked at her and blinked.

"This is going to happen, isn't it?" I said. "Moving, I mean. Whether I want it or not."

"Sooner or later. But not yet and not because of me." She paused for a moment. "Do you know what our house in Camomile Street needs? A good study. Bookshelves, leather chairs, writing tables. Perhaps a nice Axminster rug."

"Ah," I said, cocking my head. "You're trying to bribe me now. But there's more, I'm afraid."

She frowned. "What is it now?"

"Mr. Barker thinks that our house is not safe either. He is taking us to Philippa's town house for the time being. We'll secure the residence later."

She crossed her arms and gave me a look that could have curdled milk.

CHAPTER 14

I regretted every mean-spirited thing I had ever said about Jacob Maccabee. Yes, he could be pompous and self-satisfied, but who isn't now and then? And true, he had enjoyed torturing me during my bachelorhood, throwing open my draperies early in the mornings with glee. However, that is nothing. I had baited him as well, moving items randomly on tables just an inch or two to drive him mad. An old legend claims that if one is pursued by a vampire, throwing a handful of sesame seeds will stop him because he is unable to continue until he had picked up every seed. That's Mac in a nutshell.

He couldn't die. I forbade it. Who would listen at keyholes to my private conversations? Who would heat our bathhouse each evening? Who would cook the meals Etienne left in our icebox for dinner? My word, who would brew his marvelous beer? It was unthinkable.

I didn't want to admit it, but there it was. Jacob was a friend.

We had worked side by side for years, and not only as adversaries. The only thing that stopped us was that I had been hired for a position he not only coveted but expected. Since then he chose to preserve the formal manner of a servant whenever we were together. At least once I'd have liked to see him unbend and sit in a chair or take off his coat. I'd even listen to him talk about his day, though I knew how crushingly boring that would be.

Rebecca and I returned to the Priory after the tea. I saw Barker's silhouette under the archway. He was smoking one of his meerschaum pipes and leaning on his stick. Rebecca patted my elbow and went inside to find Sarah Fletcher as the Guv removed the pipe from between his square teeth.

"This poisoner has shown himself able to obtain and use cyanide, arsenic, and digitalis," he said in a low voice. "What other tricks is he planning, I wonder?"

"He means to kill us all," I stated. "Doesn't he?"

"I believe he does," my partner said. "Some people have poisoned for insurance money or revenge or to spare themselves from abuse. But this fellow, or this woman, for we cannot rule out the fair sex, does it as an art, a field of study. A science, if you will. He loves his work and he is clever."

At that moment, Rebecca returned. "Sarah's been allowed to sit with Jacob, so I am giving her some privacy."

"We'll need to go to Philippa's," I said.

"But my things," Rebecca said. "What can I take?"

"Nothing, ma'am," Barker rumbled.

"Nothing?" she exclaimed. "Not a brush? Not a nightdress? How will I fix my hair? What will I wear tomorrow? This is impossible!"

"I'm afraid you must bear the hardship for the night, ma'am. Mr. Llewelyn, you must see to your wife's comforts. I have a telephone call to make."

As he left us, I took Rebecca's hand. She looked decidedly shaken.

"I can take nothing?" she repeated. "No change of shoes, no face powder?"

"Above all, no face powder," I replied. "There's no telling what he could put in it."

"Thomas, this would not happen if you sold ties in Savile Row or ran a bookshop."

We live in a modern age now, where even a few stables had telephone sets, and matters could be dealt with from a distance even late at night. However, only one cabman could be found in the street at that hour. Rebecca ascended first on the right, then Barker on the left, and then I climbed aboard and squeezed in between them. It was a hard squeeze, the Guv being such a large man.

"Holland Park!" he bawled to the driver, and we were off.

"Is Philippa in town?" Rebecca asked.

"Alas, no," he answered. "But she said we can make do in her house for the night. I'm sure Lady Ashleigh has nightdresses and everything to meet your temporary needs."

"Oh, good," my wife said. "I was expecting . . . Well, I don't know what I was expecting. Have you ever faced such a crisis before, Mr. Barker?"

"I have not, Mrs. Llewelyn," he admitted. "I've only dealt with a poisoning once and that was long ago. The only advice I can give is to be incredibly cautious."

Lady Philippa Ashleigh's pied-à-terre in Holland Park was a tall white mansion with marble columns flanking the door. When we arrived and stepped down from the vehicle, the entire street was abed. The gas lamps lined the street like pearls in a necklace, but there was not a soul to be seen. I consulted my watch. It was just nine o'clock.

I'd only been to the town house once or twice, and Philippa's personality is so compelling that I really did not take it in. It was one of a row of houses, each resplendent in stone and brick, but having its own design. Hers was most pleasing. The brick was glazed snowy white. The house itself was larger than most row houses there, but they were all elegant.

The Guv reached into his pocket, retrieved a key, and unlocked the door. I raised a brow while Rebecca looked scandalized. A gentleman possessing the key to a gentlewoman's home? It wasn't done! Well, it was, I suppose, but not openly.

"Keep your eyes in your heads," the Guv said to both of us as he opened the door. "Philippa anticipated we might have need of her London home should an emergency arise. She gave me the key ten years ago. I have had no need to use it since."

I heard a rasp as Barker lit a lamp on the wall by the entrance. It was a large hall, but I could spy a drawing room behind it. All the soft furnishings were shrouded in linen. Rebecca was especially curious, although trying not to show it. She and Philippa were friends now, but she was still in awe of her. One doesn't generally have baronesses as personal acquaintances.

Barker turned and put the box of vestas in my hand.

"Light such lamps as you need," he instructed. "The two of you may choose whatever room you like for the night. I have a few telephone calls to make."

He carried himself off to the darkened room beyond. How the man could see in the dark with black lenses always puzzled me.

Rebecca and I looked at each other. A mischievous smile spread across her face.

"Let's explore," she said.

"You mean snoop."

"Semantics," she argued. "And that's such a vulgar term."

We lit a candle and climbed the stair, and while we ascended, I heard the rumble of Barker's voice on a telephone below. The ground floor consisted of parlors, dayrooms, and a library. The first was full of well-appointed bedrooms, including one that obviously belonged to our hostess. The second floor had less well-appointed bedrooms on one side and servants' quarters on the other. The kitchen was belowstairs, I reasoned.

We chose our room on the first floor, then my wife turned to me.

"I must borrow a nightgown from Philippa. I hope she will not mind."

I followed her to the master bedroom, but felt I could not go in. It was sacrosanct. Rebecca had no such scruples.

"Spy," I chided from the doorway.

She sat down in front of a mirrored vanity and lifted the lid of some sort of powder and sniffed it.

"In her way," she remarked, "Philippa is as private as your 'Guv.' I've got about a dozen questions about her and I'd like to have at least two of them answered by the end of the night."

"You will tell me afterward, won't you?" I asked.

"Certainly not," she said. "They are women's secrets. What sort of person do you take me for?"

I returned to our chosen room and got ready for bed, such as it was. There were no nightshirts there for me. I'd be scandalized if there were.

Half an hour later Rebecca entered in her nightgown, modeling it for me. Lady Philippa has a fine figure, but she approaches Barker in height, while my wife is but an inch above five feet tall. She looked like a child wearing her mother's gown. I laughed as she hitched up the skirt, which dragged the ground behind. Then we climbed into bed, and I turned down the gas.

The next I knew there was a tap at the door. I turned up the gas and consulted my watch. Then donning my jacket, I rose and answered it. Barker stood in the hallway fully dressed. I directed him down the hall, knowing how loud my partner's voice can be. He's never mastered the art of whispering.

"What's going on?" I asked. "It's only five o'clock."

"Your wife may sleep late if she wishes, but you and I have a good deal of work to do today, so we must start early."

"Very well," I said, relinquishing my last hopes for a few more hours' sleep. "It should only take me a few minutes to get ready."

CHAPTER 15

We took the earliest Underground train to the Elephant and Castle and arrived before six, but men already awaited us at our door: six Chinamen, Etienne, and a fellow who looked faintly familiar. He and Etienne were having some sort of argument in French, though if one knew our cook well one would say it was hardly an argument when compared to his usual temper.

The stranger was over thirty, wearing a morning coat and a homburg. He had black hair so severely pomaded that it looked as if it were painted on the back of his head. He had large gray eyes and an aristocratic nose. I'd never seen such a fastidious-looking man. It was as if he dressed with an angle and a draftsman's T square every morning. I hazarded that the set of his hat was exactly 80 degrees, and not a degree off either way. He held a square black box with a handle. When I tried to shake his hand, he stepped back and held the box in front of his chest, almost in a manner of self-defense.

"Wolfe," Barker said. "It is good to see you. I regret the early hour, but I thought your being here was necessary. This is my partner in the agency, Thomas Llewelyn. Thomas, this is Saxton Wolfe."

We bowed to each other.

"Barker, let us get started. You are paying me well enough for my time."

Etienne Dummolard did not have the same need to observe the niceties of society. He smote our front door with the back of his hand.

"I must get to my kitchen!" he bellowed.

Barker reached forward with a key toward the front door, but Wolfe stopped him. He went down on his knees and examined the lock.

"There are no scratches," he pronounced, standing. "Good. You may open it."

My partner turned the key, but Wolfe stopped us again. Opening the door slowly, he inspected the hinges, then turned and looked up over the door to the window above. Only then would he allow us over the threshold.

Wolfe and Etienne entered first. The Frenchman would have barged down the hall without a thought if Wolfe hadn't called and stopped him in time. He pointed out a wire on the floor connected to a small brass box, containing who knew what.

"That was not there when we found Mac," I said.

"No, Thomas," Barker replied. "I suspect our poisoner has worked through the night to do us harm."

Wolfe examined every inch of the hall before allowing the gardeners to go out the back door and Etienne into his domain. Then he proceeded to open his bag and retrieve a magnifying lens. Inside the bag I spied bottles and scientific equipment. He was just about to say something when we heard a cry from the garden. We stepped carefully over the wire and hurried outside.

Barker's prized koi fish were lying belly-up in the pond. The Guv stepped to the edge of the wooden walkway that flanked two sides. He squatted and dipped two fingers in the water. Raising them to his nose, he sniffed them and then shook them dry. I gave him an enquiring look but he only shrugged his shoulders as if to say "I am no chemist." He rose again and began to inspect his pen-jiang trees in the southwest corner of the garden. The gardeners returned to him after a brief inspection of the grounds. Everything they were responsible for appeared to be in order, the fish being of little concern to them. Barker fed them himself in the early morning hours while the crickets chirped and the day began to dawn.

They were just fish, I thought. But I was only trying to convince myself. I knew these fish; the orange-gold one, the albino, the piebald, the spotted one, and the black one, an aquatic twin of Harm. I counted them whenever I stood by the edge, making sure all were accounted for. Dead, all dead. And why? Merely to taunt Cyrus Barker. I turned and looked at him.

"The Pie Man . . ." I began. "Sorry, the poisoner. He killed the Burkes but spared little Bridget, although she was drugged."

Barker held up a finger. "We haven't proven he doped her. It could have been done by her parents for a night's sleep."

"Perhaps," I admitted. "Anyway, Mac was poisoned, but Harm was given laudanum. Why? Why poison the fish but spare the dog? In fact, why did he not kill Harm first? He must have put up a fight. He takes his guard duties very seriously. Is the man a dog fancier?"

"I can only imagine our poisoner put opium in a piece of meat and tossed it over the fence" Barker said. "It's the only thing that would entice him."

"Interesting," a voice said behind me.

I nearly jumped into the water. Wolfe was there, standing behind me. I thought there was something alien about him.

Wolfe dipped his fingers in the water and then put his hands behind his back. "The pond was tainted with an organic concoction. It contains walnut shells, if I am correct. It asphyxiates the fish. This is not merely a pond. The water appears to be pumped from underground and recedes again. The poison will wash out in a couple of days without any lasting effects."

"This man is playing some sort of game," I said.

"A game, yes, but we don't know the rules," Wolfe said. "Mr. Barker said his dog was drugged or poisoned. Has it died?"

"No, he hasn't," I replied.

"But a servant has been poisoned?"

"Yes," I said, nodding. "With digitalis."

"It seems to me, Mr. Llewelyn, that this killer is playing with you," Wolfe said. "Or rather, with Mr. Barker. It would be far easier and final if this poisoner simply shot the lot of you. Coming in here, setting up little traps, working long into the night. It's become a labor of love, if you will. Tell me how it all started."

I did as we watched the Guv take a pair of scissors and trim his precious pen-jiang tree.

"Fascinating," he replied when I had finished. "And your client actually died in your office?"

"He did," I answered, kicking a stone into the stream among the dead koi. "Less than a minute after he arrived."

"Then that should have been an end to it," Wolfe said, frowning. "Why go after you and Mr. Barker?"

"That is what I would like to know."

"It sounds to me as if the killer, having finished his plan, still has unresolved feelings. His anger has led him to you. You have become a part of his quest."

I shoved my hands in my pockets and looked at our bumptious visitor. "I thought you said he wouldn't kill us."

"Oh, he'll kill you all right, but he'll play with you awhile first," he replied. "He's like a kitten with a mouse. He'll tire of you eventually, but he isn't going to let you go."

"You are an imaginative fellow, sir," I noted. "Let us leave my partner with his grief and go into the kitchen."

We returned to the house. In the kitchen, we found all the food in the larder, the icebox, and even the spices and base ingredients such as flour and sugar stacked upon the breakfast table. I would have supposed that Etienne had been working himself into one of his infamous tirades, generally followed by a broken window and a vow never to return, although he always did. However, our cook looked calm enough.

"You are correct, Monsieur," he said to Wolfe. "Poison, la la la la."

He pointed to each of the canisters one by one. Then he tapped his turnip of a nose.

"This, monsieur, is a fine instrument," he said. "It knows when an ingredient is not pure or a finished dish has been trifled with. This nose, it is ugly, yes? But it is a gift, and I would not trade it for one as handsome as yours."

"Bien sûr," Wolfe said. He gestured at the mess before us. "The canisters will have to be replaced, and any pans, silverware, and kitchen tools must be soaked and rinsed thoroughly."

"Oui," Etienne said flatly.

"Monsieur Dummolard," Wolfe continued. "This is your kitchen. May I have your permission to search it for traps, like the one I found in the hall, and collect samples?"

Their eyes locked, the large, bearish man and the thin, crane-like one.

"As you wish," Etienne replied.

Our visitor went to retrieve his bag and I nipped out the back door to find Barker. The gardeners were already at work with hoes and shovels, talking quietly among themselves, glad the garden had avoided a catastrophe. Barker was giving them instructions, still waving his scissors in the air.

"Excuse me, sir," I murmured. "Who is this fellow I'm squiring about? Currently, he has Etienne pacified, but he's come close to giving orders once or twice and you know how Etienne blusters when told what to do in his own kitchen."

"Is he being heavy-handed?" Barker asked, still watching the gardeners.

"No," I admitted. "But the possibility exists. Who is he? I've never heard of him before. What is his trade?"

"He is a detective who works only for other detectives," the Guv explained. "He can't abide clients. He's insufferably rude to them. I suppose you might consider him one of our watchers, though I've used him rarely. He's well-read and anything involving traps and gadgets fascinates him. When I explained our dilemma and asked him to come 'round, he jumped at the chance, though he had to arrive early. Generally, he sleeps until noon. You have not recognized him? He used to be in our antagonistics class in Scotland Yard."

"That's where I saw him! I knew he seemed familiar."

Barker turned and spoke to the gardeners in Cantonese, then turned to me. "Run along and keep an eye on Wolfe."

"Yes, sir," I answered.

"And if Etienne cuts up rough, tell him if he breaks the picture window again, I shall send him the bill."

"I will."

"By the way," he called out as I reached the back door. "Wolfe was one of the applicants for your position."

"Why didn't you hire him?" I asked.

"Like I said, he's insufferably rude."

I turned to the kitchen. Etienne looked distinctly uncomfortable since the coffee had been poisoned and he had accomplished nothing but to throw everything away. Together we watched Wolfe work, his square bag open. He filled a test tube from each of the canisters and a sample from the pies and dishes left from the night before. He corked each vial and wrote the contents on a label attached to the test tube.

"Is that a library across the hall?" he asked, looking over his shoulder. "Oh, I can't wait."

I glanced at my partner. At least someone here was having a jolly good time.

"Are you telling me the library might have traps, as well?" I asked the Guv.

"Let us hope not," he said.

The very thought made me cringe.

CHAPTER 16

Fitzhugh's funeral was that afternoon at St Mary Matfelon in Whitechapel Street. Father Michaels officiated at his friend's funeral. Autumn was settling in and showing no signs of leaving soon. The first red and yellow leaves were doing cartwheels through the air as if seeking our attention for the denouement of their brief lives. Acorns dropped by twisted and lichen-spattered oaks crunched underfoot in front of the church. Soon it would be time for overcoats, and could scarves and gloves be far behind?

Inspector Poole was present, along with a half dozen officers. The plainclothes squad kept to itself, a distinct part of the CID. It was the division Rebecca had wanted me to join, but she didn't know what she was asking. It had an unsavory reputation. The typical Englishman, criminal or citizen, believed that it somehow wasn't fair that a policeman should go about in disguise. The rank and file of the Met thought it unwholesome.

"Llewelyn," a man said in greeting beside me.

"Sparks, isn't it?" I replied.

He was one of the plainclothesmen I'd been introduced to once. I remembered his name simply because it was a memorable one. He was of average height, average weight, and had a face it was difficult to describe and easy to forget. He wore a mustache that I suspected was false. They could do wonders with spirit gum and crepe wool these days.

"I hear you lost a client the other day. Hard luck," he ventured.

I sighed. "He barely got a word out before he dropped dead."

"Killing an entire family to cover one's movements is cold," Lieutenant Sparks said. "We want this killer. We're not all bachelors, you know."

I tried to picture Sparks sitting down to dinner with a wife and an infant in nappies, but I couldn't. It was utterly impossible.

I noticed Barker talking to Poole. I nodded to the plainclothesman and joined them.

"I'm not saying you should step back entirely, Cyrus," Poole was saying. "But this Pie Man has it in for you. He killed your client, poisoned your butler, and drugged your dog, which I find a crime all in itself. Say the word, and I'll put a watch 'round your neighborhood."

We stepped aside as people passed us to go into the old church.

"I'll consider it, Terry," Barker said, though both Poole and I doubted he would. As a rule, he's not good at taking advice other than his own.

We entered the church, where the organist was playing something a little too heavy and German for my taste. Everyone seemed lost in their own thoughts, and there was little conversation.

The chapel was full. Fitzhugh was an MP, after all, even if only for a little while. Gladstone would be in the audience somewhere, with his entire constituency. It was required of him, of them all, to be there. There would be reporters, people who knew him at one time or another, members of the Tower Hamlet Council, men who worked with him in the law, perhaps some whom he had represented. Somewhere out there, there was the Pie Man gloating.

How many would come to my funeral, I wondered suddenly. Nothing like this many. My obituary would be no more than a paragraph or two, but I was comfortable with that. I didn't need predatory reporters loitering around my service or people attending out of curiosity. I had no need to be famous. Luckily, that was not an issue.

"Card, Thomas," the Guv said, holding out his hand.

I reached into my waistcoat pocket and handed him our business card. We wended our way to the front to where an elderly couple sat. Fitzhugh's father was looking fragile and his mother snuffled into a handkerchief. People should not outlive their children, though it happens every day.

"Mr. and Mrs. Fitzhugh," my partner rumbled, removing his bowler hat and bowing. "I am Cyrus Barker and this is Thomas Llewelyn. We were the last people to speak to your son, if only for a few seconds. He passed into the beyond in our offices."

Mr. Fitzhugh's eyes looked glazed. He might have been a wax effigy from Madame Tussauds. Not so his wife. She put down her handkerchief at once and put out her hand.

"Mr. Barker," she said. "I was hoping you would come. I understand you did everything you could to try to help our son. Tell me, are you investigating his death?"

"I am, madam," the Guv replied. "I vowed to him that I would."

There was an intelligence and a spark in those watery blue eyes. Whatever had made her son what he was came through her bloodline.

"I'm trying to piece together my son's last hour," she continued.

"I can help you with that, Mrs. Fitzhugh," Barker said. "I'll introduce you to Inspector Poole, who spoke to him before me and may have more information."

She touched her husband's sleeve. "Thank you, Mr. Barker."

"Have you spoken to your son's former servant, Ogilvy?" my partner asked. "He must have seen him leave for Whitehall."

"There is some sort of problem there, I believe," she answered. "We have not been able to reach him. Something must be done with Roland's furniture and personal possessions before the flat is sold. Ogilvy has the only key."

"This sets a bad precedent, lad," Barker murmured as we left the couple to grieve. "The fact that he died in our offices and that the matter was written about in the newspapers may keep some clients from coming to our door."

He looked about, craning his neck. "I wonder if that rascal Ogilvy is here."

We found a pew as the service began. I scanned the crowd surreptitiously looking for Ogilvy's bald head and ginger side-whiskers but could not spot him.

After the final dirge had ended, a young man approached us.

"Sirs," he said. "Mr. Gladstone would like to speak to you."

He led us to a corner of the chapel where the Liberal Party was standing. There were MPs and clerks, even some from the Conservative Party who came out of respect for Gladstone. When the Old Lion roared, many still listened.

"Mr. Barker," William Gladstone said.

"Sir."

The former prime minister was helped to his feet by the young man who had approached us. A second stood on the other side. It would not do to have a symbol of Liberalism fall, but he was quite old.

"How is the enquiry coming along, sir?" Gladstone asked.

"We must be hot on his heels, Your Lordship," my partner replied. "Else he would not have attacked our household."

The old prime minister's bushy eyebrows raised. He looked at Barker, then turned to me.

"Is this so, sir?" he enquired.

"Yes, sir," I answered. "Whoever killed Mr. Fitzhugh is definitely intent on adding us to the list."

"I'm very sorry, gentlemen," he said, shaking his head. "I did not intend to place your lives in danger."

"Not to worry, Your Lordship," the Guv replied. "It is part and parcel of our occupation. We've been working with Scotland Yard. With your permission, I shall give them the credit when the culprit is found."

"When?" Gladstone echoed. "Not if?"

"We have five, perhaps six suspects," Barker continued. "I'm convinced the poisoner is among them. We are currently winnowing the list."

"While the fellow is trying to kill you?"

Barker gave him one of his cold smiles. "It isn't sporting if only one of us participates."

Gladstone cocked his head to the side, as if trying to work out why the man he'd hired was so tenacious, if not cavalier about the danger.

"Mr. Barker," he said, stretching the syllables to the breaking point. "I wanted you to know that I put my best man on the question of whether young Fitzhugh's tragic passing has influenced any bill put forward in the House of Commons. Normally, such work is beneath Joseph's attention, but he understands that the boy's passing has affected me greatly and the party must be certain that no one has attacked one of us, because in doing so, he has attacked all of us."

"I'm pleased to see that you have taken this matter with the seriousness it deserves, Your Lordship," Barker said. "What was your conclusion?"

"You young fellows are always in such a hurry, sir. Allow an old man to give an answer at his own pace."

The Guv's mustache twitched. Perhaps he liked being referred to as a young man.

"Most certainly, sir," he said, bowing again.

"This brain of mine may grind slowly, but I assure you, it grinds exceedingly fine."

"I have no doubt of that, sir. None at all."

I looked at my partner. Gladstone had certainly put him in his place and not only about the trifling matter of being rushed. Barker actually ran a finger inside his collar as if it were too tight. I could see what power the Old Man held and the tricks he used to keep his constituency in order and the enemy at bay.

"As to the matter of the Navy bill," Gladstone said. "It is fully between Prime Minister Rosebery's teeth and he shall ride it as far as it can take him. One cannot develop a war chest without first creating a war. There is nothing like the rattling of sabers to rouse the patriotic spirit of the Conservative Party from its slumbers. It is a drum Lord Rosebery thumps quite well. One junior MP's vote in such a conflict means little. If we speak, we are either cowards or traitors. Any use of logic would be better spent whispering in the ear of a cow. It has more sense."

The gentlemen on either side of him smiled and one of them scribbled his words on his cuff with a pencil.

"Not the Navy bill, then," Barker said. He showed no emotion despite the fact that he was one of the Conservatives the Liberal leader was disparaging.

"No," the former prime minister said. "On the other hand, the town council bill appears to be very promising. It throws small decisions into the hands of the local government to whom it matters most, while reducing the duties of Her Majesty's government. Some decisions have been made by ministers without even considering the opinions of those who will be required to implement them."

Barker nodded without response. He dared not risk Gladstone's wrath a second time.

"So, Mr. Barker, in answer to your question, young Fitzhugh's opinions would have mattered not at all. His vote could not have possibly influenced either bill."

"I see," the Guv said.

"I do not believe his death had anything to do with his duties as a member of Parliament. He was no more than a minnow as far as politics are concerned. It would have been years before he could stand before the opposition and propose a bill himself. I believe, no, I strongly believe, that you must look elsewhere. I hope this does not weaken your resolve."

Barker straightened his spine and set his shoulders until he looked as if carved from limestone.

"No, Your Lordship, it strengthens it. I do not mind telling you that I hoped for this answer, but I needed to ask it lest Mr. Llewelyn and I were baying up the wrong tree."

"Then I free you both to track whoever killed poor Roland and sink your collective teeth into him. Keep me informed."

Barker and I bowed. Gladstone nodded.

"Thank you, sir," the Guv said.

"Good hunting," he replied.

We were dismissed. Gladstone did not show any sign of it, but his aides did. The two of us bowed to his bald and spotted head and passed down the aisle.

My partner glanced at me. "Did you spot Mr. Ogilvy in the crowd, Thomas?"

"No, sir," I said. "He wasn't here."

"Was anyone on our list among the mourners?"

I nodded. "Just one, sir. Mr. Lindsay. If this were a horse race, I would say he was pulling into the lead," I answered.

"Would you put a wager on that horse, Mr. Llewelyn?"

His mustache bowed. It was Barker's idea of a joke.

"Not until I see how the others run, sir," I demurred.

"Ah," he grunted.

I knew what that grunt meant: *Not good enough, Mr. Llewelyn.*

We were walking up the aisle toward the entrance when Barker abruptly stopped. I looked around him to see what had impeded our progress and found an angry little impediment by the name of Miss Gwendolyn Halton.

"Sir!" she said in a low voice. "How dare you attend my late fiancé's funeral? You desecrate this place with your very presence. You, Mr. Barker, have been sacked!"

The Guv raised the hat that he had just clapped to his head.

"Miss Halton," he pronounced. "How nice to see you again."

"If you think you can wheedle your way into finding a client here you are mistaken," she said. "I shall not allow the two of you to upset Roland's parents!"

A young man stepped close behind Fitzhugh's former fiancé as if he were there especially to protect her. He put a hand on her shoulder.

The Guv raised his hat again and smiled. "My name is Cyrus Barker, of the Barker and Llewelyn Agency. This is my partner, Mr. Llewelyn. And you are?"

"Gerald Halton," he replied, narrowing his eyes. He looked confused, which I'm sure was Barker's intent.

"I assume you are Miss Halton's brother, then," my partner stated. "She spoke of you when last we met."

"Thrash him, Gerald," she urged. "Thrash the brute!"

"Gwendolyn . . ."

"Your sister is under the mistaken impression that we are seeking a client," the Guv said. "I assure you we already have one. In fact, he is coming up the aisle now."

I turned to see the two young men escorting William Gladstone. One was holding his arm to steady him. He nodded at us as they passed. Gwendolyn Halton was too caught up in her own tempest to notice, but the glance did not go unnoticed by her brother.

"Punch him, Gerald, right on that ugly nose!" she continued.

Halton pursed his lips. "Gwendolyn, we are in church."

The young woman pointed a finger at my partner. "Roland died in his offices. He must have had something to do with it. It cannot be coincidence!"

"You're causing a scene," her brother murmured in her ear.

"It is a matter of family honor!"

The young man looked to the heavens, perhaps for divine help, and then turned and followed Gladstone up the aisle, leaving his sister to fend for herself.

"Very well," she said. "I shall fight you, then!"

She swung a tiny fist at Barker's chest, which bounced off it like an acorn. At most, Barker was bemused.

"Tomorrow I shall hire a real detective," she continued. "I'm sure he shall find my fiancé's murderer within twenty-four hours."

"Craig's Court has several, miss," Barker said. "Let me know if you require a recommendation."

She could bark and nip at him, but she could not ruffle his feathers whereas the more polite he was the more it infuriated her. Finally, she gave a strangled screech of exasperation and followed after her brother.

"Excitable girl," I noted. "Very accustomed to having her own way."

"I wish her luck in her quest, but we are already days ahead of whomever she hires."

"Are we making headway?" I asked, as we turned and strode up the aisle, the last to leave the church.

"We are," Barker replied. "I know how and why these murders occurred and I know where and when. When I find who killed Roland Fitzhugh, the case will be complete."

A constable met us at the door, holding out a note to the Guv. He read it and folded it, putting it into his pocket.

"It's from Terry," he said. "Edward Lindsay has just been arrested. We're heading to Scotland Yard."

CHAPTER 17

Edward Lindsay was awaiting us in the interrogation room when we arrived, he and his solicitor, a fussy man with a tiny square mustache on his lip that looked like a smudge. Lindsay had crossed his arms defiantly, but he must have suspected Poole had an ace up his sleeve.

"This is ridiculous, Inspector," the barrister barked. "I told you all I know in my offices last week. Why have I been arrested?"

"Mr. Lindsay, you were seen last year in the front rooms of your offices violently arguing with the deceased," Poole replied calmly. "Yet you failed to mention the altercation to Scotland Yard. Did you forget, or were you deliberately hiding the fact, hoping there were no witnesses? I assure you there was."

"I did not consider our argument important," Lindsay answered. "Partners in law firms disagree all the time. We are passionate men."

He looked ready to stand and argue as if in a court of law, but

it was himself he was defending. Poole sat down in the chair opposite the suspect, while we stood. There were too many of us in
this one little room, It was hot and stuffy. I wanted to take off my
coat, but I'd have menaced everyone with my elbows.

"Mr. Lindsay," Barker counseled. "We are busy men. Tell us
what we want to know, and you can get back to whatever case you
are preparing. This should not require much of your time."

Lindsay gave him a cautious look that I'm certain worked well
in many a courtroom.

"That is immaterial," Lindsay insisted. "We were old friends.
What we argued over was forgotten the next day."

"I think otherwise, Mr. Lindsay," Poole replied. "I believe the
little tiff in your office led step by step to your former partner's
death. Tell me what the fight concerned. I already know; I'm just
giving you the chance to cooperate. It's what you would counsel
a client."

Edward Lindsay sniffed. "Forgive me, Inspector, but you have
no idea what I would counsel."

Poole raised a brow at him. Then he turned to us.

"I'm getting a bit peckish, gentlemen," he said to Barker and
myself. "Is it too early for a pint?"

"It is," the Guv replied. "However, a cup of tea would not
come amiss."

"The Shades makes a reasonable cup," I added. "And the coffee is good as well."

Poole stood and we turned toward the door.

"What are you doing?" Lindsay asked, his dark eyebrows
meeting over his aristocratic nose.

"We're going out for some tea, obviously," Poole replied.

"Release me, then," Lindsay said. "I have cases this afternoon."

"Yes, well, you should have thought of that before you made remarks about me in my own place of business. I'm working here, but
if you don't wish to communicate about the subject in question, you

and Mr. Mustache here can cool your heels for an hour or two." The inspector turned to me. "Thomas?"

"Yes?" I asked.

"Do they have buns at The Shades?"

"Better," I answered. "They have seedcake."

"Now you're talking. Let's—"

"Very well!" Lindsay cried. "I don't want to sit here all day. I'll tell you what you need to know. However, I shall speak to the commissioner when this is over."

"That's fine," Poole said evenly, as unconcerned at the threat as he could be. "He has no love for barristers. He considers you to be obstacles to our work. Every time a suspect is released after hundreds of man hours wasted, he takes it personally."

The air seemed to have gone out of Lindsay's sails. He sagged and deflated.

"I'll cooperate," he grumbled. "Ask your ruddy questions."

Poole tipped his scarred chair back and crossed his arms. "You were seen arguing with your late partner last year in the front room of your chambers. What did the argument concern?"

"It concerned a number of things," Lindsay replied. "The dissolution of our partnership had been long coming."

"Did your quarrel come to blows?" the inspector asked.

"No, of course not," Lindsay replied. "We're not savages. One can have a disagreement without resorting to fisticuffs."

"A disagreement over what precisely, Mr. Lindsay?" Barker asked in that purring rumble of his. "Or should I ask over whom?"

Lindsay looked away, toward the wall. He appeared to me like a chess master who had just lost his queen.

"Very well," he said. "I will admit it. It concerned Miss Halton. It occurred before they were engaged."

"You were hoping to have her for yourself?" Poole asked.

"If by that you mean that I wanted to marry her, the answer is yes. The worst mistake I made in my entire life was to introduce the two of them."

"Had you courted Miss Halton?" the Guv asked.

"I had visited her home a few times," he answered. "We met at society functions and walked together in Hyde Park. There was no impropriety. Her parents were aware of my intent and did not seem to find my attentions objectionable."

"What of the young woman herself?" I asked, curious.

"She seemed satisfied with the arrangement." Lindsay paused and looked at us. "I know what all of you are thinking, that I'm twice her age."

"One cannot argue with the truth," Poole said.

The barrister smiled. "Oh, but you can. I've made a fine living at it for decades."

Terry frowned. No doubt he was thinking of all the criminals Lindsay had gotten released with that silver tongue of his. Poole and his compatriots had probably been hoping to get a barrister in their clutches for some time.

"Fought over a girl, then?" he asked, without a trace of sympathy. "An old duffer like you?"

"Go ahead and laugh at my expense," Lindsay said bitterly. "I'm sure I deserve it."

Barker cleared his throat. "Was an understanding reached between you and the young woman's father?"

"It was imminent."

Arrangement, I thought to myself. It was not a word I'd have chosen for my marriage. I'd have died without Rebecca. Without her, I couldn't eat or sleep. I'd have pined away. But I had no particular question to ask of Lindsay. I was merely there to take notes.

"Sir," Barker intoned. "The question I put to you is whether she was too old for you. She was not young by marriage standards. From what I've seen of her she must have come out to society four years hence. Why was she not married already?"

The lawyer twisted his mouth to the side, as if searching for a word. The gaslight in the chamber made him look pale and his hair even grayer.

"She is high-spirited," he said at last. "Some may say challenging. Her father has provided for her financially, but she has no mother to teach her the ways of the world, so she has been forced to learn for herself."

He looked satisfied with that, a barrister for the defense. As a man who was thrown over he had every right to call her the harridan that she was, but he did not take advantage of that. Was it to his credit, or was he trying to make himself seem noble?

"High-spirited, is it?" Poole asked.

When Lindsay sat up in his chair ready for an argument, if not a fight, the crafty Scotland Yarder changed topics.

"How and where did you introduce Miss Halton to Mr. Fitzhugh?"

"It was at a party given last year at the end of the season, when everyone had returned to London. It was a soirée given by Lady Carlotta Binghampton. Gwendolyn and I had not yet finalized our engagement, and I was testing the waters, so to speak."

"Excuse me, sir," Barker interrupted. "I do not wish to be indelicate, but wouldn't a young woman in her specific circumstance look for a husband who is titled, thereby enlarging her merchant father's reputation and sphere of influence?"

"I thought so, too," Lindsay replied, looking wistful. "I'm the second son of Lord Paxton. There was a chance that I might inherit someday. My elder brother, John, is widowed and without an heir, not that I wish him a short life. In this one matter, I had it all over Fitzhugh. But I was naïve, you see."

"Did Miss Halton inform you that her intentions had changed?" Poole asked.

The chief inspector was in the heavy cream now. He'd bagged a barrister and an aristocrat at once. He looked pleased with himself.

"She did not inform me, no," he replied. "But I blame Fitzhugh for that. He should have been honest in his attentions toward the woman I was about to ask to be my wife, but no, I had to learn from a friend his deceit and despicable behavior."

"According to the information you gave Mr. Llewelyn two days ago, Mr. Fitzhugh was a model of propriety. Why do you believe he would betray you in such a way?"

Lindsay turned to his silent associate and asked for a cigarette. He lit and puffed it, holding it between the very tips of his fingers as he grappled with the answer.

"Status," he answered. "He was climbing the social ladder and I believe he didn't give a damn about the girl. As Shakespeare said, 'Though those that are betrayed / do feel the treason sharply, / yet the traitor stands in worse / case of woe.'"

"*Cymbeline*," I murmured under my breath.

Barker was unmoved. Poole, however, didn't think a murder enquiry should be punctuated with quotations from the Bard. It's all well and good for the Old Bailey, but not an interrogation cell in New Scotland Yard. There are standards. Poole crossed his arms.

"What is worse," Lindsay continued. "Many people in society I've known for years knew what was going on but didn't feel the need to inform me."

"How did you find out that you were being played false?" Poole asked.

The suspect knocked his ash onto a dish on the table.

"I was invited to the Regatta by Lady Maricot," he said. "But just as quickly, she rescinded the offer. In doing so, her eyes were on Gwendolyn. That's when I realized I was being flanked, by my own partner, no less!"

"Did you say anything at the party, in front of witnesses?" the inspector asked.

Lindsay puffed on his cigarette.

"No," he replied. "We both knew we would discuss his base betrayal the following morning."

"So there were no indications from your would-be fiancée that she had transferred her affections to another?" Barker asked.

The lawyer stabbed his cigarette fiercely into the glass ashtray.

"Not a one," Lindsay said. "I'm glad I learned of her feckless-ness before the wedding rather than after."

"Tell us about the argument itself," Poole said, scratching his nose. "I assume it occurred the morning after the event you both attended."

Lindsay shook his head. "It was two days after, on a Monday. I believe we were both churlish to our secretary, avoiding each other but snapping at the poor man. Finally, Roland came into my office and apologized for the 'way things went,' as if he were not involved in the matter, but was somehow caught up in it by accident, as if he wasn't kissing my fiancée on the balcony or meeting her for a tryst behind my back."

"And what did you say?"

"I scarce can remember. I called him a swine; I know that. A thief, a bounder, a cad. I believe I told him he was lower than a snake. I asked him why he had stolen Gwendolyn from me, and he said she had been looking for some way to dissolve our relationship for months, and then had prevailed upon him for my sake. For my sake! Apparently, I have one foot in the grave and no one had taken the trouble to inform me. At fifty-one I am in my decrepitude, and the idea of her marrying me was patently absurd. She had gone along with the charade for her father's sake and didn't care two figs about me. Then I introduced her to Roland, and he was the Lance-lot to my Arthur. I couldn't stand in the way of true love. It came to blows after that."

Terence Poole raised a brow, almost with a degree of satisfac-tion.

"Blows? You admit it, then."

"Yes," Lindsay said. "One or two. Nothing decisive. Neither of us are fighters. Mostly we grappled about, knocking over hat-stands. He was larger than I, but I was more angry. Finally, I pushed him out into the street and knocked him down. I told him our partnership was at an end and that I never wanted to see him again."

Poole blinked at him. "Is that what you said?"

Lindsay frowned. "Yes, as near as I recall. Why?"

"A witness claims you said, 'If I ever see you again, I'll kill you.'"

The lawyer blanched.

"Which is it, Mr. Lindsay?" the inspector continued. "Did you threaten to kill Roland Fitzhugh?"

"No!" he sputtered. "That is, I don't think so. I don't recall saying those words."

"But you may have," Poole persisted.

The barrister hung his head. "I may have."

"Mr. Lindsay, I charge you with the murder of Roland Fitzhugh. After you have been charged, your associate may post bail."

Lindsay looked the epitome of misery. The solicitor he had brought with him, the one with the absurd mustache, said nothing.

CHAPTER 18

The next morning, we arrived at our offices at seven-thirty as usual. Barker was poised with his key in front of the lock when he stopped and turned his head. Then he inserted the key and we stepped inside.

"What's wrong?" I asked in a low voice.

"We're being watched," he answered.

I put my hands in my pockets. "What shall we do?"

"Carry on, lad," he said. "We have a case to solve."

I turned on the electric lights and looked about, trying to decide whether or not to light a fire. The morning was cool, but *The Times* had predicted the afternoon would be warm. True, the newspaper's weather predictions were wrong half the time, but one could never seriously fault so august a publication.

Jenkins came in to report back to the Guv. He was still soldiering through the casework we had given him but he appeared to be enjoying his work. Within ten minutes, he was out the door again.

"He practically has a spring in his step," I remarked.

"Did he not?" Barker commented.

Five minutes later, a man entered our chambers. I assumed he was the one who had watched us enter the building. I recognized him from the funeral. He was Gwendolyn Halton's brother, Gerald. The man was tall and muscularly built, with tanned skin and pale hair. His jaw was set, and he appeared to be serious. I read the fellow correctly he was trying to puff himself up to look threatening.

"Mr. Cyrus Barker," he demanded.

The Guv sat back as if he found our visitor entertaining. "Yes, Mr. Halton. Good morning to you."

"I understand you insulted my sister when she visited your offices the other day."

I reached into my pocket and retrieved my notebook.

"No, actually," I interjected. "I took notes of the conversation. Your sister accused Barker of being an inferior fellow and claimed she would have him sacked, but Mr. Barker was not rude in his reply. She would not answer his questions, so he let her alone."

"That's not what my sister told me," Halton continued. "She said you were hard and rough and you frightened her. She told me you ordered her from your office without revealing anything of your investigation into Roland's death. She feared for her life. In fact, she claims you are a villain."

"I've been a deacon of my church, Mr. Halton. I have many philanthropic endeavors in the East End. This agency is warranted by Buckingham Palace, and I am investigating Mr. Fitzhugh's murder at the request of Lord Gladstone."

"Nevertheless," our visitor said. "I would have satisfaction."

Barker's brows crept up over the lip of his black-lensed spectacles like a pair of spiders.

"You challenge me, anyway?"

"I do, sir," Halton said.

"Fist, blade, or ball?"

Halton cleared his throat. "The choice is yours, sir."

Barker leaned back in his chair. "Turn in a circle, then, if I may ask."

The fellow shrugged and then slowly turned for my partner's inspection. For mine, as well. I estimated he was taller than Barker, but nearly the same weight. His physique was excellent, but that had little to do with being a fighter. Some men one thinks have gone to seed can lay one out on a canvas before you know it.

"Boxing, I think," the Guv replied after the inspection.

The man's manner brightened, or more likely he was gloating. He found this answer to his satisfaction.

"Bare-knuckle," Cyrus Barker continued. "If you don't mind."

"I think you'll find your choice a mistake, sir," Gerald Halton said. "But it isn't my place to convince you otherwise. Here and now? I saw some kind of outdoor court by your offices."

The Guv shook his head.

"I prefer proper conditions," he replied. "Thomas, write down this address for Mr. Halton: 1123 Mile End Road."

I copied it down with the silver pencil I kept in my notebook, then ripped out the sheet and handed it to our visitor.

Barker retrieved his repeater watch. "Let us say forty-five minutes. You are certain you wish to do this?"

"I am," the young man answered stoutly.

"It goes to your credit to support your sister's reputation. Good morning, sir. I'll see you in Mile End."

Halton nodded and left.

"Confound it," Barker said when he was gone. "We are wasting precious time fighting over a young woman's vanity. I'm certain Mr. Halton has better things to do and so do I."

"She is merely a show horse," I commented. "A rich young woman cosseted by society, held up as an ideal, with an inflated opinion of her own self-importance. In her defense, the life she leads was chosen by her family. I doubt she and Fitzhugh were a love match."

"Let us go, Thomas," he said. "I have not asked permission to use the ring."

We put a card in the window, locked the door, and hailed a cab. The ring in question was a professional boxing ring kept in Mile End Mission, the charity Barker funded with the stipulation that the ring be kept there. It is not generally known to the public, but it is visited from time to time by boxing enthusiasts and members of the fancy. It was a shrine of sorts.

Halton was waiting impatiently when we arrived, his hands thrust into his pockets and the lapels of his coat about his ears. The wind was stronger here, making it seem colder.

"I suppose you consider this some kind of joke," he remarked.

"Patience, Mr. Halton," the Guv rumbled.

Barker led us to a padlocked door and opened it with a key, leading us inside to a professional training gymnasium. There were Indian clubs and medicine balls, weights, barbells, and other *disjecta membra* of the boxing trade. In the center of the room was a raised platform with a regulation boxing ring. The room was lit by skylights, and motes hung in the air. All was covered in a thick layer of dust.

"Wait here," Barker ordered, before disappearing through a door.

"What is this place?" Halton asked, looking about.

"It was Andrew McClain's private boxing ring," I replied.

"Handy Andy?" he asked. "Heavyweight champion of all England?"

"Yes," I answered. "Mr. Barker was his sparring partner."

The young man's eyebrows raised. "I don't come to the East End often. What's that odor?"

"It's a mixture of bleach and carbolic they use here to clean and delouse everything," I said. "There is a laundry on the premises. Most of the secondhand items at Petticoat Lane are washed here."

He wrinkled his nose. I imagined his father began in a back-street in Bethnal Green, or someplace like it. Now the son was trying to extricate himself from such humble beginnings. Having a daughter marry a promising MP was a start.

"Your sister is very forthright," I remarked. "She seems to know her own mind."

"She does that," he answered, but did not volunteer any more information. I'd hoped I could get him to talk about her, but the attempt was unsuccessful.

After a few minutes, the Guv returned with a couple of men carrying mops and rags. While they cleaned the ring, Halton took off his jacket and shirt and began to beat a heavy bag in his singlet. Barker glanced his way, studying his opponent. He sighed and reached for his collar. A few minutes later, they both climbed into the ring. Barker had replaced his spectacles with a pair of green-lensed goggles I'd seen him wear in the ring before.

The Guv is a large man. However, Gerald Halton was even larger. He was perhaps two inches taller and well muscled. His shoulders were wide and his hips thin. Barker is broad-chested and solid, but he'd gained a stone of weight at least since his knee injury. I wondered if they were fairly matched. This upstart was half his age. He must know how Lindsay felt.

I'd always felt sorry for the other fellow. In the past, I'd seen the Guv take down many a capable opponent. I'd seen him fight a half dozen men in the street or our antagonistics classes. But now, I had a pain in the pit of my stomach.

Barker and Halton circled each other, examining their opponents' potential strengths and weaknesses. They were using the old London Prize Ring rules, although I suspected Halton had only fought using those written by the Marquess of Queensbury. He was aggressive, what is known in the trade as a "swarmer." Such men are fast on their feet, and often have a strong chin. No uppercut would bring him down.

The Guv was more difficult to classify. He does not move around much or waste energy. He is cagey. He also carries tremendous power in his hands and a pocket of dirty tricks, some bare-knuckle, others from his days fighting in Canton.

I worried about Barker's knee. It had been crushed two years before when the floor went out from under him during an explosion in our chambers. His speed was slower and his power limited. I had not seen him fight anyone of any caliber since then. I wasn't worried about him physically but being embarrassed was hard enough with Gwendolyn Halton involved.

My worst expectation came true. Halton broke Barker's nose within the first five minutes, making him the first to spill claret. The blood dripped down the Guv's chin. I tossed him a towel, assuming that he'd been caught flat-footed. He'd relied upon his reaction and hand speed, but Halton was faster still.

Bare-knuckle boxing is not like wearing gloves. A single punch can break bones for either fighter. Punching a man in the face can shatter the metacarpals. There are many small bones in a man's hand with barely enough sinew holding them together. There were groups in England trying to ban bare-knuckle sport entirely, declaring it dangerous. Men had died, some by a single blow. I began to wonder if I should join such a group myself.

Now, it was sprightly youth versus the wiles of age. Halton danced about the ring, circling Barker, who remained for the most part stationary. It was how my partner was taught to fight in China, but to this fellow he looked old and slow.

Barker wiped the blood from his mustache with the back of his hand. It was not a good forecast for the Guv, but then I'd never seen the man lose before at anything. I wasn't even sure if the man was capable of losing.

Barker began to move a little, shuffling left and right. He kept his fists up by his ears and his elbows together. One can protect the head, or one can protect the body; one cannot do both. He was exposing his stomach and kidneys, but then I've hazarded a guess that his stomach was the hardest substance on earth. I'd sprained a wrist on it once.

"Come on, old fellow," I muttered. I dared not voice the weakness he was presenting and risk drawing attention to it.

Halton saw his advantage and took it, punching the Guv full in his stomach, which, as expected, gained him no ground. However, Barker pivoted and threw a hook punch that caught his opponent over the left eye and sent him staggering across the ring. He fell against the lower rope, landing on one knee. He was young and strong, however, and soon pulled himself up and returned for more.

"Very nice, sir," he admitted, looking at Barker. "A thing of beauty."

"Your punch to the nose was classic form, as well," my partner stated in return.

I noticed there was the smallest cut over Gerald Halton's brow. I knew without asking if I saw it, my partner saw it as well.

"Are you all right, sir?" I asked Barker in a low voice.

"Of course I'm all right," he said. "What a question! How are you, Mr. Llewelyn?"

"Not bleeding currently, sir."

He snorted. "Oh, this? A trifling matter."

The two men surged forward and met in the middle with a crash as a flurry of blows were exchanged. I believe each hoped to force the other into a corner where the coup de grace could be delivered but each fighter thought otherwise.

Then Barker and Halton went into a clinch, what they call in bare-knuckle parlance "chancery." I suddenly realized I was the de facto referee. I climbed into the ring and pushed my way between them.

"Break!" I shouted.

They both stepped back and retreated several steps breathing hard. I began to understand what it must be like to be a native *mahout* herding pachyderms. Being between two giants was not where I wanted to be at the moment. Barker could fight his own battles, thank you.

They were both bleeding now. The small cut over Halton's brow had been opened wider and soon blood would trickle into his eye. He hoped he would lay Barker out on the canvas first.

The Guv looked much the same, though a ghastly sight. His shirt was stained and blotched and I noted he was shaking his left hand from time to time. He must have injured one of his knuckles on his opponent's square jaw.

Fine, I said to myself. Let them kill each other. When I fight, I fight to survive. There is no sport to it. Nor the need to slake one's bloodlust now and again, either. Calling it a sport and creating rules was merely a way to make it presentable to the public.

I watched them circle each other warily. Barker dropped his braces and ripped off his bloody singlet. Halton was not loath to follow. Each bore a sheen on his arms and chest. The Guv's hair spiked in that way it does when it is wet. His opponent wiped his brow. It could go either way now, I thought. Better yet, they could stop. Both had drawn blood. Halton was still bouncing about, but it seemed my partner was reduced to shuffling, hopping from one foot to the other so low that it seemed both feet were touching the ground.

I could sense that Halton was going to attack again. He leapt forward, but as he landed Barker swept his foot out from under him and he went down. It would be the perfect time for my partner to end the fight, but while kicks and tripping were legal, striking a downed opponent was not. Barker's move only succeeded in making his opponent more wary.

"Welcome to bare-knuckle boxing, Mr. Halton," the Guv growled.

I wondered how much longer this could go on. These were two stubborn men. It could end with one or both needing to go to London Hospital, which meant I would have to get them there.

They charged at each other, and another flurry of fists was exchanged. For a few seconds, Barker was cornered, and he hunched his shoulders as blows rained about him. I wanted to see what was happening. Perhaps if they clenched again, I could stop it and push Halton back. I crossed to the ropes and leaned in to get a better look.

I saw it just in time. Barker endured a hook punch that slid up and over his head and boxed his ear. Then his right fist came out straight and true like a javelin. It caught Halton just under the nose. A punch to the jaw tugs the head down. To the brow and the head rocks back. But there, you see, in that one spot beneath the nose the energy has nowhere to go. The brain shorts like a fuse in an electric lamp. I watched the light go out.

The man fell flat on his back, unconscious. I went down on one knee to examine him, finding the pulse on his throat. A powerful enough punch could snap his neck.

"He seems to be all right," I stated after a minute, looking up at the Guv. "I can't guarantee he'll be awake anytime soon. Are you well, sir?"

Barker wiped his nose with his bloody handkerchief, not bothering to answer me. He moved to a corner and gingerly lowered himself into a seated position on the canvas.

"Lad," he rumbled. "Could you go to Three Colt Lane? I have a room in Bok Fu Ying's house. Bring me a change of clothes."

"Yes, sir."

I left one man seated and the other unconscious and didn't bother to take a cab. Three Colt Lane was not far and I reached the residence in a couple of minutes. Bok Fu Ying opened the door at my knock. Harm was at her ankles barking. He seemed to find it humorous that I was visiting his other place of residence.

"Thomas," she said. She wore a pink silk Chinese robe, a perfect contrast to her beautiful black hair and eyes. "Come inside."

I stepped across the threshold and bent down to stroke Harm's head. When I stood, I looked into Fu Ying's curious eyes.

"Is everything all right?" she asked, frowning. "Where is Sir?"

"He's at the mission," I answered. "He's been in a bout there and bloodied his nose. I came to fetch a fresh suit."

She nodded. "I must go to him."

"No," I insisted. "Everything is in order. He just requires a change of clothes."

"Did he lose?" she demanded. "I've never seen his nose bloodied."

"No," I assured her, but I wasn't going to tell her how close he came.

She left the room and returned a few minutes later with a change of clothing but she narrowed her eyes and put her hands on her hips.

"You must take care of Sir," she said, as if the bloody nose was my fault.

I nodded. "I will. And Harm looks well. I see he is recovering nicely. I'll tell the Guv."

"I'm still coming with you," she insisted.

"That would be against his wishes. He would lose face if you saw him with blood dripping down his chin. Besides, you have a baby upstairs. Who will take care of her while you are gone?"

She frowned and considered the matter. Then she pushed me and Barker's suit of clothes into the street and closed the door.

When I returned to Mile End Road, both men were awake and leaning against the bottom rope. It appeared they had even been talking.

"Mr. Halton has agreed to bring his sister tomorrow for questioning," Barker said as I approached. "He is a solicitor and will answer our questions about Mr. Fitzhugh."

Halton turned his attention to me.

"What happened?" he asked.

"When?"

"One minute I was standing, ready to throw an uppercut, and

the next I found myself staring at the ceiling and lying flat on the canvas."

"Oh, that," I answered. "Straight punch just under the nose. I knew you hadn't a chance as soon as I saw it land. It was an excellent match, though."

Gerald Halton turned to Barker. "I thought I had you on the ropes. I should have realized you were playing with me."

"It was closer than I care to admit," the Guv replied.

"You're being modest. By god, that was a fight!" the young man declared.

Normally, my partner objected to hearing the Lord's name taken in vain, but he wanted this man in his good graces, and anyway, he was too done in to argue.

"Someone help me up," Halton said. "I could use a cup of water."

Barker tried to budge but could not even struggle to his feet.

"You gentlemen rest," I said. "I'll bring the water to you."

An hour later, we were back in our chambers. Barker made no mention of any pain from the bout and I knew better than to ask. He rose from behind his desk and crossed to the bookcase where his smoking cabinet stood. He pulled a meerschaum from among its brothers and stuffed it with tobacco. When it was lit, he sat back in his chair, deep in thought.

Belatedly, I went to Jeremy's desk and seized *The Times* from that morning. I sat on the edge of the desk and flipped through the pages for anything about the Burkes or Roland Fitzhugh. Terence Poole was named in an article, which would make him insufferable for a few days. Scotland Yard had announced a connection between the two events and requested anyone with information to please come forward. That was a risk, I thought. They'd have to winnow through gawkers, madmen, and self-important people to find one possible witness who saw anything.

Then there it was, at the bottom of the article:

The youngest of the Burke children and only survivor of their fate, Bridget, aged 1, who until yesterday was being cared for by the Alexandra Orphanage for Infants, has been relinquished to the custody of Mrs. Burke's sister, Helena Linford, of Swansea.

My shoulders sagged. I was glad that I hadn't gone to Rebecca with the news that a beautiful little girl who coincidentally looked like both of us might be available for adoption. It would have crushed her. Swansea, I thought. That was nice. She'd be by the sea. Perhaps she'd learn some Welsh. She'd be safe there, far safer than if she were adopted by an enquiry agent and his wife. That would have been a rough-and-tumble life for her at best.

I remembered the baby reaching out for me. If I'd held her, I wouldn't have been able to give her up. It was better this way, I told myself. We'd have a child of our own someday, perhaps, and if not, we could adopt then. It was a perfect solution. So why did it require all my fortitude not to step out the door, go to the Silver Cross down the street and swallow half a bottle of whisky?

The telephone set on Barker's desk jangled, along with my nerves, and I watched as he pulled it to him and lifted the receiver.

"Ahoy," he said. After a moment, he began to speak. "Yes, it is. Excellent! Thank you very much, sir."

He rang off and banished the set to the edge of his desk again.

"That was an attending physician at St John's Priory. Mac is awake and wishes to see us at our earliest convenience."

"Good," I said. "Are you going to tell him how close he came to dying?"

"He may already suspect something occurred by the time we arrive. Let's allow him to lead the conversation and keep him as calm as possible. If he looks well enough to travel, we'll discuss moving him to Eastbourne."

As we surmised, Mac was in a panic when we arrived. He demanded a new nightshirt as if it were a life preserver. He was in mortal fear that Miss Fletcher would arrive at any moment, with his hair disheveled and his chin unshaven. The orderly did not look capable of performing such duties and I was trying to recall if there were a barber nearby when Barker spoke.

"Hot soap and water, man," he growled at the orderly. "And a proper razor. I'll shave the man myself."

I was alarmed and so was Mac, or he would have been if he wasn't overwhelmed. He was still deathly pale, but he is such a naturally good-looking fellow, it suited him. With his dark eyes and cultured features, he looked Byronic. I would have simply looked ill.

"Now, Mac," Barker ordered from the edge of the bed. "Report!"

"There's nothing to report, sir," he answered. "I'm sorry. One moment I was working and the next I woke up in here. What is the day and the time?"

I told him and he looked dazed.

"As long as that?" he said. He still had some trouble breathing. "Has anyone seen me in this condition?"

"I'm afraid so," I replied. "We did our best to keep her out, but Miss Fletcher was frantic to see you. But you have bigger problems than that. You understand you have been very ill. You still are."

He turned and plumped his pillow, but the effort exhausted him.

"The doctor exaggerates out of an abundance of caution," he said. "I assume Dr. Applegate will give him a dressing down."

"Mac, Applegate agrees with him," I insisted. "You have to have time to recover. When you are safe to move in a day or so, we are taking you to a sanitarium for a while."

"For how long?" he demanded. "I have a schedule to maintain. I was going to sharpen all the knives this week."

"Forget your schedules," Barker said. "They are merely soap bubbles. Ah, here we are."

A tray was brought containing a straight razor, a cup and a brush with soap, a towel, and a bowl of water. Mac was as frightened as I would be, but Barker seized him by the shoulders and turned him around so he was peering over Mac's shoulder. Before his factotum had a chance to object, he had a face full of suds. That didn't stop the Guv from peppering him with questions.

"What was the last thing you recall doing?" my partner demanded. He put the blade to Mac's bared throat and shoveled a furrow of suds under one side of his chin.

"I was gathering material to wax the floor, sir. I always start with a good block of beeswax."

The blade made a scraping sound across Mac's neck.

"I had a cup of tea, that's all."

"Was it the breakfast tea we always purchase?" Barker asked.

"Yes sir."

"Then it's gone. Every perishable in the kitchen has been destroyed. Turn your head."

I found the sight of Barker shaving Mac highly entertaining. It reminded me of a time when he took me to a Chinese physician who filled me full of pins.

"How did you feel after you drank the tea?" the Guv persisted.

"Weak, sir," Mac answered. "My chest pounded, and my breath was short. What's happened to me? The doctor hasn't answered any of my questions. I gather he's deferring the duty to Dr. Applegate."

The Guv swiped the blade up Jacob's throat again.

"I still have questions for you, Mr. Maccabee. Tell me, are you in the habit of leaving any of the doors unlocked?"

"The front is always locked, and the back door is secured as long as I'm in the house. It's only open when I'm in the garden, or when Harm is out."

"There, I'm done," Barker pronounced. He took a towel and wiped the foam from Mac's chin and ears. "Someone bring me a pair of scissors. This man needs a haircut!"

"I'm fine, sir," Mac interjected, paler than ever. "I'll get my hair cut in a day or two when I'm better. I have a barber I've used since I was a boy."

"Jacob, look at me," Cyrus Barker said, bending over him. "The possibility exists that you will not get better. You've been poisoned."

"Poisoned?" Mac cried. "Surely there is some mistake. I'll be right as rain in a day or two."

"Mac," I said. "Your heart has been damaged. The tea contained digitalis. Your heartbeat is irregular. If you're feeling weak, that's why."

"I know," he murmured. "The doctor said I was an invalid. What a horrible word!"

"It should have been me," Barker said. "The poison was meant to be for me."

"I drink coffee and you the green tea," I said. "The poison could just as easily have been intended for my wife. Excuse me, sir, but I'm going to find this blackguard and kill him."

The Guv turned, seized a wooden chair, brought it to the edge of the bed, and sat.

"I'm afraid there is more ill news, Mac," he said.

"More, sir?" Jacob asked, looking at him warily.

"The poisoner broke into the house while we were at hospital. He set traps. He poisoned our food and set traps. I brought in a man to find them. Poisons are a specialty of his. One or two may still be there. When you return, you must be very careful."

"If I return," Mac grumbled.

"Of course you'll return," I chided. "You'll be back at your post soon, but until you are ready, you need to go somewhere to rest and recuperate."

"The seaside," Barker rumbled.

"Why not London?" Mac asked. "What is so therapeutic about the seaside? I'd rather rest in the back garden."

"No," I said. "You'd find something to do in five minutes. Then you wouldn't recover. You'll just work."

"But work is how I recover!" he insisted.

"You have no choice in the matter," Barker stated. "You are going to Eastbourne. That is final."

CHAPTER 19

The next morning Jacob Maccabee was released from the Priory. His temporary residence would be the Pevensey Sanitorium, once a country estate listed in the Domesday Book and converted to meet the needs of the infirmed and aged. Mac was ill, but he was also depressed and without hope. He'd grown silent and morose. Exertion put him out of breath. He'd been poisoned in his own house and in his opinion, he'd let everyone down. He'd even allowed Harm to be drugged. He thought his illness a punishment for his failings, considering it less convalescence than exile.

Looking back, I wished we had requested orderlies from Pevensey to come and take him. It would have been less personal. He thought of it as a court-martial: shriven of his uniform, his position, his autonomy, and his dignity. Sitting in his bath chair, locked within himself, he could not see that he was only a part of a larger picture. Was he feeling sorry for himself? Of course he was. Would I have done the same in such circumstances? Probably more so. We Welsh are sensitive creatures.

"Are you comfortable?" Rebecca asked once we were on the train.

We all accompanied him: Rebecca, Barker, Sarah Fletcher, and me. We had the best intentions, but it was a tactical mistake. It only plummeted his mood further.

"I'm fine, thank you," he snapped. He was even surly to Sarah Fletcher.

Barker and I retreated behind our newspapers for the duration of the journey. For once, there wasn't something in the press about the murders. The train arrived in Eastbourne an hour later and the Guv and I helped Jacob into a vehicle. We took two landaus, having so many in our party.

The sanitorium was beautiful as sanitoriums go. It was located close to Beachy Head and had wide windows overlooking the Channel hundreds of feet below. Gulls and fulmars wheeled about the cliffs making raucous cries that reminded me that we were at the seaside. I'd have joked that Mac had come for the waters were he not in such a somber mood.

From my point of view, it looked like a restful holiday. I'd have enjoyed lying about for weeks looking at the sea with no one shooting at me or trying to poison me. I could wake whenever I wanted, spend my hours reading, and for once have time to think. Mind you, I'd have to sneak Rebecca in. Perhaps I could convince a doctor that she was a form of therapy.

"Here we are, Mac," I said, trying to sound positive. "Nice digs, eh?"

I found his room Spartan, but not nearly so in comparison with the cell at the Priory. I once compared him to Michelangelo's statue of David, but now he was pale and drawn. His eye sockets were hollow, and his robe looked too large for his frame. The trip so exhausted him, he fell asleep almost at once.

"I've taken a room nearby," Miss Fletcher stated when we went outside to examine the grounds. She looked as if she expected a challenge. Instead, Barker nodded.

"Charge the room to me," he said.

"I can pay for my own expenses, thank you," she replied. She folded her arms and glared into his dark spectacles.

"He is my butler," the Guv growled. "I am paying for his room here. I need him well as soon as possible. I require someone to look after him whom I can trust. Have you an enquiry pending?"

"No, sir."

"Then I shall have Jenkins make a sign informing potential clients that you are out of London temporarily. Will that be satisfactory?"

Miss Fletcher nodded. "Thank you, Mr. Barker."

I could not tell if she were mollified or just too weary to argue. She and Mac were one of the most mismatched couples I knew, and they never showed a sign of devotion publicly, yet I knew they cared for each other. Whether they were friends or something more intimate I could not say, and anyway, it was none of my business.

We stayed for an hour or two until Mac awoke in time for lunch. The meal was served on a tray: soup, a thick slice of beef smothered in gravy and mushrooms, and several types of vegetables. It wasn't Etienne's cooking, but then nothing is. At least he would not starve.

A doctor named Pillsbury came to meet the new patient and to speak to us. He suddenly took me by the arm.

"Mr. Llewelyn, isn't it?" he asked.

"Yes, sir," I replied.

"I wonder if you might consider doing something for your friend."

I looked at him, trying to divine what he might mean. He led me to a small room and I looked about anxiously.

"What is it?" I asked. "How can I help?"

"Might you consider giving some blood?" he asked. "Mr. Maccabee desperately needs to have the tainted blood in his system replaced."

"How much will you need?" I asked. "I'm currently using that blood myself."

"No more than a gallon."

"A gallon!" I exclaimed.

The doctor smiled. "A little joke. A pint will do."

"Will Thomas feel ill afterward?" Rebecca asked, concern wrinkling her brow. She had followed us down the corridor.

"He'll be a little light-headed," Pillsbury replied. "I'll have some beef tea brought in. Don't let him exert himself afterward. However, you must wait outside, Mrs. Llewelyn. This is no sight for a lady."

Rebecca took it philosophically and patted me on the arm. Then she went to sit in the corridor.

The doctor lay his tools upon a table. "Roll up your sleeve, Mr. Llewelyn."

I doffed my jacket, removed a cuff link, and rolled my shirt to the elbow. The doctor thumped my arm once or twice, hunting for a vein, and then inserted a large needle. I felt the prick of it and shortly afterward the queasy sense that blood was draining from my body. I'd have gladly given blood for Mac, but I didn't care for the doctor taking it without a by-your-leave before I was prepared.

Mac and I enjoyed our relationship, the pranks and the banter. I didn't want that to change. But now, things would be different. We were becoming blood brothers. Literally.

"You're done, sir," Pillsbury said, interrupting my thoughts.

After he put sticking plaster on my arm, I rolled down my sleeve and returned my cuff link. I refused the beef tea and stood too quickly, tottering a bit, but I donned my jacket and walked into the corridor to see Rebecca.

"Was it painful?" she asked.

"It certainly was," I answered. "They jabbed a piece of metal into my arm."

She sighed as we stepped out of the building into the bracing, salt-scented air mixed with the scent of thyme. The air was cold and bracing as we looked out toward the edge of the cliff. It was over five hundred feet to the beach below. Somewhere down there I knew was a lighthouse, but I didn't want to get close enough to see it.

"What is it, Thomas?" Rebecca said at my elbow. "You're awfully quiet."

"I'm worried about Mac."

"I'm certain he will recover," she replied. "It would be too tragic otherwise."

We were near Seaford, I realized, not more than a couple of miles from Philippa Ashleigh's estate. That must have been the reason the Guv chose Pevensey for Mac's recovery.

"I suspect we're not going back to London today," I remarked. "If I know the Guv, we're staying at Mrs. Ashleigh's estate."

"Of course we are," my wife answered, as if she knew it a week ago rather than a few hours.

"Philippa will be glad to see you."

"And I her," she said. "We are fast friends, but Mr. Barker keeps her to himself. She comes to London far more often than we hear about."

"Really?" I asked. "Have you any new impressions of my partner today?"

"He seems tense, like a coiled spring," she replied.

I gave her an expurgated version of the boxing match. She gritted her teeth when I grew too graphic.

"What is it about men and fisticuffs? You'd think they'd outgrow it."

I had no response to that, being an antagonistics teacher.

Barker came out of the building and joined us, nodding at Rebecca.

"Mrs. Llewelyn," he said. "Mrs. Ashleigh has invited us to her home for dinner. In fact, she would prefer that we stay the night. Is that inconvenient?"

"Well, I don't know," Rebecca replied. "I wasn't prepared to stay overnight. I still haven't got any things with me."

"Mrs. Ashleigh informs me that she can provide you with the necessary items you require. Or we can return to London, if you prefer."

"Naturally, we must stay," she answered. "I'd love to see Philippa again."

The foregone conclusion was decided then. We boarded the hansom cab and were taken through the charming town to the outskirts where Lady Ashleigh's house looked down over the village and the village looked up to it. Tulsemore is a beautiful estate, a large Tudor home that had been added to as recently as ten years ago when she'd had a conservatory installed. I'd been shot there, as I recall. It was another reason I don't like gardens. If I needed one.

"Mr. Barker, how pleasant to see you," Frost, the butler, said when we arrived at the front door. "And the same can be said for both of you, Mr. and Mrs. Llewelyn. Come inside. Her Ladyship is expecting you."

The lady of the manor glided in, swanlike, in a dress of pale blue, which set off her vibrant golden-red hair. She kissed us both on the cheek and took Barker's arm. Philippa Ashleigh was a few years younger than Barker, in her fourth decade, but in the full bloom of her beauty. She had pale and flawless skin and eyes as blue as the Channel.

"Come into the parlor," she said. When we were seated, she turned to the Guv. "How is Jacob?"

"Rather low," Barker replied. "But Miss Fletcher is there to look after him."

"You've told me about her, haven't you?" she asked. "She's taken the office above yours, if I am correct. She sounds like a spirited young woman."

"I wish Mac was spirited," Rebecca murmured. "I'm worried about him."

"I'll visit him in a day or so when he is settled," Philippa said. "What do the doctors say?"

"Dr. Pillsbury believes he will recover with rest," the Guv replied. "I cannot be certain whether he is truthful or merely optimistic."

"He will heal," our hostess insisted. "Fresh Sussex air and sun will do him well and Pevensey has a fine reputation. Poor Jacob has to recover. I insist upon it!"

Philippa Ashleigh was a baroness. When she insists, who would dare refuse her?

CHAPTER 20

W e awoke the next morning in Lady Philippa Ashleigh's home. Philippa had sent a maid, a footman, and a cook to see to our needs, so we sat down to a true English breakfast. Normally, I make do with a brioche or a *pain au chocolat*, but we were "roughing it," as the American, Twain, put it, so I consoled myself with eggs, sausages, white and black pudding, grilled mushrooms, fried tomatoes, toast, and coffee. Over my second cup I became restless.

"Perhaps we should go back to London today," I said, placing my serviette on the table. "I dread to think what the Pie Man is up to."

"No, Thomas," Barker replied. "Our lives are in danger, and this business has proven distressing to us all. I believe a day's holiday is in order."

Rebecca and I looked at each other. I thought perhaps I had misheard him. The Barker and Llewelyn Agency does not take holidays. It had finally happened, I thought: the world had gone mad.

"Mrs. Llewelyn," the Guv continued, looking at an apprehensive Rebecca. "Might your maid be able to find some suitable clothing this morning? If you wish to purchase new things, pray do so. I suggest something nautical. Give the bill to your husband for expenses."

"Very well," Rebecca answered cautiously. An offer of free items for one's wardrobe was not to be taken lightly.

"Thomas, you and I will visit one of the local shops. The suits won't be bespoke, of course, but they have a very large selection. Something is bound to fit us."

"Where are we going?" I asked.

The Guv stroked his mustache. "Didn't I say? It seems like a good day for a sail."

"But, we're in the middle of a case, sir," I argued.

The whole holiday business smacked of a strategic retreat, the sort that generally came with a tail between one's legs. It wasn't Barker's usual method, unless one considered that he always did the unexpected.

In lieu of an answer, he rose and left the table. Perhaps he felt the killer was too close and we required some distance. Perhaps he felt, as I did, that Rebecca's life was in danger in London. Barker sent the maid with Rebecca, offering her protection, and the Guv and I went to buy suits.

Although most of our suits are made for us by R & R Kraus's Tailor Shop, we would have to forgo our usual habit. We found ourselves in a shop along Seaford's Esplanade. where we each purchased a blazer with linen trousers. We met Rebecca in the High Street when we departed the shop. She was in a fine mood, as any woman would be who had just purchased a new dress and a hat. It was that color that men called white, but women called "eggshell" or "ecru." It was wide brimmed with a swath of blue silk that tied under her chin. She looked fetching and I told her so.

Ten minutes later, we were back at Lady Ashleigh's house where she and Frost awaited us at the entrance.

"What is the plan for the afternoon?" she asked.

"I am taking the *Osprey* out into the Channel," Barker replied. "It is fine weather for sailing. It has been half a year since I was aboard, and I want to feel as if there is not someone looking over my shoulder."

"I've never been aboard the *Osprey*," Rebecca told the Guv. "In fact, I have never been on a boat at all."

"Then we shall rectify that problem this very day, ma'am."

The door opened and a man came in, very tanned and thin, with hair bleached blond by the sun. I recognized him at once. It was Beauchamp, the man who cares for the *Osprey*. I knew him very little, though I suspected he was in the employ of my partner, even though his name was not in our books. He lived in a former coast guard's home with his wife and three sons. He removed his cap and gave Barker a nod, then the Guv bowed to us and left the room with him.

Philippa watched him leave and then turned to my wife. "Did he just call you 'ma'am'?"

"He did," Rebecca said, nodding.

"Sometimes he calls her 'Mrs. Llewelyn,'" I added. "But then, he calls me 'Mr. Llewelyn' at times, generally when he is displeased with me."

"That man," Philippa huffed. "He is so old-fashioned. I suspect he learned his manners out of a book printed in Jane Austen's day. I'll speak to him."

"No, don't," Rebecca said, holding up a hand. "Let the two of us work on our relationship together. I haven't dared call him Cyrus yet, either."

"Perish forbid," I muttered.

Just then the Guv opened the door and stepped in. "Paul assures me that all is in readiness. The sea is calm and there is a light breeze. It is ideal sailing weather."

Soon we clamored into Lady Ashleigh's carriage and journeyed a short distance to Seaford harbor. Rebecca was in an excellent mood and therefore, so was I. Barker looked away as we travelled down the hard-packed chalk road. I thought about it a minute or two and then it came to me. We were seated as couples. It was an acknowledgment of their unspoken relationship. Old-fashioned indeed, I thought.

At the harbor, we alighted from the carriage by the *Osprey*. She is a lorcha, something in between a Chinese junk and a European barque. There were sails as well as a funnel for steam if required. She was an odd vessel, particularly in a Sussex seaside town, but she gleamed white as a gull and the brass on board was polished to a high gloss.

"Request permission to come aboard," Barker boomed.

There was silence for a moment, and I wondered if there was anyone aboard to answer the call. Then a sturdily built man came to the side and glared at us. I had to look twice to reassure myself what I was seeing. It was Ho.

"Granted!" he bellowed and disappeared again.

"Who is that?" Rebecca asked, moving closer to me.

"He is Barker's best friend," I replied. "His name is Ho. As I recall, he used to be first mate when this boat was a merchant vessel in the China Seas."

"Didn't you tell me last year that the boat once had a diving bell for salvage work so that, like an osprey, it was able to dive deep?"

"That's right," Philippa said. "One day they found a wreck in the Pearl River full of gold and jewels. I think it was a pirate vessel. It was enough to make all of them wealthy men."

"Mr. Barker has led a very unusual life," Rebecca observed, looking at me. She'd have elaborated if Lady Ashleigh were not present.

I won't go into the complexities of heaving two women in voluminous dresses up a rope ladder, but it was eventually accomplished with only a minor affront to their dignities. I gave

my wife a brief tour of the vessel and then the women disappeared into the hold. I believe there was some question about
whether the hat Rebecca brought could survive a sail in the
English Channel. I returned to the deck.

"You gonna work or powder your nose?" Ho said practically in
my ear. I ignored the remark.

"It's to be the English sail, then?" I asked.

"We don't want to frighten the natives," he replied in his posh-
est voice.

I removed my blazer and tie and began climbing the ratlines
to untie the ropes that held the sails. Blazer or not, I should have
realized this would not be a pleasure sail for me. It was no more
than twenty feet to the deck, but shimmying along a swaying
mizzenmast has its challenges. I didn't want to split my skull on a
Saturday outing, particularly when that gargoyle Ho was watching. It would give him too much satisfaction.

Beauchamp was adjusting lines while Barker tested the knots.
Ho pulled on a rope like he was attempting to hang someone.
I helped him wrestle it to the side where I tied it in a passable
clove hitch. Ho grumbled because he could find no fault. I was
learning slowly but surely.

Air filled the sails. One of Beauchamp's sons untied the ropes
from the cleats, and we slipped out of the harbor with the Seven
Sisters on our left, one of the prettiest bits of coastline in the whole
Channel. We tacked toward starboard, the Guv at the helm of
his own ship, as the breeze picked up the *Osprey* like a kite and
pushed her along.

I've never really understood sails as a means of reliable trans-
portation. I'm a steam man, myself. I could fill a train's boiler
with coal and the funnel with smoke and we'd chug along steadily
at whatever speed Barker desired. But a vessel powered by air
at the caprice of force winds? I didn't trust it. What if the wind
ceased and one was stranded mid-ocean for a week? I'll reckon
you'd want a full coal bunker then.

Rebecca came up on deck with a small tin in her hand and offered it to me.

"Sweets?" I asked.

"Pastilles," she answered. "For *mal de mer*."

Appropriately enough, they were Halton's Pastille Sweets. The lid assured the customer of its healthful benefits.

"You're not seasick already, are you?"

"No, no," she replied. "Philippa said I should have them if I needed them. I think this is rather exciting."

"It is," I admitted. "Especially if you aren't required to climb the rigging."

"If you fall and kill yourself, I'm never speaking to you again."

I could not argue with that logic, so I went to speak with Barker. He was at the helm holding a wheel that looked more European than Asian. He wore a shirt as I did, but he'd tied a red neckerchief about his throat. He didn't seem to mind the cold wind and he was crooning to himself in a tuneless way, like a cat purring.

"Why did we waste the summer, Thomas?" he asked. "We could have been out here every weekend."

"Commerce, sir," I replied. "Cases to be solved."

"We are becoming too popular," he growled. "Our caseload is heavy and we haven't even received our royal warrant."

"We could hire more agents," I suggested. "Or we could even open another office. A branch in Liverpool or York. Or even Edinburgh."

"Perhaps," he said, but I wondered if his mind even recorded the suggestion.

Once a boat is under way, it is all rope-work. Loosen this one, tighten that one. Is that one fraying? Often the ropes were as tight as bowstrings.

I was standing by the ratlines when I felt something hot against my elbow. Someone was holding a tin of coffee out to me. It was Etienne Dummolard, once the galley cook aboard this very vessel.

"Etienne," I said, surprised. "What are you doing here?"

"Monsieur Beauchamp *et fils*, they eat all the food from the pantry. I have been stocking it full again. Where are we?"

"I believe that's Worthing just ahead."

"He is banking. We are leaving the coast soon, I am thinking."

The sails protested for a while, but finally capitulated to Captain Barker's demands.

I took a sip of the coffee. The tin was so hot I nearly burned my lip.

"Etienne, you make the best coffee in Europe," I said.

"No, no, monsieur. No, I assure you. I make the best coffee in all the world."

"*Tout le monde?*" I asked.

"*Oui!*"

"*Bien sûr.*"

I moved to where Rebecca stood by the port bow. I wondered if she had become seasick, but when she turned her cheeks were pink.

"This is wonderful, Thomas! I'm having the most marvelous day."

She was right, I thought. Until that moment I hadn't thought of poisons or poisoners once. I hadn't awakened that morning with my jaw clenched. We were not trying to stay alive. We were busy living.

"Look!" Rebecca said. "Is that France there, that line of gray?"

"It is," I answered. "You said you've never been on a boat before, but we honeymooned in the Mediterranean, if you recall."

"Oh, a ship, a steamer," she tutted. "That's not the same thing now, is it?"

"Of course not," I said, shrugging. "They say a ship can carry a boat, but a boat can't carry a ship."

She smiled. "Then you concede my point."

"Of course."

I stepped closer and held the rail beside her. "Have you had any inspirations about the Guv today?"

She considered the matter.

"He is in an excellent mood," she replied. "It's as if the ship were part of him. Philippa is enjoying herself as well. They seem eminently suited to each other, but I suspect she is humoring him today. Only, I don't know why. This sudden gathering of old shipmates must have some meaning. Was Mr. Beauchamp a member of the original crew?"

"He was."

"Interesting."

"You have questions, but no answers."

"All in good time," she said.

"We should be in London interviewing witnesses and suspects," I complained. "This is not like him."

"Aren't you having a good time?" she pressed.

"Me?" I said, tucking my hands into my pockets. "I suppose, but this puzzles me, and I hate things that puzzle me. What is he thinking of, gadding about when there is a poisoner after us? I don't understand him. I am not in possession of all the facts."

She patted my hand.

"You sound more like Mr. Barker every day."

"There's no need to insult me."

"You'll work it out, darling," she replied. "You always do. You must, or it will drive you mad."

Three hours later, we had breached the gap. France was before us and England a row of far distant cliffs. We were in the shipping lanes. When we boarded the Osprey, it seemed large, but now it was dwarfed by freighters and steamers.

"Where are we, do you think?"

"I see something up ahead," I answered. "Perhaps it is Le Havre."

I heard the wheel creak in Barker's hand and within a moment the boat drifted into the harbor. The docks bristled with vessels of all sorts. The people looked different, or at least, they dressed differently. A man rowed by wearing a white and blue knit jumper that I would shoot myself before wearing.

My wife hopped once and clapped her hands.

"I didn't imagine I would be in France today," she exclaimed.

We found a berth and as soon as the *Osprey* was moored Rebecca went down to retrieve her hat. Meanwhile, Etienne brushed by me and disappeared into a crowd of tourists and mariners. A moment later, Ho did the same, but in another direction. My wife returned looking like a woman in a Renoir painting.

"I believe Etienne has gone off to find a meal for us," I said. "Ho left, too, but I have no idea what for."

"Perhaps he did not feel comfortable. Did you invite him to dine with us?" she asked.

"No, I didn't. But he looked determined to go somewhere, as if he had an appointment. He and Etienne are not overfond of one another. I don't believe they would willingly sit together over a meal."

Barker and I donned our jackets again. With no waistcoat or hat and the kerchief about his throat, he looked positively Gallic. Philippa appeared a few minutes later, having resettled any locks that had been disturbed by the wind on the voyage. Her ensemble was peach colored.

It was market day in Le Havre, and there were booths in the center of the streets full of flowers and produce. I stopped trying to work out why we were there and began enjoying myself. Rebecca was having a fine time and she chatted with Philippa as though they were the best of friends. It had indeed become an impromptu holiday.

We heard a whistle ahead and I looked to see Etienne waving at us by the door of a restaurant. He led us inside and as I passed, he murmured in my ear.

"I believe the owner here is not a complete idiot."

"At least no one is trying to poison us," I replied.

"I will tell you after I sample his *tripes à la mode de Caen*."

The sea air had given us an appetite. We started with escargot and the women ordered omelets. I had the meadow salted lamb and Barker a simple steak de boeuf, but then a large platter of seafood was served, full of cold oysters, shrimp, lobster, scallops, and clams, with lemon wedges scattered among them. Etienne and the owner argued about the wine, but the two got on well enough. Eventually we finished with coffee and *teurgoule*, a kind of rice pudding with cinnamon that is baked for hours. It was ambrosia.

We did not tarry, although I had thoughts of a nice hotel. I'd eaten too much, and an afternoon nap seemed very continental. At the end of our meal the owner ripped the bill in two with a flourish. I wasn't fooled, however. No doubt Etienne had paid for the meal.

As we returned to the Osprey, I saw Ho come out of a telegraph office. He hefted a sack full of food I suspected was difficult to find in London. The sack I understood, but what business would a tea-shop owner with underworld connections have in a telegraph office? I looked over at Rebecca, who was laughing at something Philippa had said.

We were back in Seaford late that afternoon and then returned to London again before bed. Le Havre had felt safe, but we'd trespassed on Philippa's hospitality for too long. It was time to return to our home in Newington, dangerous though it might be.

"Rebecca," I said as the cab clattered toward the Elephant and Castle. "I think you should stay in Camomile Street tonight."

"We discussed this," she answered. "'Whither thou goest, I will go.' That is from Ruth, is it not, Mr. Barker?"

"Indeed, ma'am," he rumbled. "Chapter one, verse sixteen."

Barker's mouth twitched. She'd made him smile.

CHAPTER 21

The next day was Saturday, a half day off unless Barker needed me. Jeremy Jenkins had gathered his notes from the files in Fitzhugh's cabinet the day before, and they were sitting on his desk when we arrived. The Guv had given him the morning off. My partner went through the notes, taking more pains than I felt they deserved.

Around ten o'clock he rose and spoke.

"Come along," he said. "I fancy some honey."

I did my best to maintain my sangfroid as we left, but it was difficult. I didn't believe a word of it. Barker does not "fancy" anything. Food is mere sustenance to him. He had a limited palate to begin with and given the amount of tobacco he uses it is a miracle he can taste anything at all. Also, he has little interest in sweets, shortbread notwithstanding. For him to say "I fancy some honey" was patently absurd. On the other hand, one of our suspects kept bees.

"Covent Garden Market it is, then," I said.

I love all kinds of markets, the upper-class ones of the West End and the jumbled and more colorful of the East. Books, busbies, and bric-a-brac, and things beginning with the other twenty-five letters of the alphabet. Cumulatively, I've spent weeks of my life in stalls, haggling over pounds and shillings and I saw no reason to quit. Having Barker along did present a bit of a problem. For example, I lighted on a small book stall tucked in among the flower vendors that had a full set of the works of Dickens. I'd been flirting with buying them for about half a year. I wondered about the efficacy of asking the Guv to help me carry them back to the office, or better yet, straight to Newington, all twenty volumes. Some other time, I thought.

Barker's viselike hand took me by the elbow and propelled me forward.

"There it is!" he said, doubling his resolve. Before I was prepared, I was pushed in front of a table with a professional-looking hoarding above it, which read:

Mistress Elder—Herbalist
Fresh Herbs & Herbal Teas
Charms, Balms, & Potions
Comb Honey & Eggs

"Mrs. Elder," my partner said, raising his bowler. "It's good to see you again."

The moth from our first meeting had molted into a butterfly. She wore a gauzy dress of many layers and hues, and a pair of large gypsy earrings which set off her blond hair, which she now wore about her shoulders. She was onstage, if only a small one. How much of her costume was natural, and how much designed to entice customers to take home something prepared by an actual witch? Oh, well, I thought. Witches must pay rent too, I supposed.

"Mr. Barker," she said, stepping back, as if he were a dog about to bite. "I thought myself shed of you on Thursday."

"Aye, you would have been if you hadn't lied to me in almost every particular. Now, we can either hold our conversation across this table for all potential patrons to hear or you can invite me into your booth, where we can discuss matters at a more reasonable volume. The choice is yours."

Her jade-colored eyes were not on us, but on the customers and stall mates, who were already eyeing the exchange. My partner can easily draw a crowd, but it wasn't the kind of attention Zinnia Elder was seeking. She invited us behind the table.

"A wise choice," he stated. "I've been going over some notes from your trial. Did you really curse Mr. Fitzhugh after you were found guilty? That would have been most prejudicial to your case."

"The newspapers claimed I said, 'I curse you for what you have done.' What I said was 'Curse you for what you've done.' It has an entirely different meaning. It was neither the time nor the place to discuss witchcraft."

"What had Mr. Fitzhugh done to you that you hadn't done to yourself?" he asked. "No one forced you to administer pennyroyal tea to Ellie Flanders. You understood what the sentence would be if you were arrested. Fitzhugh did no wrong. That is, he did no wrong to you."

The woman frowned and shrugged her narrow shoulders.

"Were you acquainted with the late Mrs. Fitzhugh?" Barker continued.

"Alice Fitzhugh and I were at school together," Mrs. Elder replied. "She was a dear, but we weren't close. She was a retiring sort of person, and I was anything but. However, a few years after we left school, I met her by chance on the street and took her to tea. I assumed we would reminisce, but we soon found ourselves discussing another matter entirely. Each of us had marital troubles and it helped to talk about them."

Cyrus Barker crossed his arms, a danger to the fabric, and cocked his head to the side.

"What sort of troubles would those be, precisely?" he asked.

"Troubles common to a pair of young brides, I suppose," she answered. "Our husbands were young, barely even adults, and our dowries presented them with more money and more responsibility than they had ever faced before. Mine speculated with ours, hoping to double it. He halved it instead. By the end of the year, he took the rest and went off with another woman. Good riddance to bad rubbish, I say."

"And Mrs. Fitzhugh?"

"Young Mr. Fitzhugh was buying into a law partnership, which requires capital and long hours. She was a naïve little thing, always willing to believe the best of him."

"You were not that generous," I observed.

She frowned at me but did not deny it. "Perhaps my own experiences had colored my judgment. I did not trust him."

"We have heard from other witnesses that he was a libertine," Barker said. It was a lie, but he was drawing her out.

Zinnia Elder turned her head and gave him a puzzled look. "Alice didn't mention it. In fact, she said she couldn't get him out of his office. He was very ambitious. He'd have worked 'round the clock if she didn't beg to see him. She told me it wasn't chivalrous, and that she should be his first love."

"That stands to reason," I said.

"Sadly, it comes down to money," she continued. "It is a man's world and there is little protection offered to women. In a way, we are property, we and everything we own. Excuse me, gentlemen."

She stepped forward and held a conversation with a woman interested in some jewelry she had made. I began to count her skills in my head. She raised hens and bees. She made charms and jewelry. She mixed her own balms. Goodness knows what the potions were made from. She grew and brewed herbs. It was a tremendous amount of work.

She stepped back again after giving the customer change.

Barker pounced immediately. "You put yourself in a good bit of trouble over that poor girl and her baby."

"I did," she admitted. "I was stupid. I allowed myself to be drawn into it personally. I felt I had to help. No one else would, certainly not that dolt of a husband of hers. He was barely nineteen and had to quit university."

That dredged up some bad memories for me. I'd been a husband at nineteen myself, and not much of one. I was both attending lectures and working as a batsman at Oxford, while my young wife, Jenny, was recuperating from tuberculosis. Things were already tragic, and they became worse when a student I worked for accused me of theft. I was sentenced to eight months, a warning to all Welshmen and coalminers' sons that they are not welcome at university, scholarship or no. Jenny died of consumption alone, while I languished in Oxford Prison.

"You are an unofficial advocate for your sex," Barker continued.

I could see Mrs. Elder start to defend herself, but then she let it go.

"I do what I can," she said. "There are so many women who have needs far more desperate than mine. There is a rip in the system, a hole. A child will be dressed and fed by a charity, a husband will be given a situation, but a wife is promised nothing and expected to keep her family safe and together. She must fend for herself and her family with no support. It is ever thus."

I noticed a change in her tone, then. She sounded more cultured. It was easy to forget that she was educated and from a good family, before her life was ruined. She had started high and been brought low.

"Another customer," she said, stepping forward to speak to a well-dressed woman and her husband. Her speech became more cultured still. She had developed a way of working out what someone wanted to hear and to mimic it back to them. She was clever, Mrs. Elder; and could very well be our poisoner. If she admitted to being an advocate for her sex, what of the other? Would she have been a danger to Fitzhugh if his wife, her schoolmate, complained about him?

"Another question or two and Thomas and I will leave you to your commerce. How did you feel when you heard about Mrs. Fitzhugh's mental collapse?"

"I was surprised," she said. "As I told you, I didn't know her well, but I had the impression that she was fragile emotionally. I hoped a visit to a spa might do her some good. However, I never thought she would break down completely. That came as quite a shock."

"Did you form an opinion of Mr. Fitzhugh then?" the Guv continued.

She frowned in thought and tapped her cheek with a forefinger. "I had not met him, and I was not the cynic I am now. Quite the contrary, the two of us had the optimism of all young brides. We were convinced our futures would work out splendidly, and these minor dowry matters would come to naught once our husbands became successful. We'd live in large homes and would never have to suffer want."

"Tell me," Barker said as the woman began wrapping candles in paper. "What did you mean when you said, 'Curse you for what you have done'?"

She turned and narrowed her eyes. "Alice was long dead then, but she had been so concerned when I met her about his ambition and drive. I thought him hard-hearted. I also suspected that she'd mentioned my name to him, because when I stopped at their door to ask after her one day, a rough-looking matron informed me that she had been sent to Baden-Baden for her nerves. I suspected he was prejudiced against me. I think it more than coincidence that of the hundreds of barristers in London he should be the one to prosecute my case."

"Thousands," Barker intoned.

"I find it unfair and even dangerous that a girl should be tethered to her dowry, and yet have no say in how it is spent," she continued. "It was the ruin of me. I wish I could have saved Alice, poor thing. But as I told you, I hadn't met the man. Perhaps he attacked every case with such obvious relish. I admit it was my fault for getting myself into that nasty business, but I must admit I felt Ellie's plight as well. Women are not taught or prepared for making their own decisions or looking after their personal interests. It's why I involved myself in both these situations, to my own detriment."

"Indeed," Barker murmured.

"Take poor Alice," she said. "She was sweet and naïve. Her father was a surgeon, so she had a proper dowry. I suspected it was like catnip to a tom. She was not prepared for being an adult. Every decision before marriage was her father's. Afterward it was her husband's."

"Did you attend her funeral?" the Guv asked.

Mrs. Elder greeted a customer and talked with her for a few moments. Then she turned to us again.

She shook her head. "I'm sorry. What did you ask?"

"The funeral," I supplied.

"I did not," she said. "It was for family only. I wanted to go, but did not want to cause a disturbance. I lit a candle for her at home instead. It was a personal remembrance of sorts."

"Thomas, do you have any questions?" the Guv asked.

He enjoyed putting me on the spot, but then I wasn't there simply to follow him about.

"Mrs. Elder, were you aware that when he died Roland Fitzhugh was engaged to be married?" I asked. "It was in the society columns."

"I was not aware, sir," she replied. "And I most certainly do not have time to lay about and coo over who married whom and what they wore."

"Ma'am, it would have been better had you answered our questions truthfully the first time," Barker chided.

"But how was I to know?" she asked. "My experience with Scotland Yard has been 'slip-the-darbies-on-her.' The two of you are gentlemanly. The CID is not. They are not gentle at all. One clouted me on the ear with his billy."

"Have you no family to go to for advice?"

"None to speak of. My aunts have washed their hands of me. I am disgraced. Not for being a witch. For losing a husband. I don't expect a man to understand."

"You should," he replied. "We are not all ravening wolves. One must expect compassion from both sexes. Do you represent a particular charity or organization?"

"No, sir, I do not," she stated.

"Then form one," he said. "You are obviously organized enough to do so. Set up a charity and I will have Mr. Llewelyn write a cheque."

I began adding in my head, always a headache-inducing proposition for a classics scholar. The late Mr. Fitzhugh would not be paying our expenses. Mr. Gladstone had offered to pay, but I wasn't certain Barker would send him a bill. Jeremy had been given money for clothes and an allowance. Barker had given a hundred pounds to a failing public garden and cat sanctuary, and now he was offering to fund a charity for poor women, led by a possible murderess.

Rebecca can attest that I am an impractical man, but often I feel that I am the only practical member of our agency when financial matters are concerned. I wondered how generous Cyrus Barker had been when he was a ship's captain in the China Sea. Still, the man was wealthy, although I didn't know how wealthy. That little morsel of knowledge he always kept from me.

"Are you having me on?" she asked, probably expecting another trick. It is not good to be cynical in one's thirties. It gives one little to do in one's forties.

"Here is my card," he said, taking one from his waistcoat

pocket. "Remember, if one is going to do a public work one must not be fainthearted. You must see it through!"

Mrs. Elder's eyes traveled to mine to make certain he was serious. I nodded in return. If Barker is anything, he is a man of his word.

"Thank you for speaking candidly to us," he rumbled. "We actually came to purchase some honey."

Barker raised his hat again, and after the transaction, so did I. I was lost in thought as we pushed our way through the crowd like gondoliers in a canal.

"It was difficult enough for me to find work when I came to London with nothing but a prison sentence to my name," I remarked. "I don't think a woman in her circumstances could find work at all, certainly not something suitable. You know what that means."

"The streets," he replied. "And all that entails. However, Mrs. Elder changed her own course through determination and industry."

"If someone told me by the end of this enquiry, I'd be feeling sorry for a witch, I wouldn't have believed him."

"Are we nearing the end?" he asked, handing me the jar of honey, as I suspected he would.

"Lord, I hope so," I answered.

For once he did not correct my small blasphemy.

CHAPTER 22

I'd forgotten the inquest into the death of Roland Fitzhugh was to occur that afternoon at two o'clock at the Dove Inn, the very establishment in which the entire case began. The room was filled to capacity, not merely by the inquisitive public, but by the twenty jury men, twelve of whom would be required to return an accusation of murder. The tables and chairs had been shuffled about and Dr. Vandeleur sat at the best table left, with a notepad and a glass of sherry. Most of us had stout. The proprietor was doing a brisk trade and had even brought in more staff to accommodate the crowd.

Vandeleur explained the purpose and procedures of the inquest in a voice that was simultaneously gruff and elegant. He was in his natural element. This is what a degree from the University of Edinburgh in general medicine and another from Oxford University in law will get one if he is willing to apply himself vigorously for his entire life.

Here I will provide a transcription of the proceedings, which I took myself for our permanent record.

Coroner: I call Mr. Geoffrey Beeton to the stand. Mr. Beeton, what is your occupation?

Beeton: I am an innkeeper. The innkeeper of this establishment, as a matter of fact.

Coroner: Were you acquainted with the victim, Mr. Fitzhugh?

Beeton: Yes, sir, I was. He came in here of a morning, two or three times a month for a year or more.

Coroner: You have visited the body in the Metropolitan Police morgue in the company of most of the jurymen here. Do you hereby identify the body you viewed as being that of your customer, Mr. Fitzhugh?

Beeton: I do, yes.

Coroner: Let the jury know that Mr. Fitzhugh's former business partner Edward Lindsay, his manservant Alexander Ogilvy, and his father, Chester Fitzhugh, have all identified the body as being Mr. Roland Fitzhugh. Jurors, if you agree that the body belonged to Mr. Fitzhugh, please raise your hand. [Pause.] We have received our vote of twelve. In fact, let the record show it is unanimous. Now, Mr. Beeton, what did Mr. Fitzhugh eat at your inn on the morning he died and at what time did he break his fast?

Beeton: Seven o'clock, sir. He had an egg, a rasher of bacon, and a bun. It was his usual order. We wouldn't stay open long if every customer ordered as he did.

Coroner: Confine yourself to the questions, sir. Did you prepare the meal yourself?

Beeton: I did, sir. That's why I remember it.

Coroner: Did you deliver it to his table?

Beeton: No, sir. It was carried by Meg Turner. She's new, so I watched her take it to him. I wanted to see how she treated our regular customers.

Coroner: And what happened next?

Beeton: He came up to the counter for a tumbler of water. After ten minutes he returned and complained the water was off.

Coroner: And what did you do?

Beeton: I took a big swallow from the pitcher. It didn't taste off to me, but I'll admit we were down near the bottom of the barrel, sir, and had not opened the next. Twenty minutes later my stomach started to hurt.

Coroner: Did Mr. Fitzhugh seem satisfied with your answer?

Beeton: No, sir. He was agitated. I apologized and helped him to a cab. Then I poured out the pitcher and filled it again. No one complained about it for the rest of the day.

Coroner: Was there any point when Mr. Fitzhugh's food was unattended?

Beeton: Not at all. I gave it to Meg and she took it 'round to him.

Coroner: So you did suffer an ill effect after drinking the water?

Beeton: Yes, sir, but by then, Mr. Fitzhugh had gone.

Coroner: You may step down. I call Mr. Klaus Steiner. [Mr. Steiner came forward and sat.]

Coroner: You are the owner of the Old Vienna coffeehouse, is that correct?

Steiner: It is.

Coroner: On the sixth day of October, two men entered your establishment, did they not?

Steiner: A lot of men enter my establishment.

There was general laughter at the answer. Steiner looked discomfited. He didn't understand the humor. Vandeleur quelled the laughter with a hard look.

Coroner: One of the men was a priest. Did you note the second one?

Steiner: I didn't note his appearance, only his actions. He

purchased the coffee. I remember him setting a cup in front of the priest.

Coroner: Did either of the men get up from the table after that?

Steiner: *Ja.* I mean, yes, sir. My daughter was just cutting the Sacher torte, which requires precision and a few minutes to slice properly. They both came to the counter for a piece and then returned to their table.

Coroner: Was it a large table?

Steiner: No, a small round one that seats two chairs. The room is full of them.

Coroner: Would someone at another table be able to reach out and put something in a cup of coffee?

Steiner: I suppose so. One could certainly touch another's table.

Coroner: Was it busy that afternoon?

Steiner: We are always busy.

Coroner: When did you next notice the two men?

Steiner: The priest leaned over and was helping the other man. The second man went into the water closet. He was there for some time, I believe. A queue formed. Finally, he came out and the two left.

Coroner: You noted his movements but not the man himself.

Steiner: He wore a hat, and I was busy making coffee. I don't have time to watch customers. I have duties to perform.

I recall that Vandeleur gave him another hard look, but the café owner did not notice.

Coroner: You may go. The priest who accompanied the second man to the café is Father Anthony Michaels of St Mary Matfelon. It is not expected that a clergyman speak at an inquest or trial. However, Father Michaels has provided the following note: *"I affirm that I visited the Old Vienna coffeehouse on October sixth in the company of Roland Fitzhugh, a friend of mine. We stayed for about half an hour. Roland began to feel ill. I helped him outside and put him in a cab.*

I called on him the following day to see how he was doing and found him much recovered. He was about to go to the House of Commons."

Here I leaned over and murmured in Barker's ear. "I don't see a motive, but I think the Father might have been able to put something in Fitzhugh's coffee at some point."

"That is certainly possible," he replied.

A gavel came down on Vandeleur's table and he eyed us critically.

"Silence," he ordered.

Coroner: Let me state that ipecac was found in Mr. Fitzhugh's digestive system three days later. However, there was no way to determine how many times he was subjected to it. His actions were consistent with receiving a dose while in the café.

"So, he wasn't poisoned that day," I said to the Guv. "Ipecac is not a poison."

Barker lifted a finger.

"That has not yet been established," he replied.

The coroner called Detective Chief Inspector Terence Poole. Steiner rose from his seat and Terry Poole made his way to the front of the room.

Coroner: Inspector, when did you first meet Mr. Roland Fitzhugh?

Poole: The morning he died, sir, at approximately eight o'clock. I received a message from Sergeant Kirkwood at the front desk that an MP was there to see me and came down to see what he wanted.

Coroner: What was your first impression as a seasoned detective?

Poole: He was agitated, but also embarrassed. That is, he feared he was being poisoned, but he was also afraid he might be wrong. He said he'd had a cup of coffee at a nearby coffeehouse two days before and was ill afterward. Then he drank some water at the Dove Inn that morning and was ill again. I thought it more likely he had some kind of ulcer. Men don't get poisoned very often.

Coroner: Did he name someone he believed might have poisoned him?

Poole: No, sir, he had no idea.

Coroner: Did you tell him you would investigate the matter?

Poole: Yes, I did. Aside from him being a member of Parliament, he was a barrister and I supposed he knew what he was about.

Coroner: When did you next see Roland Fitzhugh?

Poole: In the offices of Barker and Llewelyn, Private Enquiry Agents at 7 Craig's Court. It wasn't more than half an hour later.

Coroner: And how did you find him?

Poole: Stone dead on the floor of their office, sir, with his shirt torn open. There was no obvious sign of what had killed him.

Coroner: Have you continued to investigate the matter?

Poole: Yes, we have interviewed many people, but it is still an ongoing investigation, and I am not prepared to talk about it.

Coroner: Very well, Inspector Poole. You may go. The court calls Mr. Thomas Llewelyn.

I felt that shock one gets under such circumstances, as if someone had tossed a bucket of water over one's head. I stood and lurched to the stand. I had been given oral exams by a tutor at Oxford and it still made me nervous when I recalled it. This was very similar.

Coroner: Mr. Llewelyn, when did you first see Roland Fitzhugh? Me: He entered our offices at 8:30 and spoke to our clerk. The man seemed in some distress. At first I thought he'd been running. He entered, but then he started to choke. He asked for a glass of water, but by the time I had poured it he had collapsed on the floor, insensible.

Coroner: Why was his shirt found open?

Me: Mr. Barker hoped to bring him around. He was unsuccessful.

Coroner: Did you send for Scotland Yard?

Me: I went for them myself.

Coroner: I understand there was an incident in Great Scotland Yard Street.

Me: Yes, sir. I passed the Clarence Public House into the street when I encountered a boy offering samples from a tray.

Coroner: What was the boy offering?

Me: Tarts, sir. Raspberry tart, to be precise.

Coroner: Did he offer you a sample?

Me: He did. The boy was quite insistent.

Coroner: Did you eat the tart?

Me: Yes, sir. I did.

Coroner: Did you have any ill effects?

Me: None, sir.

Coroner: You went into Scotland Yard, you say. Was the boy still there when you returned?

Me: He may have been. I had no reason to notice him again.

Coroner: When did you see him next?

For all his dryness, Vandeleur has a touch of the showman within his own personal theater.

Me: In his house in The Highway. Stone dead. He was Tommy Burke, the lad who was recently poisoned with his family.

There was a gasp from the crowd. Most had not connected the two crimes. Vandeleur looked pleased with himself. He had just caused a sensation, certain to be reported in the newspapers the following day.

Coroner: That will be all, Mr. Llewelyn.

Vandeleur shuffled papers about and studied his notes, but I knew who would be called next.

Coroner: Cyrus Barker, please take the stand.

The Guv stood and swelled in that way he has as if he were going to engulf the chamber. He pushed his way through the crowd and settled into the chair by Vandeleur with a protest from the wood.

Coroner: Mr. Barker, what is your occupation?
Barker: I am a private enquiry agent.
Coroner: Do you often receive clients that have first visited Scotland Yard?
Barker: From time to time, yes. The brave men of Metropolitan are underpaid and overworked.

Vandeleur wouldn't have let me get by with voicing such an opinion, but he did not belabor the point.

Coroner: Tell us what happened that morning.
Barker: We arrived at seven-thirty, to find our clerk, Mr. Jenkins, in residence. We had finished an enquiry and Mr. Llewelyn was preparing our final statements and a bill. I was reading the morning edition of *The Times*. Then I heard someone enter the outer offices and speak to Mr. Jenkins. Roland Fitzhugh came into our office before our clerk brought his card. He was trying to remain calm in front of strangers but seemed to be in some kind of distress. He asked for water, and Mr. Llewelyn crossed the room to get it. I came around the desk, because Mr. Fitzhugh's eyes were starting from his head and his face was turning red. He tugged at his collar, begging me to help him, then made a retching sound and collapsed. I eased him to the floor. Mr. Llewelyn came with the water, but it was too late.

Coroner: He was dead?

Barker: No, but he was dying. I must admit that at the time I did not think of poison. I assumed it was a heart attack or apoplexy, so I attempted to restart his heart.

Coroner: Do you have medical training, Mr. Barker?

Barker: I volunteered as a surgeon's assistant occasionally when I was in China. Their methods are far different from ours.

Coroner: What did you do to Mr. Fitzhugh, precisely?

Barker: I massaged his heart.

Coroner: How?

Barker: I put one hand on his breast, the other on top of that, and then pushed on his chest rhythmically.

Coroner: Is that how heart attacks are treated in China?

Barker: Aye, sir. I hoped to get his circulation going again, but my diagnosis was wrong.

Coroner: Two of his ribs were cracked.

Barker: That would have meant little if I were able to start his heart again.

The two men exchanged looks. Vandeleur was wondering whether to continue this avenue of questioning or go on to another.

Coroner: Did you feel his pulse or listen to his heart?

Barker: I did. He was gone to his maker. Alive one moment, clay the next.

Coroner: What did you do then?

Barker: I sent Mr. Llewelyn to Scotland Yard. At the time I was unaware that Mr. Fitzhugh had been there first.

Coroner: Did you move the body?

Barker: No, sir, I did not. I am aware that sometimes Scotland Yard inspectors take photographs, and it is preferred not to move the body in any way.

Coroner: What happened when Mr. Llewelyn returned?

Barker: He brought Chief Detective Inspector Poole. We explained all that had happened to him. Then a constable arrived with a hand litter and the body was taken away.

Coroner: Mr. Barker, at the time were you aware that the man who entered your office was a member of Parliament?

Barker: I did not see his card until after he was dead.

Coroner: Tell me, Mr. Barker, are you actively investigating this case?

Barker: I am, sir.

Coroner: Who is your client?

Barker: Mr. Fitzhugh himself. He said, "help me," so that is what I am doing. Even if he hadn't asked, I'd have taken the enquiry. I cannot have potential clients dropping dead in my visitor's chair.

There was a chuckle in the audience, but Vandeleur killed it with a look.

Coroner: Thank you, Mr. Barker, you may step down. I will now call Dr. Eustice Penfold to the stand.

A young man stood and came to stand in front of Vandeleur. He was about my age with dark hair and a grave demeanor. He took the chair promptly.

Coroner: Dr. Penfold, where do you work?

Penfold: I am a general surgeon working at Charing Cross Hospital.

Coroner: Is it not true that you were on duty when Mr. Fitzhugh's body was wheeled in by the constable?

Penfold: It is, sir.

Coroner: And how did you find him?

Penfold: There was no sign of life. He was deceased.

Coroner: Could you ascertain how he died?

The young doctor looked nervous. I suspected either Vande-leur had a reputation as a great physician or a tartar. That is, unless he were both.

Penfold: No, sir. There were no obvious wounds about his person. I did not make any judgment of how he died without information. When Inspector Poole arrived, he said it was a police matter and that he would take the body to New Scotland Yard. I wrote some general notes and sent them with the inspector. No one notified me that the deceased was a member of Parliament, not that a man's profession should dictate how much time a surgeon should spend with a patient.

Penfold stopped and stared at the coroner. Perhaps he'd said too much or went on too long. Perhaps he had been too frank with his opinions. He looked discomfited.

Coroner: Quite right. Thank you, Dr. Penfold. You may step down. Gentlemen, I received the body of Roland Fitzhugh at ten-thirty on the morning of Wednesday, August 8, 1893. A comprehensive postmortem revealed that he had indeed been poisoned. The cause of his death was cyanide, concealed in a bite of raspberry tart. Cyanide is a fast-acting compound. He must have eaten it in front of Mr. Barker's chambers. Gentlemen of the jury, we have engaged a room for you to discuss matters. As I said, this is not a trial. The only purpose is to decide whether there is enough evidence to recommend a trial. Is that understood?

There was a wait of perhaps half an hour while the coroner's jury deliberated. Barker and I nursed pints of stout and discussed the case. Finally, the twenty men returned.

Coroner: Have you reached a verdict of twelve or more votes to accuse?

Juryman: We have, sir. We return a verdict of willful murder by a person or persons unknown.

Coroner: Thank you, gentlemen. Let the verdict be noted. This inquest is finished.

CHAPTER 23

Gerald Halton had requested an appointment for his sister at two o'clock the following afternoon. He would accompany her, and I hoped he might be a calming influence upon her. From what I'd seen, she was a volatile young woman. My professional instincts were correct.

"Is that the chair Roland died in?" she asked, pointing to one of the deep yellow leather seats in front of Barker's desk.

"Aye, Miss," the Guv replied.

"Oh, I cannot sit in that chair!" she cried. "In fact, I cannot be in the same room with it."

"Jeremy, bring in another chair," the Guv called into the outer chamber.

Our clerk brought a chair from the waiting room, then the two of us carried the offending one into the back hall. By the time we returned, Gwendolyn Halton was seated in the second chair, while her brother made do with the Spartan wooden one from our antechamber.

"Thank you for coming to answer questions for us, Miss Halton," Barker said. "You must understand that your fiancé spoke but two words to us before he passed, and we know very little about him. Who should know more about a man than his betrothed?"

"Gerald believes I should apologize for my behavior at our last meeting," she said. "I told him everything I said to you. You must forgive me. Roland said I am remarkably forthright for a woman." She paused. "Tell me, please, what were the last words he said?"

"He said, 'Help me,'" the Guv replied. "I have vowed to do just that. You may be instrumental in my goal. Mr. Fitzhugh was in physical distress when he arrived, so we had no way to know what sort of person he was."

"The best sort," she said firmly. "Better than I deserved."

I put a tick in my notebook. The two of us agreed on something. However, she was contrite.

"We met at a party at Lord Bainsworth's home here in London," she continued. "I thought him handsome and well-spoken. However, he was too impressive to waste his time as a mere barrister. I was the one to encourage him to run for the vacant seat in Shoreditch."

I couldn't help adding a note in the margins that the daughter of a throat lozenge maker thought herself above a "mere barrister."

"And what attracted you to him, if I may ask?" the Guv replied.

"He was most impressive," she said. "Handsome, knowledgeable, and serious. He was attentive as well and his manners were excellent. I thought him the best man in the room and I believe I wasn't alone in that opinion."

"Would you call him a pious man, Miss Halton?"

"We attended St Mary Matfelon every Sunday morning together. It's down-at-heel and in a terrible neighborhood, but his constituency was there. I'd have preferred St Paul's. If I may say it, he was more concerned with the practical aspects of helping one's fellow man, rather than any reward he might receive after."

"Commendable. Did he ever show signs of a temper?" the Guv asked.

"Temper?" she repeated. I could see her start to bristle. In fact, her brother put a hand on her wrist.

"As I said, we did not know Mr. Fitzhugh," Barker said, "but someone felt cause to wish him harm."

"I have all the particulars surrounding his death, culled from newspapers and Scotland Yard, and I have an opinion," she replied.

I watched a corner of Barker's mustache raise. This slip of a girl was going to solve the case.

"Pray express it, then," he said, leaning back in his winged chair and tenting his fingers over his stomach.

"I believe it was chance," Miss Halton stated. "Someone—presumably whoever hired that boy, poisoned one bit of tart and placed it among the others merely to cause a sensation. Roland's choosing that bit of tart, or having it chosen for him, was a random act. Obviously, someone was to die, but poor Roland was simply in the wrong place at that moment. What do you think of my theory, Mr. Barker?"

"I believe your theory is a possibility, Miss Halton," he answered. "I must work from the opposite theory if only to prove yours, but I commend you for your insight."

She looked at him with those large eyes of hers, as if trying to work out if he was having her on.

"Did you see him the week of his death?" he asked.

"I did," she replied. "Twice."

"Did he say anything to you about poison?"

"No, but he did say his stomach was upset, and he ate little at his supper." She stopped and looked at the Guv. "Now that you ask, he didn't drink anything at all. Not wine, tea, or even water."

The thought occurred to me that he must have chosen water in the Dove Inn because he didn't trust the coffee.

"Did he ever speak of having enemies?"

"None, sir. That is, none save Mr. Lindsay, but then that was imagined. Edward wouldn't do such a thing."

"Am I correct in my assumption that the rupture between these two gentlemen was over you?"

"Mr. Lindsay was of the opinion that his many charms could outweigh my concerns about him," she replied. "He is over twice my age. Now, I understand that some young women are not overly concerned about such matters, but it has an air of grasping about it that I find distasteful. Why marry an old man when there are handsome men like Roland about?"

Barker and Lindsay were of a like age. I don't believe he was comfortable with the concept that a middle-aged man could be considered old by those of a younger generation, but that was mere speculation.

"You never considered Mr. Lindsay a viable candidate for marriage?"

"I most certainly did not," she said primly. "I understand a girl's need to marry well, for personal comfort, for alliances, for matters of business, but my father is a wealthy man, therefore I can marry whom I choose. Mr. Lindsay's argument with Roland was mere pique. He could never have induced me to marry him."

My partner looked toward his smoking cabinet. I'm certain he was in need of a good pipeful. He turned his chair to the left of the swivel, facing the spot on the corner of his desk where he perched his boots in contemplation, but again he was thwarted by the expectations of polite society.

"Had you much opportunity for conversation with Mr. Fitzhugh?" he proceeded. "I understand some affianced couples are kept apart during their courtship."

"Oh, Daddy wasn't that way," Gwendolyn Halton replied. "He said he never could do anything with me, didn't he, Gerald?"

"Oh, yes," her brother said, nodding. "He's said it many times."

I studied Halton while he sat. He, in turn, was watching Barker intently. I believe he was still sullen about losing the bout to the Guv and observing him for signs of weakness. Perhaps he hoped to challenge him again. I wondered idly if a man would poison his sister's beau if he found the man unsuitable, but no. Halton might beat him within an inch of his life, but he wouldn't poison him. However, I wondered which of the siblings was eldest. If it were Gwendolyn, part of his inheritance would have gone into the hands of Roland Fitzhugh.

"Miss Halton," the Guv said, breaking the moment of silence. "Were you at all involved in his political life?"

"Oh, there isn't anything I have found to be duller," she replied. "Roland would meet with his male friends after dinner to discuss important matters, and I was glad to flee with the women to discuss more interesting things, like dresses and furniture. I hope that doesn't make me sound vacuous, Mr. Barker."

"Women require dresses and rooms require furniture," he said with diplomacy.

"Precisely."

"Were you aware if any of his opinions were contentious?"

Her wide-set eyes rose to the ceiling. So far, she hadn't gone off the handle, and she had answered each question.

"One would have to understand Roland," she continued. "He was new to politics, and he told me it had been suggested by his fellow Liberal Party members that he curtail expressing any strong opinions until he'd been an MP for a few years. Roland was an attractive candidate, unlike his opponent, and I think he won due to his charm. No, he was not contentious in the least."

"I understand he was married before."

Immediately, two pink spots appeared on her cheeks. "Yes," she answered in a low voice.

The Guv cleared his throat. "Did he speak of it much?"

"No. He was loath to talk about it with me," she said. "Whatever I learned I had to winkle out of him. He did not want to discuss it."

"What have you learned about the matter?" Barker asked.

The young woman leaned forward in her chair in anticipation of her story. "From what I've gleaned, the two of them barely spoke before they were married, and afterward he was very busy with opening a law office. She was almost a stranger to him, and he to her. He said she was prone to strong displays of emotion, very angry at times and given to screaming. He took her to Baden-Baden to see some specialists. When that didn't work, he refurbished the attic of their home and hired a nurse. Even that was not enough to quell her rage and so he sent her to a private asylum and kept her there. He was concerned not only about her welfare but his position as a barrister. If someone learned his wife was mad, no one would hire him and he wouldn't be able to pay for her care."

"Did he mention if she had a dowry?" I asked.

She looked at me as if surprised there was anyone else in the room but her brother and the Guv.

"No, he did not mention it, but I'd assume she had. He said she was from a good family. A law office near Lincoln's Inn and in the right street can be very expensive he said."

"I'm sure," I said. "Tell me, did you at any time doubt his word about his first wife?"

"Doubt his word?" she echoed. Her cheeks did not bloom anew, but they were already pink. Her slender eyebrows began to descend. Storm clouds threatened.

"It is a delicate situation describing a former wife to a future one, fraught with danger," I observed. "Even the best of men, and I include Mr. Fitzhugh among that list, may be prone to exaggerate some facts and obscure others."

"I see," she said flatly.

"Men are weak creatures, Miss Halton," Barker remarked. "Especially when in the thrall of a beautiful woman."

My partner had come to my rescue, but then he was pressing her for information. Not for one second did I believe he thought her beautiful, though she swallowed the compliment without question.

"There was a time I thought he wasn't telling me everything," she said after a moment. "She wasn't mad in the beginning, and they must have been happy for a time. He didn't like to talk about that, about the good times. It would be ungallant."

"No doubt," I said.

Barker leaned forward and folded his hands on the glass desktop.

"Looking back over those last few days, did your fiancé seem nervous?" he asked. "Was he watching people or being careful with what he ate or drank?"

"Yes to both questions, Mr. Barker," she replied. "We were walking in St James's Park, and I was talking to him but he seemed to be looking over my shoulder. I thought it might be a pretty girl he was studying, but when I turned my head it was a man simply walking by, not noticing us at all. Later, we had tea, but he refused a cup. It was unlike him. Normally he would accept it from me even if he only took a sip or two."

"Would you consider Mr. Fitzhugh to have been reserved?" my partner asked.

Just then Jenkins returned with a man carrying a tea tray. He was the proprietor of the Silver Cross Public House across from our offices. From time to time we have feminine visitors, clients, and even suspects who require a cup of tea. Therefore, we had an arrangement with the pub. I had not thought of it and neither had Barker, but Jenkins had. Hidden depths, I thought.

"Would you repeat the question, Mr. Barker?" Gwendolyn Halton asked after a restorative sip.

"I asked if you considered your late fiancé a reserved man."

"Oh, yes," she answered. "Very much so. In social situations when one is interested in meeting or speaking to a gentleman, there are certain rules. One may ask one question of a man across the table at a dinner party, but not two. One may answer a question, but not elucidate and monopolize the conversation, and even then, one must not be obvious."

"I had no idea it was so complicated," Barker admitted.

"There are chaperones and hostesses and gossips everywhere," she observed. "Anyway, poor Roland didn't rise to a single signal. When I first met him, I thought he was either a total innocent or he found me tiresome."

"Which was it, Miss?" the Guv asked.

"Neither, in fact," she said, looking at my partner intently. "I believe he had sworn off women entirely."

"He was rather thick about it, I must say," Gerald added. "She might as well have been speaking Dutch to him. I got the impression that the fellow never expected to speak to an attractive female ever again."

Barker raised a brow. "Was he more loquacious with you?"

Halton considered the question as I took his empty cup and saucer.

"We spoke, but we weren't exactly chummy."

My partner turned to me. He does not understand slang terms and those he's heard he would never repeat.

"Not friends at all, then?" I supplied.

"We were friends in the way brothers-in-law would expect to be, but he wouldn't take me into his confidence. Sometimes it seemed as if he were giving me snippets from his speeches. I can only stand a certain amount of politics in my conversation or I become depressed. Gwendolyn was right. He was very reserved. I suspected he was being on his best behavior."

Barker stood. "Miss Halton, Mr. Halton, you have been most

patient with my questions. I will not badger you further. I promise to do my best to find Mr. Fitzhugh's poisoner. When I find him, I shall inform you at once."

They rose. Barker came around his desk and bowed to her. She in turn curtsied a trifle awkwardly.

"Miss Halton, I understand this was difficult for you. I thank you for returning."

"Do you have any thoughts or opinions?" he asked when I returned from seeing them out.

"More the latter than the former. The sooner Gwendolyn Halton becomes a bride, the better for London society. I hope she has a half dozen children, preferably all boys, and is consumed with taking care of them."

CHAPTER 24

Our visitors were not gone long when the telephone set on Barker's desk jangled. Under normal conditions he'll let it ring once or twice, but now he seized it before the first ring was done.

"Cyrus Barker speaking." He paused. "Yes. Good afternoon."

I heard a voice, rather loud and strident, though I couldn't make out what the man was saying.

"You think it significant?" the Guv asked.

The voice continued for a while.

"Very well," Barker said at last. "We'll meet you there."

I stepped out to the curb and raised a stick. Barker insists that both of us are nattily, if conservatively dressed. It draws cabmen to choose us over another fare, particularly on gray days, which it was, and threatening rain. One arrived at my feet and when Barker came out to join me, I called to him and he brought out two umbrellas. He threw mine to me and we clambered aboard.

"Are you going to tell me what he said, whoever he was, or shall I guess?" I asked.

"Cheek," he replied. "It was Poole. He said Ogilvy has been acting strangely. Today is the first of the month and he's shown no sign of quitting Fitzhugh's apartment. He hasn't left the building since yesterday."

"It could be nothing," I remarked.

"Aye, but it could be something," he countered. "We won't know until we look into it."

When we arrived, I saw Lieutenant Sparks, the plainclothes policeman who shadowed Poole standing outside awaiting us. His collar was up. It had indeed begun to rain.

"Inspector Poole is inside," he volunteered. "He's having a jaw with the desk clerk."

When we entered, the clerk turned to me. "What's he doing here?"

I waved at him as if we were chums. Hail-fellow-well-met and all that.

"He's here because I called him," Poole growled.

"What has happened, sir?" Barker asked with more politeness than the fellow deserved.

"Fitzhugh's manservant was supposed to have all his effects removed by yesterday," the clerk replied. "There's been no sign of him for two days."

"Is that all?"

"I think he's been living there, as if he owned the place," he continued. "I saw him last Friday, looking for work, I suppose, but he was wearing his late master's suit. Too expensive looking for his wages. Also, there was an empty bottle of scotch whisky in the bin. Mr. Fitzhugh didn't drink, so he must've swallowed it all himself. I was going to tell him to take himself off, but I haven't seen him for two days."

"Did he have any visitors?"

"None that I saw, and nobody signed the register, but I can't be here all the time. I eat my meals in the kitchen."

"I think it's time we paid Mr. Ogilvy a visit," Poole said. "If there's one bottle, there's probably two. Give me the key."

"Here now," the clerk protested. "I don't just hand out my key."

"I can kick in the door for you, sir," Sparks volunteered.

"Thank you, Sparks," Inspector Poole replied. "A fine idea."

"All right," the clerk sputtered. "Take the bloody keys. Just don't damage the property!"

As we filed by, I gave him a pat on the arm. He flinched and stepped back.

On the top floor, Poole put the key in the lock and turned it. The door opened readily. He pushed it open, peered in, and then stepped inside to look about. We followed him. The room had not changed substantially, but it was obvious a new master was here—and a slovenly one, at that. I've heard it said that servants who look after a master or mistress are often themselves untidy at home. The remains of a plate of some unrecognizable food lay forgotten on the table. A whisky tumbler sat carelessly atop a stack of antique books. A doused cigar floated in a teacup.

Poole called for Ogilvy, but there was no answer. Barker had his nose up like a pointer. I sniffed, as well. If there was a body here, it had not decayed sufficiently enough to produce a strong odor.

"Here, sir," Sparks called from the doorway to the bedroom. We all herded toward it. There it was, that sweet, sickly stench, faint, but there all the same. Vandeleur, in a rare talkative mood, once told me how a body teems with life after death. Try as I might all these years later, I still recall every word of his enthusiastic explanation.

"Dead," Poole pronounced, putting a finger to Ogilvy's throat. The man was seated in his master's desk chair in his best suit, rigid as a statue. His jaw was locked, his forehead upon the desk. A pen lay on the carpet. In front of him was a glass and a small bottle.

"A confession," Poole said, giving a contented sigh.

We all crowded about and bent over the corpse to read the letter.

To Whom It May Concern:

I killed my master and a family I did not know in order to live a few days as my master done. It is not fair that one man may live the life of an idol dog and another cooks his meals and does his laundry. Finally, I had enough, so I poisoned him. I think now about Mr. Fitzhugh and that poor tyke and his family, that poor baby crying surrounded by corpses, because of me. It is too much guilt for a sole to bear. I deserve to swing by a gibbet, but I'm taking the coward's way out. It wasn't worth it all. My sister always said I'd end up in trouble. I'll bet she won't half laff.

"I always love a good confession," Poole said. "So heartfelt, so heartbreaking, so final. Don't touch anything, Sparks! I'm bringing a photographer in for this one."

"I believe congratulations are in order, Terence," the Guv answered. "Nice work. How were you alerted?"

"I wasn't. I began to think of the suspects and wondered what he was up to. Then I questioned the man downstairs, and he made me curious enough to give you a call."

Barker bowed. "Thank you for including me, Terry. It looks as if you've got your man. And a photographer on the way . . . very modern. Dr. Vandeleur would approve."

"Sorry about this, Cyrus," Poole replied. "I know you wanted to catch him for yourself, Fitzhugh dying in your offices and all."

'You earned it," the Guv said. "Didn't he, Thomas?"

"He certainly did," I agreed. "Congratulations, Inspector."

"Thank you, Thomas." He turned toward his men. "My god, somebody open a window!"

Over the next quarter hour Poole did not crow but he had a warm glow about him. I'd have liked to examine the note more closely, but he warned us back now to keep the body in situ. The face of detection was changing and the examination of pools of blood were giving way to finger marks and cigarette ash, more in Wolfe's province than ours. Perhaps we were all getting stale and needed to change our methods. I suppose if Poole could learn, we could, as well.

"We shall leave you to your victory, Terry," the Guv said at last. "The lad and I shall go lick our wounds. Come, Thomas."

"Cheerio," Poole said.

We descended the stair and seized our umbrellas, then launched ourselves into the rain. We walked through a few streets without a word.

"'It looks like you have your man,' you said," I observed, trying to keep up with his long strides. "Not 'you have your man.'"

"Very good, Mr. Llewelyn," he remarked. "Impressive, even."

"The letter is a fake," I added.

"The Pie Man—what a moniker for a murderer—is enjoying himself far too much," Barker said. "He is tweaking our collective noses."

"Did he write the note?" I asked. "The Pie Man, I mean."

Rain drummed on our umbrellas overhead.

"The note sounds as if it were written by an East Ender. The real Pie Man didn't know Ogilvy was a Scot. It is the same as it was during the Whitechapel killings, an educated man trying to sound like an uneducated one. Good diction and with a dash of Cockney."

"Not the Pie Man, then," I pressed. "You're certain."

We stepped over a puddle as it began to pour and then went

under an archway in the street, to watch the rain. London is an entirely different city during a downpour, just as it is late at night.

"So, what happened?" I asked.

"If he can enter our house without a by-your-leave, he can certainly break into Fitzhugh's rooms," Barker said. "Then it would be a small matter of poisoning a bottle."

CHAPTER 25

That afternoon Terence Poole entered our chambers carrying two bottles of Watney Ale by the neck, one in each hand. He placed one on Jenkins's desk and another on mine. From his pockets, he withdrew two more bottles and set them on the Guv's, retrieving a bottle opener from yet another pocket and removing the caps. Then he sat back in the visitor's chair and sipped. I touched the bottle on my desk. It was cool, fresh from the Rising Sun's cellar across from Scotland Yard. They were the local distributor of Watney's brewery. I pulled my hand back and waited.

It was four-thirty, rather early for a drink if one were puritanical, which Cyrus Barker could be, but only sometimes. He stared at the beer as if an affront, then he reached across and lifted the bottle to his lips and drank.

"Thank you, Terry," he said. "To what do we owe this beneficence?"

"I just want to talk over the case," Poole replied. "It's thirsty work."

In the outer office I heard Jeremy Jenkins belch and give a sigh of satisfaction. For once, the ale had come to him. I saw the Guv's mustache twist in amusement.

"Very well," he continued. "What are your thoughts?"

The inspector put the bottle down on the floor beside the chair. He began to pace with his hands in his pockets, jingling coins as he did so.

"I would like very much to believe that Alexander Ogilvy killed his master," he stated. "It's neat. Justice is met. Ogilvy confessed. He'd been drinking steadily, dressing in his master's clothes, and not answering the door when the landlord knocked. He got a taste of the good life and got to play MP for a while."

"Then believe it if you wish," my partner replied.

"No, the motive is weak," Poole countered. "Why would a steady servant suddenly go mad, poison his master, spend all the money in the flat, write a confession, and then poison himself? And then there's the obvious."

"Aye," the Guv said. "The man was neither a chemist nor a gardener. How did he learn so much about poisons?"

I swiveled my chair toward Barker's desk. "I would assume that the Pie Man is well and truly mad and that he would ultimately either confess or kill himself. In that way it is consistent."

Poole pushed the visitor's chair closer and perched his shoes on the edge of Barker's desk. I'd have pulled my own teeth before I had the nerve to do such a thing.

"Ogilvy told us Fitzhugh was a good master," Barker said, picking up the argument. "He felt that as a servant, he'd fallen into a good harbor. Why would it end as it did?"

"Perhaps he lied to you," Poole said. "Fitzhugh could have been a tyrant. Or he could have been a good master, but Ogilvy was tired of the servant's life, one man bowing and scraping to another. Perhaps he grew more and more irritated until he couldn't stand it anymore. Who knows the vagaries of the human heart?"

"Vagaries?" I said, smiling. "Is that a word they toss around at the CID?"

"Very well, Thomas," he answered. "I'm not an Oxford scholar, but I have read a book or two besides Scotland Yard regulations."

"If it's not Ogilvy, then he's another victim," I observed. "Someone broke into Fitzhugh's flat."

"Or was already there," Barker said. "Our poisoner has a fondness for making himself at home in his victims' houses. The concierge said Ogilvy was living there and avoiding him, but Ogilvy had been dead more than twenty-four hours."

Poole reached into his pocket, extracted a cigarette case, retrieved one, and lit it with a vesta. Barker wrinkled his brow. He loves his tobacco, but cigarettes contained the cheapest and lowest quality tobacco, the dregs. However, he did not object because he understood cigarettes had become a mainstay at Scotland Yard. It kept the men going through a twelve-hour shift.

"I have no trouble imagining Fitzhugh's killer poisoning his servant and living in the home of his victim, gloating at his triumph," Barker said. "It's not madness. It's merely evil."

A thought came to me then. What if the poisoner were here even now? I looked about the room where we sat. There was nowhere for a man to hide. I stepped into the waiting room, Jenkins's domain. I stepped next door and rattled Miss Fletcher's doorknob. No one was there, and our clerk had stepped outside. By then, both men were staring at me.

"I thought perhaps the Pie Man was nearby listening to us," I explained. "He'd be very interested in our conversation."

I went into the short hall, looked in both rooms there, then stepped outside into the alley which circles our chambers on three sides. There was no sign of anyone or anything, so I returned to the office.

"Nothing," I said.

"Still, wise to look," Poole murmured.

I stopped. Had that been a compliment from Scotland Yard? I'd been called a wiseacre several times but never wise.

"Lindsay," he continued. "I'd bet my winnings on Lindsay. He was disgruntled at having the girl snatched away. He was dreaming that he'd have a chance of winning her. Jealousy is a classic motive and the core of almost every case is a strong emotion on the part of the perpetrator. I don't think it ever occurred to him that she didn't love him, that she'd prefer a younger, more handsome and ambitious man. Most motives are selfish."

"I'm sure after the fight in their office, Fitzhugh gave her a detailed account," I said. "And don't think Lindsay wouldn't have known it. It would have scorched his spirit."

"You're suggesting he'd have committed the murder over a conversation that may never have happened?" Barker asked.

"Perhaps," I answered. "He certainly had reason to hate Fitzhugh."

"What about Gwendolyn Halton herself?" Poole asked. "Or her brother? He seems to do what she tells him. A fine-looking fellow, but not much in the hayloft, I think."

He pointed to his own skull.

"You interviewed them?" I asked.

"I did," he replied. "A CID man is thorough. Were you gentlemen aware Gerald Halton was covered in bruises? I just wonder where he got those."

I thought about telling him about the bare-knuckle fight but held my tongue. It was illegal, after all.

"What motive would you attribute to Miss Halton?" the Guv asked.

"The old familiar refrain," Poole replied. "Fitzhugh was sparking another girl. I might even know what girl."

He waggled his eyebrows at me.

"No," I cried, slapping my hand on my knee. "You're not suggesting Mrs. Elder! They hated each other."

"Laugh all you want, Llewelyn," the inspector said. "She's a stunner, no mistake. You wouldn't know that being a married man and all."

"You did," I countered. "I wonder what Mrs. Poole would say about you giving a suspect the eye."

"Let's leave Mignon out of the conversation, shall we?"

"Mr. Barker certainly fell victim to her charms," I said.

"Oh, ho!" Poole laughed, putting out his cigarette and turning to my partner.

"I think Mr. Llewelyn is under the mistaken impression that I flirted with Mrs. Elder," Barker said. "I merely encouraged her to speak her mind by sympathizing with her."

Poole turned back to me.

"Right in front of your eyes?" he asked.

"So help me."

"Well, well," Poole said. "Didn't think you had it in you, Cyrus, you sly dog. It's always the quiet ones."

"Gentlemen."

"And he's got a fortune," I supplied.

"Gentlemen!"

Personally, I still thought he had flirted a little. Often, he does not choose a strategy before meeting a suspect. He goes by instinct. Perhaps that instinct had told him to string her along. It hadn't worked well, and he'd been forced to be hard with her in Covent Garden, but she probably shut up like a clam with the Yard boys.

"How do you feel about her as a suspect?" Barker asked, hoping the previous thread of conversation had come to an end.

"I think her a highly credible candidate," Poole answered. "The woman traffics in poisons. She's growing white oleander right in her front yard."

"I'm certain there are at least one or two poisonous plants growing right now in my back garden," Barker replied.

"But you don't sell them to the public," Terry argued. "She's got a stall in Covent Garden every Saturday afternoon. Herbs and flowers and handmade charms. And cups of witch's brew, toads included."

"Again, there is not a strong enough motive," the Guv answered.

"Not a motive!" Poole cried, raising his voice. "The man put her in the stir for three bloody years!"

"She knew the chances she was taking when she helped Ellie Flanders," the Guv stated. "She understood she would be prosecuted by law and convicted. The sentence was lighter than others I've seen for the same crime. I don't believe she felt strongly enough about seeking revenge, especially knowing she would be taken back to jail. She has learned to prize her freedom over anything."

Poole went to the window and looked out at Craig's Court. "She's good for it. I won't let her alone, but I'm willing to consider other options. Mallock ain't one of them."

"Oh?" Barker asked. "How so?"

"The man's only thought is of his new family," the inspector replied. "He's besotted with them all, keeps a pocket portrait of them in his wallet."

"A ready-made family," I said.

Poole still hadn't turned back to us. "His wife was a dolly-mop. She was hauled into 'H' Division for solicitation twice. Before that she turned in her last common-law husband for beating her and the two girls."

"That's not fair, you having records to consult," I commented.

"I feel sorry for you boys in your fancy chambers and fine suits," he said. "If you were to build a case, what would you say?" Barker asked.

Poole shrugged his shoulders and turned to us. "He admitted to theft already. Said he deserved to be put in prison."

"Is it possible," I asked, "that Lindsay paid him to kill his former partner? He'd be first on my list if I were in Lindsay's shoes."

Terence Poole turned and pointed at me. "Now you're thinking like a Scotland Yard inspector."

In answer, I crossed my arms. "My wife would be so glad to hear it."

"Ha," he said, turning back to the view of the Court. "Your windows need cleaning."

"Jenkins has been occupied," I told him.

"Mallock's motive is weak," the Guv argued. "Lindsay could have paid him well and consider what presents he could take back to his family, but in the end he would decline. I'm sure he's been accused of other crimes when the Met spreads its nets wide."

"Very well, we've brought him in several times, but nothing has been proven. He's claimed he's being harassed."

I raised my shoulders. "Perhaps he is."

"You jailbirds flock together." He turned back to us and came to the desk, where he looked over the Guv's box of Dunhill cigars, but ultimately decided against them.

"What about Chumley?"

"That broken-down gardener?" I asked. "Don't make me laugh. Could you imagine him creeping around someone's house? His knees and ankles would crack loud enough to wake the dead."

"Because of his age, he is not a likely suspect," Barker replied. "And I would like to think that gardening would soothe his soul enough to give up any sense of revenge."

"Good luck there," the inspector said.

"Terry, you are becoming a pessimist."

"The question is, Cyrus, why aren't you? You've remained as sunny as these ugly yellow chairs of yours."

Barker looked insulted. That is, he looked the same as he always looked, but I inferred that he was insulted.

"They are not ugly," he stated. "I happen to like yellow."

"Very well, Cyrus, we've discussed every suspect with ayes or nays. Who's your winner?"

"None of them," the Guv growled. "At least not with the information we have so far."

Terence Poole blew the air out of his cheeks. "Agreed. I've prepared a statement for the press about the suicide of the Mad Pie Man, but I'll only use it if I don't find someone in the next twenty-four hours. Mind you, it'll work out nice. Ogilvy's not around to deny it. However, if another murder occurs, I'll look like a fool."

Poole looked at me, but I looked back at him seriously. One doesn't need to be glib all the time, and I considered him a friend of sorts. I've eaten at his table and met his wife. We'd worked together and though he'd tossed me in the cells at Scotland Yard many times, it was generally at the behest of the commissioner, who despised private enquiry agents.

"Very well," my partner said. "We will keep digging until we turn over the right rock. Thank you for the ale."

The detective chief inspector left, rueful that our meeting hadn't been more successful. When he was gone, Barker sat behind his desk in the big green leather chair with one hand scratching the skin under his chin, a sign he was thinking. I let him do so for half an hour. Thinking is always a good thing.

CHAPTER 26

Jeremy Jenkins came into our offices near closing time with a
stack of papers. He looked a bit chagrined.

"Sir," he said, looking more solemn than I believed I'd ever
seen him. "I have gone through all of Fitzhugh's files. Every one
of them. If it isn't in the notes I've written down, I shall need to
go through them all again or the information is simply not there.
I'm sorry I failed you. I know you were certain we would identify
the killer there."

"You're not to blame yourself, Jeremy," Barker said. "It was
merely a hunch. You've done very well. The thought occurred to
me that we might look into whether Fitzhugh had any personal
cases or judgments either for or against him. Tell me, having
gone over his professional career in its entirety, what impressions
did you gather?"

Jenkins shifted from foot to foot. Reporting to the Guv was not
generally a part of his duties.

"Speaking as a man who has been in the dock," our clerk said. "I'm glad he wasn't my barrister for the prosecution. He was a tiger. He put a lot of men and women in stir. Some, I'm sure, were innocent. I even knew one or two of them. It was a blessing the day he became an MP and left off the work he'd done before. Many of his sentences were what you might call heavy-handed."

"Thank you," Barker answered. "If I find any other avenue of investigation, I shall let you know."

I looked at Jenkins. "'Pon my soul, you're looking natty today." He resettled his tie, looking embarrassed.

"Thank you, sir," he said. "I reckon I've bought Mr. Smoot enough ale to fill a barrel. A motive against Fitzhugh didn't appear in his cabinet. I'll go to the public records office."

"Yes, do so," the Guv told him. "Before that, however, I'd like you to go to the *Times* building and place an advertisement in the agony column. We are looking for a Mrs. Pomeroy, who worked for the late Roland Fitzhugh."

"Right," Jeremy said. "Pomeroy. Will there be any kind of reward?"

Barker sat back in his chair and thought for perhaps half a minute debating the question.

"I think not," he answered. "But I don't mind frightening her a bit if she yet lives. Also, Mr. Llewelyn is of the opinion that we have spent too much money on this case."

"Only if Mr. Gladstone doesn't pay us," I stated. "I'm not naturally penurious."

"I'll be off again, gentlemen."

"Enjoy your evening, Jeremy," Barker said.

I nodded to our clerk. "Cheerio."

We were just locking up for the night when we heard someone running in our direction. I turned immediately, my nerves already overwrought from the last week. I saw a top hat dodging through the pavement traffic. It was Dr. Applegate. When he reached us, he stopped, a trifle winded.

"Cyrus," he said to the Guv. "Someone got into my surgery last night. He broke the lock on my cabinet and rifled through my files."

"We'd love to help you, John," the Guv said, "but as you know, we are in the middle of an enquiry."

"No, you don't understand," Dr. Applegate insisted. "Whoever it was took your files, yours and Mr. Llewelyn's. He has all the details of your personal health."

"When did this happen?" Barker asked.

"At lunch, I suppose," the doctor replied. "I didn't notice the cabinet lock was broken until an hour ago. Somehow I thought of you and hunted for your files."

"Was the door to your office locked when you returned from lunch?" my partner asked.

The doctor's eyebrows rose. "It was, come to think of it. I hadn't thought of that."

"Shall I come and look at your offices?" Barker offered.

"No, thank you, Cyrus. I moved everything back into place already."

"Was the office a mess?" I asked.

"No, just the lock broken on the cabinet." He raised his hat. "Look, I've got to run, but I wanted to warn you. Take care of yourselves, gentlemen!"

"Thank you, John."

Barker stepped into the street and waved for a cab.

"He's taunting us," he stated as we watched the doctor bowl off.

"Dr. Applegate?"

"The poisoner, lad. If he could break into a surgery, he should have no difficulty picking a cabinet. He is being intentionally heavy-handed. It's as if he is saying 'You're not up to scratch. I'll have to be more obvious. Or more devious.'"

"Blighter," I muttered. "Was there anything in your personal file that might be used by him?"

"Not that I'm aware. And you?"

"Nothing, unless he can train wasps to sting on command."

"Ah, yes," he murmured. "You were stung in the garden last year. Your face swelled like an aubergine."

"Don't remind me," I said. "Let's go home."

"Very well."

"Do you think we should carry our pistols?" I asked.

"They wouldn't be helpful if we're poisoned," Barker rumbled. "However, it most certainly wouldn't go amiss."

An hour later, Rebecca was frustrated. We had tickets to an Edvard Grieg concert to hear *Peer Gynt*, but Barker had forbidden it, or at least discouraged us from going.

"I was so looking forward to it," she said, kicking an innocent ottoman.

"So was I," I replied. "You know he's one of my favorites."

"What are we to do with ourselves all night, Thomas?" she asked. "I'm tired of reading and embroidering. My eyes are weary."

"No doubt."

"I've a mind to go out and track down this nuisance myself."

"What would you do?" I asked. "Kick him in the shin?"

"For starters," she replied. "Then I'd hit him with one of your heaviest books."

I chuckled. "Only if I can choose which one. But, what if it's a woman?"

"I'd box her ears. Take away my concert, will she?"

I untied my cravat and removed my evening jacket.

"It would be no less than she deserved," I said, tying on my dressing gown. I put my hands in my pockets and looked at her.

"Sir!" I called out to Barker's aerie.

Rebecca looked at me and frowned. "Is something the matter?"

"Sir!"

"Coming!" came a gruff cry in return.

"The door is unlocked."

I heard his heavy tread on the stair, and he burst into the room.

"My apologies, ma'am," he said, not looking in her direction. "What is it, Thomas?"

I pulled my hand from my pocket. It was studded with wasps. Dead ones, but still dangerous. There must have been a dozen in my pocket. My hand had already begun to sting.

"Shake it, Thomas," Barker said. "Shake your hand. Wasps have no barbs."

I shook it and at least half of them dropped to the floor.

"Mrs. Llewelyn," he said, turning to Rebecca. "Do you have a small pair of tweezers?"

"I do," she said, hurrying to a drawer in the bureau, making certain to avoid the wasps on the floor even though she was wearing shoes.

"Sit here, Thomas," she said, indicating the edge of the bed.

I sat. By then the strange feeling passed my elbow and I could feel it reaching to my shoulder. She took my wrist and began extracting them one by one. I watched her, unable to feel what she was doing, as if the hand she held belonged to someone else. When she was done she returned to the bureau and brought a hand mirror and comb. She pushed the dead wasps onto the face of the mirror with the comb. She crossed to the window.

"How are you feeling, lad?" the Guv said.

"Peculiar," I answered. "But no pain yet. How did he get in?"

"I am a dolt," he said. "It was so obvious that I overlooked it entirely. When the killer broke in last week, he must have thrown drugged meat over the fence for Harm, entered through the back gate, came through the door, and poisoned Jacob's tea. Then he pocketed Jacob's keys. He's been able to walk in and out of the house since the very beginning."

My hand had begun to swell. It looked jaundiced and had begun to shake.

"I'll call for an ambulance," Barker said, hovering over us.

I felt queer all over after that. I remember the ambulance arriving but nothing between Barker going to call for it and its arrival. I vaguely recall being lifted into the back of a vehicle on a stretcher. The next thing I remembered was waking up the following morning. Rebecca was sitting next to me, watching me with concern.

I tried to speak, but just as my hand had felt like someone else's the night before, my tongue felt as though it wasn't mine.

"Mirror," I finally choked out, my speech slurred.

"I'll get one," Rebecca said.

I wondered what new catastrophe had occurred since I had been asleep. I lifted my hands and inspected them. The left one was swollen, but not particularly worse than the night before. My right looked serviceable enough. Rebecca returned with a small mirror, holding it out for me to see. My lips and cheeks were red and swollen. I was no beauty, but it was better than I expected. For one thing, I was alive.

When she returned it, Cyrus Barker came into the room and stood at the foot of the bed.

We'd speculated that Mac's poisoned tea was meant for the Guv, but the wasps were definitely intended for me. I supposed that made sense to the killer. It was our agency. I'd been a witness to Fitzhugh's death, and even tried to bring him water to save his life.

"It smells like salad in here," I muttered.

"Your wounds have been dressed with cider vinegar," Barker replied. "You have had a severe shock to your system. It was touch and go last night, so you must rest today. Mrs. Llewelyn and I have discussed this, and we both agree you should be moved to Camomile Street. There are only two keys, and they are both here now."

"The case," I said.

"The case is under control, Thomas. I'll inform you of any changes when I return this afternoon."

I attempted a sentence and somehow, he got the gist of it.

"No, I won't finish the case without you, but neither will I allow you to malinger. I need you up and ready in the morning."

"Yes, sir," I said.

I waited. There was no response. When I opened my eyes, Barker was gone and Rebecca standing in his place.

"He's gone, isn't he?" I asked.

"Yes, dear," she replied. "I'm afraid I have to go as well. I'm wearing yesterday's dress. I must go to the City and change."

I looked up into her brown eyes. "You stayed all night?"

She put her hands on her hips. "Of course I did. What sort of wife would I be otherwise?"

She kissed my brow and was gone, almost as quickly as Barker. As for me, I lay in bed and stared at the medieval beams overhead until finally, I fell asleep again.

When I awoke, Dr. Applegate was there. He had his back to me reading the doctor's notes and turned when I moved.

"Thomas Llewelyn," he said. "You lead a charmed life. You should have died last night and yet you live."

"Sorry to disappoint my many detractors," I answered. "Barker wants me out of here by tomorrow. Is that possible?"

Applegate narrowed his eyes and looked at me.

"Could I? Should I?" I asked.

"The toxins in your blood will dissipate quickly," he said. "You should be well enough to be shot at in the morning."

"The Guv'll be glad to hear it," I said. "He thinks I'm a lie-abed."

"There's a lot of that going around these days," he said. "Take care of yourself, Thomas. Don't let Barker run you off your feet. Tell him I said no dangerous activity."

"I will."

"As your doctor, I should make you aware that there are less-dangerous occupations."

"My wife is of the same opinion."

"Sensible woman," he said. "Give my best to your partner."

"I shall."

He, too, left me. My copy of *The Woman in White* was back at home on my bedside table. I'd have much rather read Mr. Collins than think of the case, but it was all I had at the moment.

I'd put my hand in a pocket full of wasps and nearly died.

Roland Fitzhugh ate a poisoned tart and died.

The Burkes ate a pie and also died.

Mac drank poisoned tea and nearly died.

What was the Pie Man's modus operandi? What did all these attempts have in common? It took a few minutes before it came to me. Everything was self-administered. They weren't shot, stabbed, or beaten by someone. No one forced the poison down their throats. In a small sense, they had killed themselves. The killer didn't hold a gun to their heads and make them drink the poison. In fact, he or she may have been miles away, which in other sorts of cases would make the perfect alibi.

I still felt that poison was a woman's weapon. Generally speaking, men attack. They seize something randomly and beat one over the head, often in a moment of anger. Women plan. They have a cooler temperament, and they understand their own fragility and plan accordingly. They don't outweigh us, and therefore must outthink us. And there was only one female suspect in this enquiry.

Zinnia Elder was both intelligent and sly. She had played the Scotland Yarders like a violin. She was watching me and gauging my reactions during our first interview, while deflecting Cyrus Barker's questions. It was tantamount to fighting two opponents at once and besting us both. The Guv worked out that she was lying, but only after he left her house and gave it some thought.

When we approached her in the stall the day before she had

played the wounded bird. *Yes, sir, I knew Roland Fitzhugh, but I'm just a woman.* She'd even provided herself with a motive unbidden. He'd stolen her old school friend's money.

That left me with only one question: Why would she target us, who had such a tangential connection to the murder of Roland Fitzhugh? I fell asleep before I could divine any answers.

CHAPTER 27

The next morning, we were on the Underground going to Charing Cross and our offices, which technically were in the Charing Cross district but only by a few yards or so. We rode in silence. What could one say? My face was still swollen and the Guv's nose had been broken a couple of days before. He'd had a couple of nosebleeds since.

"Sir, I think you should have that nose examined," I remarked.

"It looks worse than it feels," he replied. "I'll be fine in a day or two."

We reached the station and climbed the steps to the street. It was a blustery afternoon and we had to hold on to our hats. The Guv unlocked the door to our offices, and we stepped inside.

Barker crossed to his smoking cabinet and took out his morning pipe. He stuffed tobacco into it from the jar with the faded gold lettering that read *TABAC*.

"Bring me the newspapers, Thomas."

I turned and went to get them from Jenkins's desk. The Guv sat in his chair and puffed, He immediately coughed. The smoke went down the wrong pipe, I thought. He coughed again, louder, and then louder still. He was choking. His face flushed and he began thumping on his own chest.

"Sir!" I cried, rushing over beside him. "What can I do?"

Barker continued his racking cough but pointed behind him to the decanters on the table behind his desk. But which one, I wondered, the water or the brandy? The water might clear his throat, but brandy was medicinal, at least to a Baptist's mind. I chose the brandy, splashed it into a tumbler, returned to the Guv's side and placed it in his hands. He brought it to his lips. Then I slapped it out of his hands again.

It was the wrong color, the brandy in the decanter. Too dark. Good brandy looks like liquid gold. This was brownish and I thought I saw some sediment in the glass. The tumbler was made of stout crystal and bounced across the floor, spilling its contents onto the carpet. Immediately, I returned to the table. Did the water look safe to drink? I couldn't tell. No, I wouldn't risk it.

Barker was choking so hard his forehead was smudging the glass of his desktop. He was honking like a goose and beating the glass with the fist.

"Sir!" I cried, bending low so he could see my face.

"What in blazes?" he managed to squeak.

"The brandy, sir. It was tampered with."

"Outside," he said, in little more than a whisper.

I lifted him out of his chair as best I could. Then I dragged him toward our back door. Halfway down the hall he pushed himself away from me and went into the water closet, where I heard him being violently ill. I waited outside anxiously. He did not come out for five minutes. By that time, I was beating on the door.

It finally opened and he lurched into the hall again. His face was covered in sweat and he could barely stand upright. I seized him bodily and carried him outside. No sooner were we out the door and onto the flagstones that his knees gave out and he sprawled prone upon the ground. I rolled him over onto his back.

"Sir, speak to me!"

"My heart is beating fit to burst."

I pulled off my jacket, rolled it in a ball, and put it under his head.

"If you started choking, naturally I'd get you a drink," I said. "But it reminded me of Fitzhugh and how he'd been herded along until he reached Whitehall. The Pie Man would have put something into the tobacco merely to make you need a drink."

"Clever," he muttered hoarsely.

I helped him back inside into his chair, though it took a few minutes. Then I called Scotland Yard.

"Poole," a voice crackled from the other end.

"Llewelyn," I barked. "Barker was just nearly poisoned."

"I'll be right there."

He was, too. The inspector came into the offices, noted the pipe on the rug, the spent match on the desk, and the tumbler in the corner. Then he stepped over to Barker's side. Like Ogilvy, the Guv's forehead rested on his desk.

"Cyrus?" he asked. "Can you hear me?"

"He's out, I think, Terry," I replied.

"I'm awake," my partner murmured.

"What happened here?" the Chief Inspector asked.

"We'd just come in," I said. "He crossed to his cabinet, stuffed a pipe, and lit it. Then he began to choke. He pointed to the decanters, so I poured him a brandy, but as soon as I gave it to him, I noticed the color was off, so I knocked it out of his hand."

Poole crossed the room and lifted the brandy bottle.

"There's something in it, all right," he said. "It's too dark. And look, there are some crystals on the bottom of the water, as well. It looks like the Pie Man's been playing in your offices. I'd call that friend of yours. What's his name?"

"Wolfe," I said. "Saxton Wolfe. Not that he's a mate of mine."

"I'll bet you a penny to a pound your Guv will take the room you just vacated at the Priory."

"Take me home," Barker said.

"Sir, no," I protested. "I insist. Your heart is racing. You said it yourself."

"I've got to bring my squad in," Poole said. "I'll be back in a few minutes."

I nodded. "I've got some telephone calls to make."

"Home!" the Guv barked.

"But the Scotland Yard boys should be here in a minute, sir. I'm going to call Lady Ashleigh."

I rang the Ashleigh estate. The butler, Frost, answered the telephone.

"Frost, this is Thomas Llewelyn," I told him. "Mr. Barker has met with an accident. I wonder if I may speak to Her Ladyship."

"Hold the line, please," he said.

"Tell me," she ordered urgently when she came on the line, with a voice that warned me she'd been through too much already, thank you.

I explained the situation with as few words as possible.

"Does he have the same symptoms as Mac?" she asked.

"No, Mac's heart was erratic," I explained. "Mr. Barker's is beating strongly. Something was put in his tobacco, I think."

"I'm coming," she said. "I shall be there in two hours." There was a pause. "Thomas, do you think he will be alive in two hours?"

I heard it then. The minute she hung the phone on the receiver, she was going to cry.

"Yes, I think so," I told her. "I'm sure of it."

It was a bald-faced lie. I had no idea what condition he would be in two hours from then.

"I'm leaving now," she stated. "I'll be there soon."

"Yes, ma'am. He insists that I take him home."

"I'll meet you there."

I hung up the telephone, my heart racing nearly as hard as Barker's. After a moment, I called Rebecca to tell her the news. Afterward, I thought of calling Mac, but he was fighting battles of his own.

"Still here, eh?" Poole asked when he returned. "My men are coming. You two nip along."

"I'll take you home, sir," I said to Barker.

I helped him up. Suddenly, Poole was on the other side of the Guv and helped me heft him to the cab. When we had him seated in a cab Terence Poole did something he'd never done before. He shook my hand.

"Good luck."

"Here now," the driver called from his perch. "What's wrong wi' him?"

"He took ill," I said.

"I don't want him getting sick in my cab."

"You won't want me pulling your license, either," Poole snapped. "This is Scotland Yard business."

"All right," the cabman grumbled. "Keep your shirt on."

I waved at Poole as we bowled toward Westminster Bridge. Then I turned and looked at Barker.

"Still with us?" I asked.

"Just," he replied. "Handkerchief?"

I gave him mine and he mopped his face while leaning against the window on the right side of the cab. He was awake, but for how long? I didn't speak to him for the rest of the journey. However, I eyed him every minute or so to be certain he was still among the living. We arrived home and I was relieved when the cabman helped me lift Barker into the house, earning himself an excellent tip.

Once in the parlor I stripped the Guv of his jacket and shoes, then opened his collar. I helped him to the sofa and he turned away.

"At least let me call Dr. Applegate," I said.

"I'm fine," he rumbled like a bear in his den.

Knowing both Rebecca and Philippa would be there soon, I went upstairs and changed. Then I washed my face and combed my hair. As I looked at my swollen face in the mirror, I thought how much I wished this enquiry was over before we were all murdered in our beds.

I took a chair from the dining room and carried it into the front room. I assumed the Guv was asleep. That or much worse, I didn't want to find out which.

"Nicotine," Barker suddenly rasped. "Nicotine."

He pushed himself up to a sitting position. "It is the drug in tobacco that makes it so potent. I tasted nothing but tobacco, but it was too strong. Our poisoner boiled or reduced it, then mixed it with the tobacco in my jar. It wouldn't kill me, but it would send me reaching for a drink."

"You're sure you are well?" I asked.

"Not well, Thomas, but I'll live."

He repaired his collar and donned his cutaway coat again, just before Rebecca arrived. He was in the act of buttoning his collar when she stepped inside.

"How are you feeling, Mr. Barker?" she asked with genuine concern in her voice.

"A wee bit under the weather," he admitted. "But a good nap and I'll be fine."

"I'll make some tea for you," she said. "Wait, we have no tea, and Philippa is coming! I must go to a grocer nearby. Heavens!"

Rebecca ran out the door again. She hadn't so much as kissed me on the cheek.

My partner sat back and rested his head against the top of the cushion.

"I can still fetch the doctor," I said.

"He's one of the busiest men in London," Barker replied. "We've already interrupted his day more than once this week. We cannot afford to wear out our welcome."

He lay in that position for another five minutes. Then he moved to lay on the pillow, turning away again.

"Another few minutes," he said.

An hour later, Philippa arrived in a flurry. By then, Rebecca had returned and prepared tea.

"How is he?" Lady Ashleigh asked, finding him still asleep. He was lightly snoring. I've heard him rattle the rafters at times.

"He was up and talking an hour ago," I told her.

"Poor dear," Philippa said. "He brings it on himself, you know. He takes on too much in order to prove a point no else cares about."

"Thomas," Rebecca said, bringing in a tray. "I believe we've been patient long enough. Or, at least, I have. What happened?"

Barker woke then and pushed himself into a sitting position with my help.

"I'll tell you what happened, Mrs. Llewelyn," he said. "Nothing more or less than this: your husband saved my life. If it weren't for his deductive skills, I'd be stretched out on the office floor only a few feet away from where Roland Fitzhugh took his last breath."

Rebecca put a possessive hand on my arm. Meanwhile, Lady Ashleigh took my other hand and squeezed it.

"Thank you, Thomas," she said. "You don't know what that means to me. Now tell us what happened!"

I explained everything. The odd thing is that I didn't embellish. I told it as Barker would have. Frankly, I was embarrassed. I'm not a hero. Far from it, in fact.

"I recognized a pattern, that's all," I said, looking at the Guv. "Anyway, you've saved my life a dozen times over."

"Who is this killer, Mr. Barker?" Rebecca asked. "What sort of man is he?"

"To begin with, Mrs. Llewelyn, it's possible he isn't a man at all. Your husband is of the opinion that our killer is a woman, and I have very little concrete evidence to disprove it."

"Do you have a suspect?" Lady Ashleigh asked, as if she would find her and then scratch her eyes out.

"Her name is Zinnia Elder," Barker said. "And she is an herbalist."

"Say it plain, sir," I protested. "She is a witch."

That caused a sensation. We talked about her for the next quarter hour. The women offered some insights that we hadn't thought of, such as the fact that spiritualism had made the occult more palatable to the sophisticated London public and that her motley home with its chickens and bees were just the sort of abode they would expect. It was like a stage and if nothing else proved it. The grimoire and candle certainly did.

"Is she a fake, then?" I asked.

"Do you believe in witchcraft?" Philippa asked bluntly.

"Well, no," I said. But we Welsh are raised on tales of magic and mysticism. I wouldn't admit it if I did.

"She might be false," Barker said. "But she would act accordingly, which might be the same thing. Particularly if she felt justified."

The Guv was nearly back to himself, though his tie was crooked. He was able to take a deep breath without coughing.

"Thomas, in an abundance of caution, has brought you to London for little reason," he said to Philippa. "However, let us make the best of it. Mrs. Llewelyn has purchased tea but there is little food in the house. I propose a meal for all of us at *Le Toison d'Or*. Etienne will be glad to see us, and we will ignore poisoners for one night."

"All the same," I remarked, "I'll watch my food."

CHAPTER 28

The front door of our offices opened the following morning and I heard people talking in our waiting room. Father Michaels and an elderly woman appeared at our door. The woman was almost gnomelike, no more than skin and bones. She was sour-faced and hard-looking, but she held fiercely to the good reverend's hand.

Barker rose from his seat. "Father Michaels, it is good to see you again."

"Excuse me, Mr. Barker," the clergyman said. "There's someone I thought you should see right away. This is Mrs. Mabel Pomeroy. She saw the advertisement you placed in the agony column."

"Please come in and have a seat," the Guv said, stepping around the desk to pull out a chair.

"Mrs. Pomeroy is one of my flock," Father Michaels explained, continuing the story. "When she saw the note in *The Times*, she was afraid, so she came to talk to me. She's got quite a story to tell."

Barker went back to sit behind his desk. "Thank you for coming forward."

The Guv and I had believed the same thing, that the woman was already gone from this world. We were taken aback by her sudden presence in our chambers. She sat and looked at us with glittering, deep-set eyes. Her face was deeply seamed and she appeared as fragile as gossamer.

"You'll think me a bad woman, sir," she said, shaking her head. "When my name was in the papers, I knew it would all come out, finally. The secret has tried my soul these many years, and him walking about like there's no consequence on this side of the grave or the other. But you know, I dared not say anything. I signed a paper. I'd go to jail if I spoke up, and then what would happen to my family?"

"What paper?" my partner asked.

"It appears that Roland had Mrs. Pomeroy sign a document of nondisclosure concerning the events she was party to," Father Michaels explained. "I've done my best to tell her that such a thing would not be legally binding if what occurred was criminal in any way. You must understand how disillusioned I am about Roland if what she says is true. I very much suspect that it is."

The Guv looked at her carefully. "Mrs. Pomeroy, I am Cyrus Barker, and this is my partner, Thomas Llewelyn. Roland Fitzhugh died in this very room last week. I suspect you know things he hoped to take to his grave. There is no consequence in speaking up now, I assure you, and you may stop a murderer by doing so. Would you care for a glass of water?"

"No, but I'll take a small dram, if I may," she replied. "My bones are so cold this time of year."

I stood and poured brandy into a clean tumbler and put it into her hand, having removed the offending brandy and water that morning. I suspected she would nurse her drink, but no. She swallowed it in one and handed the tumbler back. Then she puffed herself up the way I've seen Pouter pigeons do and began to speak.

"Well, sirs," she said. "Mr. Fitzhugh hired me in 1882 to look after his wife. They'd been married for two years, and he was busy with his court trials. The poor girl had taken ill with hysteria. She'd have periods of nervous agitation and depression. Sometimes she'd cry or faint. Other days she would act as normal as you or I and ask if she could leave the house, but Mr. Fitzhugh revealed that she had become violent in the street and could not be trusted on her own. Likewise, he had many medications for her condition, but I was not to let her near the bottles in case she'd attempt to kill herself. Such a sweet thing, too. Alice was her name."

"What did you do before going to work for Mr. Fitzhugh?" Barker asked.

"I worked with the lunatics at Colney Hatch for twenty-year, sir, and as a wardress with the workhouse at Bethnal Green. I used to be more hale then and could take any sort of nonsense a madwoman could throw my way. Looking after one woman, young and mostly docile, for more pay, seemed to be a treat. But it broke your heart. She wasn't but twenty-two or three. I hoped she'd have a child. Sometimes that relieves the imbalance in a woman's body. But that didn't happen, and it only got worse."

"Worse?" I prompted.

"Yes," she said, glancing at me. "She said she was being held captive against her will. She shouted and demanded to be freed. She claimed her father was looking for her, and Mr. Roland, he had even put extra locks on the doors and a thick screen over the fireplace lest she burn herself on purpose. She began to refuse to take her medicine, swearing her father would save her, but Mr. Roland told me the man had died not long before their marriage."

"Did it occur to you that she might not have been as insane as you thought?" Barker asked. He came around the desk and leaned against the front of it. Father Michaels sat in one of the yellow chairs and Mrs. Pomeroy in the other. The tension was such that I had to keep relaxing my muscles or I would be tied in knots. Father Michaels and Barker were the same, straining for each fresh word.

"You've got to understand, sir," she continued. "I was a poor widow woman with mouths to feed and I wasn't to know what he was doing to her."

"Which was?" I asked.

"Living on her dowry money, setting up a fine office and a partnership. Alice claimed he came right out and told her one day that he had married her for her money and had no more interest in her than a charwoman. By law, all her property belonged to him the minute they married. Now she was a burden, unnecessary, and she a pretty good thing that any young man would jump to marry. It was a sad situation."

"How long had you worked for Mr. Fitzhugh before you realized the girl might have been as sane as you or I?"

"It was longer than you might think," the old woman answered. "I'd been a matron so long and so used to all the dodges inmates try that it didn't seem likely that what she babbled might be true. Mr. Roland was a charming man and could soothe her with a word. I never saw him act violent toward her, although he could be strict. He had to be, you see."

"I see," the Guv said. He was unconsciously tapping one foot as he leaned against the desk.

I rose and refilled her glass. She was a shameless old thing and I had no trouble imagining her with two stone more weight on her bones, working as a matron in an insane asylum. As before, she swallowed the drink off. A sad end for an imperial brandy.

Father Michaels moaned in his chair.

"What a perfect fool I was!" he said, holding a hand to his head. "I counted the man my friend."

"He was a cunning devil, Father, no mistake," Mrs. Pomeroy said.

Barker grunted. "You began to suspect Mr. Fitzhugh was keeping her, a healthy young woman, against her will. How long was it before you were convinced?"

"Six months, sir. It took me that long to believe it. He had a silver tongue and a kind word and 'Here's an extra shilling for a gin.'"

"Wait until the Men's Morality League learns about this," Father Michaels murmured.

"Excuse me," I said. "Was this at the flat in Spitalfields?"

"No, dearie," she replied. "But I seen it. This one was nothing so grand. It was by the law courts in Chancery Lane. Just a step above student lodgings, but you could see him starting to clear it out, stick by stick. He was going on to grander things."

"What happened when you became fully convinced?" Barker asked.

"By that time, he'd moved her to the attic, under lock and key. He'd found a doctor who came by once a week with vials and pills, all he could want. The doctor was a charlatan or worse. Alice began to lose weight. She lost her bloom. Once a year or so, he'd dress her up with my help and take her out into society. It wasn't to show her off, but to make his peers feel sorry for him, like. Sometimes she was doped. She always came back in hysterics."

"And did—" the Guv began.

Mrs. Pomeroy leaned forward more quickly than I imagined and clutched his hand. "I knowed I'd done wrong by then, but I was trapped, you see. She was kidnapped and held against her will and I'd been a part of it all the while. I could go to prison and here I had my children to look after."

I coughed and she turned a murderous eye on me. Children, I thought. She'd been over sixty at the time. Her wee bairns were probably lightermen and barmaids with offspring of their own. Those children probably had children themselves by now.

"Once I knew he was an out-and-out rotter, there wasn't much

I could do. He was aware of what was what. One day I came in and she was gone, just like that. Had her committed. He just needed me to testify."

"Which you did," I said.

That vulpine eye turned my way again.

"I did," she agreed, staring at me. "We both knew my work was over and it was a matter of how much I'd get if I testified to his satisfaction. The man even wrote me a script for the witness stand. I memorized it and said it in court, with that poor girl, like a daughter to me, staring me in the face. Oh, my!"

She burst into tears. The three of us reached for our handkerchiefs at once. It doesn't matter what sort of woman she is, she deserves a clean handkerchief. However, if she wanted more brandy she'd wait in vain.

"Then I run," she said, wiping her nose, an unpleasing sight. "I hid as best I could. He held all the cards, you see. I was sure if he wanted to he could search me out after the trial and have done with it. I was a . . . what's the word?"

"A loose end," I supplied.

"Right!" she said. "I hid for months. For months! I went to my sister's in Bournemouth, but I ran out of money and eventually there were no positions open for anyone with my background. So, I came back. I reckon he forgot about me."

I looked over at Barker and caught his gaze. That was Fitzhugh's only mistake. She lived to tell the tale. But he didn't.

"In the end she was committed to Bethlehem Asylum. Poor, poor thing. There was nothing wrong with her, nothing that he didn't cause. Some girls got spirit, you know, but she was sensitive and reading all the time. Bedlam is no place for the worst of women, let alone a lady like her. He drove her mad, sirs, through willfulness and neglect. He was a demon. I've never accused a man of being one before, but he was!"

Barker and I both nodded. I would not have been so quick to

help Fitzhugh with that final glass of water if I had known what a monster he was.

"I read about it all later," she said. "That after she spent six months in the asylum, Mr. Roland in his infinite mercy thought he'd bring her home for Christmas. More like he'd run out of flies' wings to pluck or dogs to kick. He was ready for a bit of excitement and he got it, by gaw!"

She broke into a spell of coughing, so I poured her a glass of water. She was not pleased and looked ruefully at the nearly full bottle of brandy.

"I don't recall the trial," Barker admitted. "But then a suicide by a woman from an asylum is not of great note."

"So, one morning," she continued. "I got to thinking. Good or ill, I'd given good service and deserved better treatment."

"What does your son do for a living, Mrs. Pomeroy?" I asked.

"He's a foundry worker."

"Strapping lad?"

She shrugged. "Strapping enough. Why?"

"I just thought you had been ill used. There was Fitzhugh, not giving you tuppence. You might have let him know how much you could reveal to the police."

"S'what I did, sir," she admitted. "I sent Jack around to jolly him up and make him pay us more, to show him what I'd done for him, and he can't treat me that way."

"Did your son crack a skull?" Barker asked.

"Oh, no, sir," she exclaimed. "Mr. Fitzhugh saw the error of his ways and paid us accordingly. But he made me sign the paper."

"Then he died," Barker said in that basso voice that rattles the furniture.

"Yes, sir," she said. "I felt terrible. I thought over everything Alice ever said to me, her kind words, her cries for help. I remembered her face as she changed from a beauty to a madwoman. I thought of how I could have released her at any time to the outside world. She didn't care about the dowry, really. She just wanted a kind husband and a normal life."

She cried racking sobs. The woman had stained her soul and then realized the damned spot could never be removed. It was not a dainty cry, but a grinding, rasping, gurgling sound that grated on my ears. Father Michaels reached out and held her.

"Then the worst of all," she finally said after catching her breath. "A few days after the trial there was a knock at my door. I opened it and there was a wealthy-looking man standing there, all in black, with riding boots like you see on a china plate from olden days. So polite, he was, but so bowed down with grief. It was her father, the one that devil had told me was dead. All that time he'd been trying to rescue the girl, but she weren't his property no more. She was Fitzhugh's now. He owned her, so to speak, and could do whatever he wished with his own wife."

We nodded. I hadn't suspected that turn of events, but now I saw it must be so. Nothing Fitzhugh said could be trusted.

"He wanted me to recant my testimony. That's the word, isn't it? Recant? He'd been suing Mr. Fitzhugh in lawsuit after lawsuit, beggaring himself, the poor man, but Fitzhugh was too wily. The thing was, I'd already spent the money and there was still that paper he had me sign, saying he'd toss me in jail if I breathed a word. So there wasn't anything left to say or do. The gentleman just raised his topper, bowed to me—to me, a matron—and went on his way."

"Do you happen to remember his name?" Barker asked her.

"No, sir. It's been so many years."

Cyrus Barker came forward and took her hand. "Mrs. Pomeroy, thank you for coming, and you, Father Michaels, for bringing her here. Thomas, give her something for her trouble."

"Yes, sir," I said, taking twenty pounds from the desk, although I knew what she would do with it.

After they left, the Guv and I looked at each other.

"That was a tragic story," I said. "Imagine the pain that father felt knowing he couldn't help his child when she needed it."

"Aye, it is tragic," he agreed. "But sadly, she wasn't the first wife to be at her husband's mercy and she won't be the last."

CHAPTER 29

We who require art for our soul's sake feel things more than other people. We are temperamental creatures. We suffer for our art, though to tell the truth what art I was destined for was still unknown to me, but I knew it must be there somewhere because I, too, was a temperamental creature. I'm certain Mrs. Llewelyn will agree with that sentiment.

We were changed by the Roland Fitzhugh case. It would be a while before the Guv took down a pipe from his smoking cabinet and I wouldn't be reaching casually into pockets anytime soon. I began to believe we were losing, that we would not simply fail to solve this case, but that it would kill us.

The Mad Pie Man was ahead of us. While we were investigating one outrage, he was planning and performing another. For all his madcap title, he was a thinking man, and therefore a dangerous one.

The door opened and Jenkins entered, looking weary. I would have as well had I been forced to read court records for days.

"Afternoon, Mr. B., Mr. L.," he muttered. I thought to myself that he'd had enough of investigation and would gladly return to wandering about our chambers like a bottle fly.

"Jeremy, report," Barker ordered. The latest attempt on his life had made him irascible.

Gingerly, Jenkins eased himself into the visitor's chair. He sighed. His eyes were puffy, and he looked sober. I thought I preferred him half-stoked. He opened a fat ledger-sized notebook on his knee.

"Poor pickings, sir, I'm sorry to say," he told us. "I've been through all of Mr. Fitzhugh's personal files, then all of the files at the law courts, every last one of them. The only people on the court records who gave cause to be removed from the proceedings were Mr. Mallock and Mrs. Elder. The one tried to get to him and the other invoked some sort of blasphemy directed at her prosecutor. Apparently, it's been a while since the courts have added blasphemy to a sentence. As for the rest, according to what I read, they were all good as angels, going cheerfully to their punishment."

He cleared his throat before continuing. "According to Smoot, we were the second at table. An eager plainclothesman named Sparks got to the records first. I've failed you, sir. I'm sorry."

"You've done your best, Jeremy," Barker answered. "I could not ask for more. I'm sure you were very thorough."

"I was, sir!" he said. "I even tracked down the coroner's inquest notes for each case."

"That was good thinking, Mr. Jenkins. Tell me, did you feel at any time that your life was in danger?"

"No, sir."

Barker leaned forward in his chair. "Did anything unusual happen?"

"No, Mr. B."

"Did anything make you feel ill?" he persisted.

"No, I . . ." Just then Jenkins broke off and looked up at the Guv. "Wait. There was one thing."

Cyrus Barker moved to the edge of his seat as the chair gave a creak of protest. He spread his hands wide and supported himself on the glass.

"What 'thing'?" he demanded. "Pray be precise, Mr. Jenkins."

"It was the sweets in Mr. Fitzhugh's private office, sir. There was a bowl full of them on the corner of his desk. It was dry work taking notes—and I don't mean dry as in temperature—"

"We understand, Jeremy. Continue."

"Well, sir," our clerk said. "Mr. Fitzhugh being dead, he had no need for them, and no one had been in his office other than me, the plainclothesman having just used the court records office. Anyway, I pinched one."

"What did they look like?" the Guv pursued.

Jeremy shrugged his shoulders. "They were just boiled sweets, sir, each wrapped in a twist of paper. So, seeing them go to waste, I opened one and popped it in my mouth."

"And?" I pressed.

"I was hoping they'd be lime, sir, or green apple. I've always been partial to green apple sweets myself. Even when I was a child."

"Who cares when you were a child?" I demanded. "What was it?"

"Licorice, Mr. L.," Jenkins said, unruffled. "Of all the tricks in the book. I can't abide licorice. I spit it back into the wrapper and threw it into an ash can."

"Then what did you do?" the Guv asked.

"Had a pint or two, didn't I?" Jenkins said. "That'll fix anything, but my lips felt strange for an hour after."

"That's probably wise," Barker said, looking downcast. He'd pinned his hopes on those records.

"Sorry again, Mr. B."

"You did your best."

"I searched everywhere," Jeremy said. "I even found a case against Mr. Fitzhugh himself."

I raised a brow. "Did you?"

"Yes, sir," he said solemnly. "It was in the death of his wife."

"A case of wrongful death?" the Guv said.

"Yes, sir, but it came to naught. Mr. Fitzhugh was exonerated. The judge ruled that it was a clear case of suicide."

Barker sat back in his chair again. He had that expressionless look on his face. I couldn't tell if he was disappointed or not.

"Who put forth the case?" he asked.

"Her father, sir."

"His name?"

The latter was in the interest of thoroughness. He would be our next person to question.

"His name . . ." Jenkins said, opening his notebook. He looked a trifle nervous. He didn't want to appear incompetent in front of Cyrus Barker. Perhaps he'd enjoyed his investigative work, but as it ended in failure he'd be glad to return to his desk, his meager work, and his nightly visit to the Rising Sun.

Jenkins turned the pages until he found the specific notes. He ran his finger along one line.

"Applegate, sir," he replied. "John Applegate."

I've seldom seen Cyrus Barker in a state of shock. His mouth went slack, dragging his mustache down with it.

"Applegate?" he demanded. "Dr. John Applegate?"

"Dunno about doctor, sir," Jenkins answered. "That was his name."

"That is our private doctor's name," I explained to our clerk, trying to absorb the shock to my system. "He was just in the offices a short while ago."

"Didn't see him, haven't heard of him. I must have been tied up with the court records when he came."

There was a groan of protest from the green leather chair once

again and the Guv stood. I immediately followed suit. We left
Jenkins looking positively elated, which in this case was perfectly
justified. Because of his diligence, a word I'd never associated
with his name before, we finally knew who had been trying to
kill us, Roland Fitzhugh, Alexander Ogilvy, and the entire Burke
family. Driven by his love of the outré and the press, Jenkins had
proven his worth at the Barker and Llewelyn Agency.

Sprinting down the stair I went to the curb and raised my stick,
but Barker pushed down my arm and ran past me. I followed at a
brisk pace. He was heading south toward the Yard and Westminster Palace, where even at that moment our other client, Gladstone, was probably debating a bill. We wormed our way through
the crowd. I did my best not to jostle pedestrians, but the Guv was
a brick wall moving forward at a great rate. Looking back over my
shoulder I saw the outraged faces he left in his wake. Still, we were
on our way to capture a fiend who had tried to kill us both.

We skidded around the corner heading to the Metropolitan Police headquarters. It was no longer raining, but the pavement was
slick. Once our shoes found purchase, we slowed our pace. Scotland Yard was just ahead and the guard at the gate was diligent
about stopping anyone who might appear violent or agitated. Barker
slowed to a stop and linked his hands behind him. I followed suit.
Just a pair of blokes cutting through to the Embankment.

Once inside the Yard lobby, we shot past the front desk. I nodded at Sergeant Kirkwood as we went by. I'd assumed we were
heading toward Poole's office, but no. The Guv reached the stairs
leading down to the Body Room, Dr. Vandeleur's private domain.
Ah, yes, I saw it now.

We trotted down the hall, the odor building at each step as we
shot into the Body Room. The coroner appeared to be weighing
a brain.

"Out!" he barked.

"Doctor," the Guv said, ignoring the command. "When did
you last see John Applegate?"

"I don't know," Vandeleur answered irritably. "Six months ago, perhaps. Why?"

"We believe he is the killer of Roland Fitzhugh and several others."

That caught the coroner's attention. He looked over his shoulder. "Do tell," he said.

"I believe he held Fitzhugh responsible for his daughter's death."

Vandeleur lifted the brain from the scale into a clean jar of formaldehyde.

"I'm not surprised," he remarked. "It was too much."

"What was?" I blurted.

"His disgrace," the doctor continued. "He was struck down nine months ago. He rather butchered a simple gall bladder removal. The victim, if I can call him that, was a well-connected shipowner. His family sued, and we had no choice but to take his license. The Hippocratic oath is to be taken seriously."

"And how did he react to ending his career?" Barker asked.

Vandeleur dipped his bloody hands in a solution in a large bowl and wiped them with a cloth. He turned and faced us.

"Poor fellow had a complete breakdown. The rumor was that he went violently mad. Everyone in the local medical community felt sorry for him. We'd known him for years. He was a good man and a fine surgeon. His daughter's death was a decade ago so there seemed to be no reason for him to break down over it, though such a wound rarely heals well. Poor girl. I suspect, but I am not able to prove, that there is madness in the family. I would like to study his brain sometime."

"The man is not dead," Barker told him.

"Not yet," Vandeleur said. "However, the two of you are pursuing him, which does not exactly assure his personal safety."

"What has become of his surgery?" Barker asked.

"Closed, naturally. I believe he sold it. There are some legal proceedings about that, as well. It's such a shame, really. We were not friends, but I admired his work. I've had bodies in here that had once been operated on by him and I can recognize his small, meticulous sutures."

"He's patched me like an old shirt a half dozen times," I remarked. "Mr. Barker more than that."

"How well did you know him?" the Guv continued.

"We greeted each other at conferences," Vandeleur said. "We spoke briefly at concerts and the like. Poor fellow. No wife, no daughter. I imagine if he is caught, it shall be Burberry Asylum for him, and once one enters, one rarely leaves."

We'd been shown around Burberry once. It takes only the violently insane. The guards wear cages around their heads, and stout coats with padding to avoid being bitten. The building, in black brick with three wings, is one of the gloomiest prospects in all England. I felt down-in-the-mouth just a few minutes inside the door. I could not imagine a night there, let alone a year. Or ten years. The ones that manage to take their own lives, or who become catatonic, they are the fortunate cases. I didn't want Applegate to end his days like them, but then I thought of poor Mrs. Burke and perhaps I did. Odd that I felt more for her than my own safety. He'd nearly killed me, too, after all. Roland Fitzhugh did not have my sympathy, but Mrs. Burke was just a poor woman struggling to feed her family.

We nodded and left Vandeleur to his work. Giving Kirkwood a nod as we left the building, we passed along Great Scotland Yard Street in the direction of Whitehall Street.

Just then Terence Poole came 'round the corner, and we seized him bodily and whisked him away.

"Oi!" I called as I sprinted to the street in time to snag a cab. We clambered aboard. I stood on the step, in front of the batwing doors.

"You can't stand there, sir," the cabman said.

"Scotland Yard!" the rest of us bawled.

CHAPTER 30

D id you suspect Applegate was the killer?" Poole asked
Barker after we'd explained the case as we knew it. Our
vehicle had reached Westminster Bridge by then.

"I thought it strange that he should be so often in our sights
at the same time the poisoner was hovering about and breaking
into our home. However, there were other, more likely suspects
and I was waiting for Jenkins to uncover something. It was to our
advantage that Mr. Fitzhugh led a life that appeared so often in
the public records."

"If it had been Barker or I reading the files, we would have
noted it immediately," I replied. "Jenkins has never met Applegate, so he could not have known."

"I counted Applegate a friend!" the Guv said. "He played us
falsely."

"Applegate predicted that Fitzhugh would go to Scotland

Yard," I said. "He expected Fitzhugh to take the tart and die there. Instead, he got it on the way to our offices."

"I'm going to have him in my grasp within the day or I shall hang up my boots!" the Guv growled in my ear.

"He must have known the moment Fitzhugh entered our doors that you would take the case," Poole said. "I have no doubt he was concealed across the street or somewhere nearby. Imagine his horror after finally seeing his former son-in-law take that tantalizing bite of raspberry tart to watch him walk through your door."

"His only choice was to come after us," the Guv remarked.

"That letter and the murder of Ogilvy was a good touch," Poole said. "If you hadn't been there, I would probably have swallowed it for the sake of expediency. I'll forgive you when you show me what you've found. Where are we going?"

"The doctor's house."

"Newington!" I sputtered. "Right by our own front door. To think we could have walked to the Mad Pie Man's house this entire time!"

"I do wish you would stop calling him that," Barker stated. "It gives the case an air of melodrama."

"Come, Cyrus. A family killed in Ratcliffe Highway, a man poisoned with cyanide, a houseful of poisoned traps, an innocent bride consigned falsely to an asylum? There is enough melodrama there for any music hall's roster!"

"Agreed."

"It's ironic that Applegate's daughter spent time in an asylum," I stated. "Old Bedlam is a few minutes stroll from his house."

"It's not ironic at all," the Guv replied. "Newington is not generally a place where established doctors live. I'll wager that he chose the property near Bethlehem Asylum in order to be near his daughter." He rapped on the ceiling of the carriage and called out to the driver. "Hurry, man!"

We skittered around a corner on two wheels, then the cab righted itself.

"Why wasn't Applegate able to get his daughter released?" Poole asked.

"According to Jeremy's notes Fitzhugh was an excellent barrister."

"Alice killed herself in front of Fitzhugh," I said. "What must that do to a man?"

"If his heart has not turned to granite, he would realize the enormity of what he'd done."

Poole nodded. "It was far too late to make amends, but what he did was not strictly unlawful."

"Just morally despicable," Barker growled. I saw the anger in the set of his jaw.

"I agree," I replied. "But if he was still redeemable after what he'd done, the only path left for him was to realize his guilt, live humbly, and try to make amends wherever he could. Which in fact he seemed to do."

"I don't believe that would have been enough to satisfy Applegate after losing a daughter," Poole stated. "Changing one's spots doesn't mean one won't be hunted."

We turned into Newington Causeway, in the Elephant and Castle district.

"Meanwhile, Applegate loses his case against Fitzhugh and attempts to bury his sorrow in work," the Guv said. "He lives a quiet life until one morning he picks up the newspaper and reads that his former son-in-law is engaged to be married. It must have been the grossest of insults to him. In his mind, it was another young virgin being led to the slaughter."

"I imagine he frothed at the mouth," Poole said.

"There it is!" I cried.

I pointed to Applegate's residence, a neat, angular mansion, smaller than Barker's, with a tower at one side. We saw a to-let sign in the window. I paid the driver and jumped down, crossing the lawn to peer in a window.

"Empty," I pronounced to Poole and my partner, who had come up beside me. "Perhaps we should call an estate agent."

The Guv made a sound in the back of his throat, a dry chuckle. He reached into his waistcoat pocket and extracted a skeleton key. A little jiggling and the front door popped open.

"Officially, I did not see that," the inspector said.

We stepped into an empty hall. A study was off to the left and a parlor to the right, where a piano was draped in a sheet. There were no other furnishings that we could see. I poked my head into an empty dining room and then a kitchen. There was not so much as a plate or a pot in either.

"Perhaps he just left the piano behind," I said.

We climbed the staircase and looked about. All the doors were open, and the rooms empty. All that is, save one.

"Sir," I murmured.

"Open the door, lad," Barker ordered. "Pistol ready."

I pulled my Webley from my pocket and slowly opened the door, my mind grasping that this room was fully furnished. There was a four-poster bed, a vanity, and screen. It was a girl's room, or perhaps a young woman's. There was a stuffed toy, a cat, lying on the bed. The trim around the walls was white, the wallpaper a berry red.

"Alice's room before she married," Barker said in my ear.

"It looks like a shrine," Poole replied.

There was no one under the bed or in the closet. We stepped back into the hall.

"Empty," Poole said. "He's done a bunk."

The Guv shook his head. "Nay, you've missed one."

He was right. At the far end of the hall there was an extension. I recalled the small tower at the corner of the building. We followed a tight spiral staircase leading upward. We climbed until we reached a landing. A door there was closed, and I opened it slowly. Applegate was there, sitting at a deal table in an otherwise empty room, as if waiting for us.

"Good afternoon, gentlemen," he said.

His voice echoed in the empty room.

"Good afternoon, Doctor," Barker answered, equally as formal.

"Alas, a doctor no longer," Applegate replied. "I have been struck off, but you already knew that or you wouldn't be here. I've been waiting for you. Oh, not long. I do not mean to insult your intelligence. No, I knew you'd come eventually, just as I knew you would not stop until you found me."

"Fitzhugh hired me, John," the Guv said. "His last words were 'Help me.' I might have refused otherwise, but not under those conditions."

On the table was a bottle of wine and a goblet. Beside it was a walking stick. Now, I know walking sticks very well. This was a novelty cane, the kind that holds something inside. I knew because I was holding one myself. Mine contained seventeen inches of sharpened steel. Some canes even contained a pistol with a trigger in the grip and a long barrel.

"Drat the luck," Applegate muttered. "If only that monster had been satisfied with Scotland Yard, you would not have been involved. I'd set the boy in the alleyway, but for all his effort, Fitzhugh refused the tart. The child tried again when he came out and this time, Fitzhugh took the sample. I watched him, concealed from across the street. He didn't eat the blasted thing. I thought he might toss it in a bin, but at the last minute, he crammed it into his mouth. Then he opened your dratted yellow door and stepped inside. It seemed like ages before Mr. Llewelyn ran out of the building in the direction of Scotland Yard."

"Why kill him now, after all these years?" Barker asked. "I believe I know the answer, but I must ask."

"He was preparing to take another bride and destroy her, just as he destroyed Alice. I've thought of killing him all these years. I pictured a hundred different ways to do it, but poisoning seemed the best option. I could lay hands on just about any kind, or even create something of my own. This was it, I thought, the fullness of time. Fate, if you will. If I could not save my daughter, I could at least spare this poor girl."

"You did not believe he showed remorse over these ten years?" Barker continued. I noticed the revolver was still in his hand, a long-barreled pistol sold in London for the Colt Company.

"I don't care about his remorse," Applegate replied. "He had to die. Alice wasn't ill, you know. At least not until she was locked away for so long it drove her mad. Afterward, I brought a solicitor and a constable to the asylum when he refused to let me see her. He stood at their door ready with proof that he was her husband and alone able to see to her welfare. I hired the best advocates demanding she be released, but again he was ahead of me. My only regret is that I was not there with you in your offices to watch him die like the dog he was."

"Your only regret?" Cyrus Barker said, shaking his head. "Come now, John. Surely you have not sunk so low."

Applegate poured wine into the goblet. I suspected it was poisoned and we had arrived too late.

"You're speaking of the boy, or rather, his family," Applegate said. "The Burkes. I assumed he was an orphan. I'd have left a tart if I knew he had a family. A final meal of sorts. He died with a full belly."

"No, John," Barker argued. "He purged it in racking pain. An ignominious death, and to a child. An innocent lad."

"I am desperate, Cyrus, and past caring, I'm afraid," Applegate replied. "Yes, that even surprises me. I, a surgeon, have truly become a danger to society. I realized this not a half hour before you arrived. I was insulted by the crass moniker in the newspapers, but am I truly mad? I wonder if I am. A second person driven mad by that horrible man."

"I hurt for you, old friend," Barker said. "I had no idea you were in pain. We've known each other for fifteen years."

"Yes, I recall the day you arrived in my surgery, bleeding from a wound. What was it again? A tiger? Only you could be attacked by one in the middle of London."

"It was a panther," Barker replied. "You did fine work stitching it."

"I've always had nimble fingers."

Barker nodded. "And a keen mind. Setting up Mr. Ogilvy to take the blame was brilliant."

I heard the click of my partner's pistol. So did Applegate, I suspect.

"Yes, well, I'll waste no guilt on him. He pampered and cosseted that devil for years. He was his lackey."

Barker could think of nothing more to say. Silence fell over the room.

"Take care of yourself, Thomas," Applegate said, looking at me. "You're a married man now and I won't be here to patch your wounds any longer."

He seized his cane, upsetting his chair. Simultaneously, I pulled the sword concealed in my cane. Barker raised his pistol. Applegate pulled the handle off the cane. There was no sword inside, just a tube of glass. It was a tipple cane, the sort in which one hides a wee dram from the missus on a country hunt. He raised the amber liquid to his lips. Prussic acid, I guessed. He would die as his daughter had, having destroyed her tormentor. There was poetic justice in it.

Terence Poole's pistol barked right by my ear. The bullet pierced Applegate's hand dead center and shattered the glass tube inside it. Then, it clipped his forehead just above the ear. He cocked his pistol again. I realized he'd been resting his wrist on my shoulder to steady his aim.

Applegate stared mutely at his hand, now a bloody mess, as if he couldn't comprehend what had happened. Poole straightened and prepared to pocket the pistol again. That is, until Applegate pulled one of his own, a small single shot, not much of a pistol at all. I doubt it could even pierce the Guv's thick hide.

Barker's Colt echoed in the small chamber. I'd be deaf for the rest of the day. The pistol kicked out of Applegate's hand, which now began dripping blood like his other. The surgeon howled.

"You'll not be getting out of your punishment that easily, John," my partner said in a low voice.

Dr. Applegate fell back until his shoulders hit the wall, then he slid down slowly to the floor staring at his ruined hands, hands that had once been renowned, now a bloody pulp. We pushed the deal table out of the way to get to him. He looked confused, as if he didn't know what had just happened. Or perhaps he'd finally lost his hold on reality.

Barker returned his pistol to the holster inside his coat, and I slipped my blade back into its sheath. Then Applegate gave a snort. He seized his left arm with his right hand, and his mouth formed a rictus of pain.

"No!" Barker yelled, seizing him by the lapels as Applegate sagged down to the floor.

He ripped the doctor's shirt open and I knew well enough what would happen next. The so-called heart massage, which managed to crack some of Fitzhugh's ribs. One of Barker's hands spread across Applegate's singlet, while the other formed a hammer which came down on the anvil of his other hand. It's a wonder that was not cracked, as well. The Mad Pie Man's body bounced on the floor. Barker's palms pressed into the stomach, rolling up to the rib cage.

"Listen!" he demanded.

I put my ear to the man's chest.

"Nothing."

He set to again, and none too gently. Applegate's body flailed about under the rough treatment.

Barker was breathing heavily. "Now?"

I listened again. "Nothing, sir. I'm afraid . . . Wait, I hear something. Yes, a heartbeat! It's weak but I can hear it."

"We'll need to call an ambulance or throw the man into a hansom cab."

There was a telephone set on the floor in the hall, having lost the dignity of the table it once rested upon.

"It works," I called. "Hallelujah!"

I made a telephone call to Charing Cross Hospital and returned to the room. Barker was seated, leaning against the wall, his head back. Applegate lay on the floor beside him. Poole made a third. I eased myself down beside them so that I sat near the Guv.

"Rebecca is right," I said to the inspector. "There must be easier ways of making a living."

CHAPTER 31

We made the doctor as comfortable as possible though he wore darbies. I inspected the tower and found what I was looking for, a closet filled with bottles, vials, dried plants, and other detritus of the poisoner's trade. It was enough to kill an army, and Barker and Poole had a grim interest in it, going through them bottle by bottle as if it were a museum exhibit. We were still examining them when Scotland Yard arrived with a Black Maria, a half dozen constables, and Lieutenant Sparks.

"Who have we got here?" Sparks asked. "He's well dressed for a Pie Man."

"This is Dr. John Applegate," Barker replied. "He is my private physician and an old friend. He's also responsible for the half dozen deaths this last week."

Terence Poole understood, I think. He made no threats to the broken man; he did not crow about the case. He merely looked at everything thoughtfully and then turned to us.

"Everything is in order here," he said. "You two look done in, so push off. I'll be by later. Walk in a park. Take in a museum. Your part is done. Nice work, gentlemen."

I wasn't going to look a gift horse in the mouth. I gave one final look at John Applegate. He was awake, but there was no way to gauge what was going on behind his half-closed eyes. We left Poole in charge and walked out the front door. He was right. We both felt stunned. It was all too much: the murders, the narrow avoidance of death, the wasps, the pipe, the brandy. Barker still had a wheeze in his chest and my face looked like a battleground.

Of course, the Guv didn't take a walk or see a museum. We returned to the office, where I began typing my notes, and he sat with his boots on the edge of the desk, staring blindly at the wall across from our bow window, deep in thought. I took Jenkins outside and let him smoke in Craig's Court and told him all that had occurred. He puffed and looked at the old cobbles lost in thought.

"You know what I'd like?" he asked.

"No, Jeremy," I answered. "What would you like?"

"I'd like to get so jiggered tonight that I can't lie down without holding on. Then I'd like to come in tomorrow like before and not talk to anyone unless it's absolutely necessary."

"That sounds marvelous," I said, nodding. "You go ahead and start early. I've got typing to do and the Guv will stare at the brick until it crumbles from his efforts."

"Thanks, Mr. L. Do you think Mr. B. will be all right? He's been out of sorts lately."

"I'll be honest," I said. "I have no idea. Whatever it is doesn't really concern us. The minute I hear more, I'll let you know."

"Right," he replied. "I'll be off, then."

I returned to the office and typed my report. I called Rebecca and told her the case was finished. Then I strolled down to the

Houses of Parliament but learned that Gladstone was not in residence. I retrieved his address from Kelly's Directory.

"Sir," I said to Barker, speaking for the first time in two hours.
"The report is done. I have Mr. Gladstone's address."

"Good work, Thomas," he said. "Thank you."

We traveled on foot to St James's Square. William Gladstone
lived in a Georgian mansion in Carlton House Terrace. The
house was grand; grand enough to intimidate me a little, but then
he had been leader of Her Majesty's government four times. If
anyone had the right to a manor house, it was he.

Carlton House Terrace is one of those boulevards in St James's
that some of my friends would call toney. One could not own a
house here unless there was some sort of title affixed to the front
of one's name. Each of the private residences in the street could
have been used as an embassy by a country twice England's size.
The street was lined with Australian hardwood blocks to muffle
the sound of passing vehicles. There wasn't a cracked paving
stone underfoot.

The house was a light tan color that looked white at noon and
almost pink at sunset. I live in a fine house myself, though it is not
mine, but I know the difference between a functioning house and
an opulent one. For example, I've looked all over Barker's house
and have yet to find a ballroom, but I would wager Gladstone had
one. Or perhaps an indoor bathhouse with a pool. Small wonder
I rubbed the toe of each pump against the back of my trouser leg,
then wiped the soles on the mat.

I notice butlers whenever I visit a house. They interest me.
It's such an odd and varied occupation, yet so coveted. It has
been my experience that most butlers are infinitely more aware
they are living in the lap of luxury than their masters, and they
are far more proud. This fellow was an interesting specimen.
He smacked of the military, a former marine, perhaps, or a captain who once marched the streets of Agra and fought rebellious

sepoys. Who better to protect a national treasure? I'd bet that the footman were all chosen from the ranks, as well.

We were taken to the former prime minister, who was seated in his library directing two servants in the packing of books. There were more books than my brain would take in, the size of a public library. Later I would learn there were thirty-two thousand volumes.

"Mr. Llewelyn," Gladstone called out. "You will be glad to hear my collection is going to St Deiniol's Library in your native Wales."

"That's quite a collection, sir," I replied, admiring the shelves. "St Deiniol's is very fortunate."

"Mr. Barker," Gladstone acknowledged.

"Sir," the Guv replied in that basso voice of his.

"Sit, gentlemen," Gladstone said. "Shall I have tea prepared?"

"No, sir," Barker answered. "We have a number of duties ahead of us today."

"Very well. How is your enquiry coming along? Are you any closer to a solution?"

We sat, but I noticed the Guv didn't settle back.

"The matter is resolved, sir," Barker replied. "The man is in the custody of Scotland Yard."

Gladstone smiled. His face was no more built for the exercise than my partner's.

"What sort of grievance did he have against poor Fitzhugh?" the Liberal Party leader asked.

"The man was his late wife's father," Barker answered. "Apparently, Mr. Fitzhugh was responsible for taking her fortune and having her put away. Her father was convinced he would try the ruse again with his new bride." Cyrus Barker looked my way. "It was painful for us both, I'm afraid. He was a friend of ours and our personal physician. His name is Dr. John Applegate."

"Applegate?" Gladstone exclaimed. "You mean the Harley Street man? I've passed his surgery a thousand times."

"Alas, he broke down and accidentally killed a patient and was struck off about six months ago. A sad end for a fine career."

"Indeed."

"Mr. Barker and I have discussed whether or not a man can change," I remarked. "Can a leopard truly change his spots?"

Barker nodded. "A leopard may change his spots as many times as he wishes, but he cannot disguise the fact that he is a leopard, and spots or no, leopards make fine rugs for clubs in Pall Mall. Therefore, the effort is wasted."

Gladstone raised a brow. "You have a unique way of expressing your sentiments, Mr. Barker," he said. "Bloodthirsty, but unique. You don't believe, then, that a man can be a scandal in his youth, learn from his mistakes, and turn about? The Church is full of such men. Many go on to become husbands and fathers, men of commerce, and clergy."

"Aye, sir, some do," the Guv agreed. "And some do not. Thomas, who was that fictional gentleman Father Michaels spoke of?"

"Dr. Jekyll, sir."

"The very one. The man walked about, a benefit to all, and none could discern the monster within. Had he run for public office, he might have become the youngest member of your constituency, as Fitzhugh was."

"Would that I could read souls as easily as voting records," Gladstone said. "I will admit to you, Mr. Barker, that I would accept a scoundrel's votes if they will allow me to push forward a bill for mankind's good. In fact, I have done it. To do so, I must hold on to the belief that there is some good in a man somewhere, even if it is only a teaspoon."

"Sir, I bow to your generosity," my partner said.

"We are fragile vessels, sir, or at least I am," the former prime minister said wryly. "You look sturdy enough."

"Your point is taken, Your Lordship, and I cannot disagree with it." Barker turned to regard me. "Mr. Llewelyn, what say you on the matter?"

"Well, sir," I said. "I have no difficulty finding Mr. Hydes. It's the Jekylls who seem few and far between these days."

The former prime minister shook his head. "Doing good is never easy or everyone would do it. We are all wayward and self-ish at times. One of the difficulties of being in charge of a political party is that we cannot scrutinize every member of the Parliament. We go through records, of course; look into backgrounds and question people who knew them, but I'm afraid our best source of information is the press. I say 'afraid,' because they often break the news first if there is a problem and we are caught flat-footed. MPs keep mistresses, swindle the poor, drive businesses into the ground after selling personal shares, the same as other powerful people. I suppose I should be shocked at Fitzhugh's behavior but I am not; merely disappointed. However, he did not deserve to die for his misdeeds."

He lifted a volume, looked at it ruefully, and put it in a packing case.

"I'm going to St Deiniol's as well," he continued. "My daughter lives near there. She'll look after me. I'm officially retiring from politics this year. I am eighty-four and my eyesight is failing. I can no longer read this treasury of knowledge I've collected over decades. Ironic, is it not?"

Barker and I agreed.

"Send me a bill for your services, gentlemen," Gladstone said. "It's the least I can do for the poor fellow, be he good man or scoundrel."

The Guv stood. "We won't take up any more of your time, sir."

"Actually, I thank you for coming," he replied. "It took my mind off this task. I find giving away books to be a painful process akin to bloodletting."

I nodded. "Hear, hear."

We bowed and were soon in the street again.

"Remember to send the bill, although his signature might be worth more than the cheque," the Guv said. "I don't always agree with his stances, but he began as a Conservative and I believe in his heart he remains one."

The residential neighborhood was free of cabs. I looked about.

"Let's find a tearoom," I said. "I need a cup of tea."

"You don't drink tea."

"Let's go, anyway."

Cyrus Barker gave me a stern look of enquiry, but I didn't rise to the bait. We walked a couple of streets and found an ABC tearoom. They serve coffee of a sort, but it is not recognizable as such. The tea was well enough. I had Earl Grey.

When we sat, Barker said nothing. He is generally a patient man.

"We must pay for Mr. Wolfe's services," I stated.

"He told me I have paid him enough already," Barker said. "Wolfe bores easily. He needs constant mental stimulation. Watching him crawl about on all fours examining minutiae is to see him in his element."

Our tea arrived and I took a sip. Normally, I put sugar in Earl Grey but in front of Barker it seemed childish. I doubt he even knows if there is cream or sugar in his own house.

I reached into my pocket and extracted a small package wrapped in brown paper tied with string. I put it on the table and pushed it toward him.

"What's this?" he asked.

"We could try to deduce it, but the quickest way to find out is for you to open it."

He stared at me again, convinced I was going mad. First I drank tea, then I began throwing presents about.

Carefully, he opened the package, as if it were a bomb, untying the string slowly. He had surprisingly nimble fingers considering how thick they are. He opened the wrapper and removed its contents. It was two pieces of wood less than three inches square, hinged together. When you opened them, one side was a compass and the other held a thin timepiece.

"Happy birthday," I said.

"This is not my birthday," he said, looking uncomfortable. He squirmed in his seat. Some people don't like receiving presents.

"No, but it will be," I answered. "Fifty years is a milestone, one I'm sure many people assumed you would not attain."

"This is fine," he said after a moment. "Where did you get it?"

"At a stall in Covent Garden. I understand it belonged to an admiral. The compass is to lead you home and the clock is set to London time, so you won't forget us."

"Why should I forget you?" he asked.

"Because you are leaving London," I replied. "You're going to China, the lot of you."

The Guv strained some tea through his mustache and paused a moment before replying.

"Am I?" he asked.

"You know you are," I answered. "Six months, perhaps a year. Ho tells me your knee still bothers you after your injury last year and so far, Western medicine has done nothing for it. I've always thought of you as a dangerous man, but there are so many younger fighters out there."

"Let us face it, Thomas," he said, "as far as the fistic arts are concerned, I am old."

"You're not old," I assured him. "However, I think I can understand your dilemma. You trade upon your ability as a boxer, but you were nearly beaten by young Mr. Halton just days ago."

"I was not!" he growled.

"I said 'nearly beaten.' I was there. I saw it."

"I was slow off the mark," he admitted. "This body I depend upon has begun to let me down. My speed, my power; they aren't what they once were."

He pushed his half-empty teacup away.

"Did you expect to stay as you've always been forever?" I asked, looking at him.

I was in choppy seas. The man hated talking about himself

and admitting he had a problem was even worse. Cyrus Barker is self-sufficiency itself. The strenuous life is everything. To admit even the smallest failing is to admit failing altogether. However, fifty would eventually become sixty and then seventy. Granted, he'd be a lithe and canny seventy-year-old, but I doubt he could run down a suspect or face a trained opponent half his age. That was fantasy.

"What's in China that you can't find here?" I complained.

"There's a doctor in Canton, a bonesetter. He's practically a miracle worker. He can help me with my knee, which has never healed properly. He's also my former teacher, so he'll know what sort of therapy and exercise I'll require."

"Dr. Wong," I said. "You've mentioned him before."

"Aye," Barker replied. "He's just a year or two younger than I. Perhaps he's encountered some of the challenges I have been facing. Also, I've taught much of what I know in our antagonistics classes. I have neglected my own learning. I cannot allow myself to stagnate."

"Sir, you are coming back, are you not?"

"Mr. Llewelyn, I have not yet admitted I am going." A waiter brought a fresh pot of tea. "If it sets your mind at ease, I cannot go to Canton or China at all, for that matter. The Qing government put a price on my head. I'd be in the country illegally."

"Exactly what is the price on your head for?" I dared ask.

"For breaking into the Forbidden City," he responded. "It was a lie, considering that the Empress Dowager invited me herself. She was being poisoned."

I couldn't help myself. I pointed at him.

"That's the poison case you were involved with before!" I said. "And the 'her' Ho mentioned was Empress Dowager Cixi!"

"Aye, it was," he said. I believe his cheeks actually colored.

"What happened?" I asked, leaning forward.

"It would be indelicate of me to say."

I clapped a hand to my face. I'd been trying for nearly ten years to get the story from him, of how he'd been rewarded with one of the Empress's own prize Pekingese, Harm (Boddhidharma, actually), and found himself fleeing the country immediately afterward. But then I always ran into that brick wall.

"Sir, we've been acquainted for ten years now," I replied. "I am thirty. Surely I am old enough now to hear an indelicate story."

"Nevertheless."

I sighed. Let me say that I consider Cyrus Barker to be a great man. Let me also admit that at least once a month I want to take him by the throat and squeeze the life out of him.

"Lady Ashleigh is going, I assume," I continued. "She won't be in any danger, will she?"

"Her husband was revered in Canton and she still has friends there. Also, there is nothing to connect her to the criminal Shi Shi Ji."

"You were a pirate," I stated.

The Guv gathered his dignity about him like a robe. "You've accused me of that before. I ran a merchant vessel, a tramp steamer. Some of the cargo may have been clandestine, but that is how things are done on the China Sea."

"Then you searched for pirate treasure," I prodded, trying to goad him.

"I searched for sunken goods along the Pearl Delta from ships destroyed by war and typhoons."

We stared at each other, almost at an impasse.

"Very well," I said at last. "But if there is a warrant in Peking for you, I'm sure piracy is listed as a crime therein."

He looked away. "Perhaps. I have not read it."

"How will you live?" I pressed.

"I have not said I am going."

"You haven't admitted it, no, but I suspect you've been planning this for a while," I said.

"Last summer I realized my knee was becoming a problem for me in the performance of my duties."

"Will you—no, wait—would you take Etienne with you?"

"No, but theoretically, I would ask him, so as not to hurt his feelings."

"What about Ho's tearoom?" I asked, running a hand through my hair. I was feeling a little betrayed, I suppose. He was about to swan off without a care about me after ten years, and it rankled.

"If we were to go, his assistant would run it in his place."

I nodded. It was the most civil thing I could do under the circumstances.

"You know, lad, you and I are very much alike."

I coughed then. That last remark was too much. He thumped me on the back and if he knew why I'd choked, he hid it well.

"How so?" I squeaked.

"We both came here as aimless vagabonds, not merely from other counties but different countries. Our ancestors had fought against English kings. Now you and I are Londoners. It's not only where my home is, it's my home itself. I never felt that way about Perth, Foochow, or Canton. I lived by chance and for work. London is a choice."

"You once said, 'She's a right raucous lass when you get to know her.'"

Barker gave a low chuckle. "Did I? Well, she is, don't you think, now that you know her?"

I nodded. "She is at that. When are you leaving?"

"Lad, I haven't said I was going anywhere," he insisted.

"Perhaps not, but Ho has."

The Guv chuckled. "He's putting foolish notions in your head."

"Are they foolish?" I asked. "Or are you put out that he revealed your little plan before you sprung it on me tomorrow morning?"

"We're only going to Philippa's estate in Seaford," Barker said. "A brief visit."

"It's to be tomorrow, then," I said. "As early as that."

"As you say."

"You don't give a man time to prepare."

Barker gave me his most adamantine glare.

"Neither does life, Mr. Llewelyn," he stated.

I could not argue with him.

CHAPTER 32

I don't know much about sailing. From what I've seen it would take far too much effort to sail halfway around the world merely so a man can poke pins in you and pronounce you healed in spite of all Western scientific knowledge. Canny people, those Chinese, full of history and wisdom, but their medical practices are a trifle antiquated, and were when Julius Caesar was sailing around this sceptered isle.

I left for work with the Guv every morning and returned with him every evening. I dined with him. We taught our antagonistics classes together. I was his right-hand man, which I supposed made him my left-hand one. We were a set, a pair. We were Barker &, not Barker or.

Who would I complain to? Who would give me unsolicited advice? Who would quote scripture for the edification of my soul? London would be dull and listless without him. It might even begin to pine.

It began to concern me that I might not be up to the duties of running the agency on my own. Working at another agency or as a detective at Scotland Yard would be easy enough and well within my abilities, but cases at our agency were different. Because of Barker's connection to powerful secret societies, our work often involved political and even royal personages, the sort who would not be impressed by a slight Welshman with half a year at Oxford and a troubling past. Barker impresses just by glowering, whereas I've had to fight tooth and nail for any shred of respect I have earned. I'd have to be as discreet in the West End as I would canny and merciless in the East. Could I carry it off? Did I actually have a choice?

What was he thinking, anyway? There was a price on his head. The Qing government could swoop down in the middle of the night and no one would ever see him again. Chinese justice is swift and it cuts cleanly. Goodness knows if his affairs were in order or if he'd even made a will. Generally speaking, I would have known of any such arrangements.

What if he stayed in the East permanently, I wondered? He was as accustomed to Canton as London. I'm sure he had friends and acquaintances there. He was part of a secret fraternity known as the Heaven and Earth Society. It's possible he could take up where he'd left off. They'd keep him concealed or try to. He's not an easy man to hide, but it was possible. He could send for his dog and disappear as if he'd never been here at all. The partnership would be dissolved. Rebecca and I would move to Camomile Street and the house and offices sold unless I bought Barker out through solicitors. Goodness knows what would happen to Mac and Jenkins. They'd be cut off without a sou. No, I wouldn't allow that. They could both work for me, I thought, though at reduced wages. We wouldn't have such deep pockets anymore.

I was quiet over dinner that evening. I don't know if the Guv noticed, but Rebecca did. She attempted to start a conversation, but Barker was as distant and preoccupied as I.

"Look!" she said suddenly, peering into the kitchen. There

was a red glow from under the kitchen door. My first thought was fire. It was not a poison, but it was the only danger left that I could think of. We all rose and went to see what it was.

The sky was still dark from the rain which had fallen for days, but now a fiery sunset had appeared and was fighting for control of the heavens.

"'Red sky at night, sailor's delight,'" he quoted to Rebecca. "It is an old sailor's adage."

He stepped into the hall and consulted the barometer that hung near the telephone alcove.

"We shall have rain tonight, but fine weather in the morning."

I frowned. I had not taken issue with a barometer before, infernal things.

After dinner Rebecca and I went upstairs, while Barker headed down to the basement. Within a few minutes we heard the steady thrum of the Guv hitting the heavy bag. It sounded like distant thunder. I tried to read *The Woman in White* again but found Collins can grow tiresome sometimes. I crossed to the desk, dipped my pen, and began to write.

"What's that you're doing?" Rebecca asked.

"Notes," I replied. "Everything is going to change. There's so much to consider. Take desks for example. I couldn't take Barker's desk. It is outsized. I'd look like a boy sitting in his father's chair. But I can't run the agency from my little rolltop either. I have no idea what to do."

"I can't imagine Mr. Barker leaving," she said. "In fact, I refuse to believe it. He wouldn't miss receiving his royal warrant, and that should bring a rush of cases. He won't have time to sail off to China to meet Dr. Wang."

"Wong," I said. "Dr. Wong."

"Forgive me," she answered. "I've had my fill of doctors, thank you."

"I'm his partner in name only," I complained. "He hasn't consulted me about leaving. I wouldn't know anything if I hadn't asked Ho about his behavior. My opinion doesn't matter to him any more than a bootblack's."

"You're bitter," she noted.

"Of course I'm bitter. I have a right to be."

I wrote notes until I worked myself into a foul mood, then went to bed. My wife is the most patient of women: little disturbs her. She fell asleep instantly, while I tossed and turned. I smacked my pillow about like an opponent.

It began to rain, just as Barker predicted. I decided that somehow it was his fault. Half an hour later there was a loud boom and thunder rolled across the whole of London. The rain set to in earnest then, as if it had been toying with us all week. Perhaps the weather would be so beastly he couldn't leave.

Sometime in the middle of the night there was a knocking on our front door. What the devil, I thought? Who'd be knocking at this hour in the middle of a downpour? I put on my dressing gown and went downstairs. I passed the standing clock and saw it was a quarter to midnight. Then I flung open the door.

A man stood in the rain, holding an umbrella over his head. He was a tall Chinaman, as tall as the Guv. His gray robe hung to his shoes, which were more like embroidered carpet slippers. I knew if he turned his head there would be a long, plaited queue down his back, like a length of rope.

There was a slapping of shoes in puddles then and Ho appeared beside our visitor, holding a second umbrella.

"Let us in, boy," he demanded.

I glanced at the stranger again. There was an incredible stillness about him, as if he could stand on our porch in the rain forever. However, Ho would not.

"Welcome," I said. "Come in out of the rain. Let me take your umbrellas."

They entered. Ho's friend looked about our hallway, taking in the furnishings: the tall hallstand where I stashed the umbrellas, the Swedish standing clock, the front room, which was used seldom. There was no way to deduce his opinion of our furniture.

"Shifu!" Barker called behind me, and suddenly I was brushed aside. He bowed before the man, who put one fist in the other palm and waved it in greeting.

"Shī Shī Jì," the man replied, with obvious pleasure.

It came to me then. Wong Fei Hung, Barker's master, had come from China.

"Wong Fei Hung?" I whispered to Ho, who stood at my side, watching the exchange.

"The mountain has come to Mohammed," he said in a low voice. "Apparently Dr. Wong left Canton as soon as I sent the first telegram weeks ago, but then, I was not to know."

Cyrus Barker suddenly took me by the shoulder and pulled me in front of our guest. I would not call it an introduction. More an inspection, I think. I was the Guv's number one student, which he has told me is important in the Oriental half of the world. Our visitor examined me for a minute, which seems more like a quarter hour when you are the one being inspected. It was highly discomfiting. I was still in my dressing gown, but then I supposed, so was he.

"Nee hao," I said, bowing. It was the only Cantonese phrase I knew. He smiled, either a kindness or due to my complete mispronunciation of a simple greeting, and repeated the phrase.

I suddenly realized I liked the fellow. I thought him cold and imperious at first glance, but he made me feel as if he had come all this way with no other purpose than to see me.

My partner spoke to him again in Cantonese and led him into the front room. The doctor sunk into the sofa cushions as if he feared he would be swallowed up by them. I suspected that, like his student, he was a stoic and unaccustomed to such luxuries. Meanwhile, Ho and I watched them from the hallway, just out of sight.

"Does this mean no one is going to China?" I asked.

"Let us hope not," he replied. "I have a tearoom to run. I can't be sailing off to China because your master is feeling old."

"You're older than Mr. Barker, sir," I said. "Did you ever have a time of crisis like this?"

He considered the question. "I did."

"How did you deal with it, if I may ask?"

"I took a wife," he answered.

I looked at him, a trifle dumbfounded. You think you know a man, then after ten years you discover he is married.

"You have a wife?" I stammered. "I had no idea!"

"I didn't say I kept her," he said, looking at me like I was simpleminded. "I didn't even say she was mine to begin with."

"I have to say I'm relieved that the Guv is not going," I admitted.

"If your boss man had gone, he would have been captured by the Qing authorities."

I happened to glance up in time to see Rebecca on the stair. To be precise, she was leaning over it, looking at us. I excused myself and went down the hall to speak to her.

"It's Dr. Wong," I stated. "He's in the front room."

"Mr. Barker's teacher?" she enquired. "Then they aren't leaving?"

"No, I don't believe so."

"What's he like?"

I searched for the word. Several came to mind, but none seemed to encompass all of my impressions but one. "Imposing."

Rebecca was in a dilemma. She very much wanted to see this imposing Chinaman, but there were strict rules in society, and she understood them even better than I. She sighed with regret and went upstairs.

The Guv turned to Dr. Wong and spoke to him politely. I realized then that Wong did not speak a word of English. In response, he replied in Cantonese and pointed at Barker's knee. The Guv rolled up his trousers and Wong examined him. He clucked his tongue at the state of it, swollen and misshapen. Ho stood and squeezed my shoulder. *Do not disturb them,* the gesture said. I saw him to the door and handed him his umbrella.

"Is there a bounty on your head in China, as well?" I asked.

"Let us say my memory is not revered there," he replied.

Ho stepped into the rain and was immediately gone. I closed the door and locked it, then turned around. I would have dearly loved to sit and watch Barker and Dr. Wong converse, even if I didn't understand a word they said. However, Ho was right. This was not the time.

"What happened?" my wife asked when I went upstairs.

I explained again or tried to. It was a muddle of manners involving two cultures different in practically every way. Like sensible people who don't have Chinamen arriving at their door in the middle of the night, we went to bed.

I woke at dawn, but Rebecca was already dressed, looking out over the garden. I pulled on my dressing gown and joined her, yawning and scratching my head. Down below, Dr. Wong and Barker were already practicing.

"It's a bit early, isn't it?" I asked. "What o'clock is it?"

"Nearly six, but they've been at it for at least an hour."

The doctor was in a spotless white tunic with a mandarin collar and black trousers gathered at the ankles. Cyrus Barker was in Western trousers and a singlet, bathed in sweat. I watched, fascinated. Wong had his umbrella and was using it to correct the Guv's position. A tap to the ankle here, a hook of the elbow there. The teacher had become the student and was having a difficult time of it. I knew what he would face soon: pins inserted all over his body, a near starvation diet accompanied by herbal teas that tasted like mud. He'd stand in the same position for hours until his knees quivered. He'd lift stone weights and metal rings and beat the heavy bag for hours. Ah, the infinite joys of physical culture.

"Let the punishment fit the crime," I remarked.

My toilet was completed within a quarter hour. Rebecca would wait until everyone was properly dressed before making an appearance. On the stair, I heard a sound. A dish had fallen to the floor. I knew what that meant before I stepped into the kitchen. Etienne was holding a meat cleaver in his hand, while across from him Ho waved a carving knife. They circled each other, their feud a long-standing one. I had the impression the winner would feed our new visitor.

They both stopped and glared at me as I came into the kitchen.

"Is there coffee?" I asked.

"Over there," Etienne Dummolard said, pointing. "It isn't made yet. You can make it yourself or wait until I've diced this Chinaman."

"Do we have cream?"

"No," he growled. "You must drink it black."

"Blast," I said, stepping between them. "Carry on, then."

They began circling each other again, waving their weapons. Neither was actually hurt during these matches. It was a ritual of sorts. They had a referee with them; Harm had returned.

Suddenly, Barker burst into the kitchen, passing between the two as if they weren't there. At the far end he lifted a pump handle over the sink and began pumping water over his head. His misery earned no sympathy from me. He had asked for this. Let him enjoy it awhile. When the coffee was ready, I poured two cups and carried them upstairs, thinking I lived with madmen.

"Have Etienne and Ho killed each other yet?" my wife asked, her mouth full of pins as she arranged her hair.

"You have good ears," I replied. "So far, it is a draw. Have you any plans for today?"

"Plans?" she said. "I thought you were working."

"I'm declaring a holiday," I stated. "Being a partner, I can do that. I've got something to do this morning, but I wondered if you'd like to try riding Juno later. We could go to Battersea Park. That is, unless you're busy."

"I suppose I could cancel a few appointments this afternoon," she replied. "But I'd need a sidesaddle."

"I purchased one," I answered. "It's waiting in her stall."

"You're thoughtful," she said, smiling. "No matter what my mother says."

An hour later I was boarding the express train to Newhaven and points south. I had decided to collect Mac. Barker was too preoccupied to consider the matter, so I took the decision into my own hands.

Once at the Pevensey, I approached Mac's doctor and spoke to him. Jacob Maccabee was convalescing, but he was also in high dudgeon. Pillsbury thought as I did that returning Mac to his familiar surroundings might be more therapeutic than lying around in lounge chairs staring at waves.

We needed him in Lion Street, and he needed us. I'd seen him lying there in abject misery convinced his life was over. He needed rescuing. I knew what needed to be done.

Mac hadn't shaved since Barker had last been there. He watched me enter with little interest or enthusiasm and he appeared to have lost more weight. I sat in front of him and crossed my legs.

"Hello, Mac," I said.

"Thomas."

"How are you feeling?"

"Wonderful," he said, his voice laden with sarcasm.

"Excellent," I replied. "I've come to give you a final transfusion and take you home."

His lips curled. "What? That's preposterous. They won't let me leave."

"They're not Scotland Yard, you know," I argued. "Look, we brought you here to heal, but I don't think you're thriving in this environment. I'm sure you've got Miss Fletcher very concerned. This place isn't helping you, so we need to try something else."

"What does Mr. Barker say?" he asked, frowning.

"He's busy," I answered. "You need to come home. We'll hire a nurse if necessary to help you recover. You need to work. I think that's what's missing, and we need you, too. Not to serve us or to clean, but just to be there. You are the soul of the house, and it feels strange not to have you there."

He just stared at a spot on the floor. I thought I'd try a different tack.

"Tell me, in the past month have you noticed a change in the Guv?" I asked.

He shrugged his shoulders. "He's been exercising, trying to lose some weight. He's eating less."

"Jacob, he'd been planning to leave for China for weeks, even months. He took the *Osprey* out into the Channel with the entire crew to practice. He was leaving, Mac. For at least a year, possibly forever."

He glared at me. "You're making this up."

"I'm not," I said. "Listen."

I told him the entire story, from Rebecca's first suspicions to the Guv's secrecy and odd behavior, the journey to Le Havre, Ho's revelation to me, Barker's confession of a sort, and the eleventh-hour arrival of Dr. Wong.

"He would have simply left us?" Mac asked.

"Yes," I answered. "He said it would be for half a year and then he'd return, but I can't help but wonder if he told his acquaintances in Canton that he was taking a brief holiday in England and would return soon as well."

Mac nodded, taking it in.

"And this is China we're talking about," I continued. "Anything can happen there. Ho claims the Guv has a price placed on his head by the Qing government."

"Where is this Dr. Wong staying?" Mac asked. "In the house?"

"I don't know, but he was ordering Barker about at five o'clock this morning, so I suppose he slept on a sofa or something."

"Is this man some kind of miracle worker that the Guv would go all the way to China to see him?" Mac asked. "Perhaps he just needs some of Dr. Applegate's energy pills."

I looked at him and blinked, a wave of apprehension coming over me. "Hasn't anyone been telling you anything?" I demanded. "Lady Ashleigh? Miss Fletcher?"

"Lady Ashleigh has visited twice, but just to see to my comfort and bring me flowers. Why do people bring patients flowers? I've never understood that. Sarah, I mean Miss Fletcher, has been here in Sussex with me. I'm not certain she's spoken to anyone from London since I've been here. Why? What's been going on?"

"Never mind that. Did Dr. Applegate give you energy pills?"

"Yes," he replied. "I was feeling a little run-down, so he brought me a bottle of pills a couple of weeks ago."

I stood and walked to the window looking at the cliffs and the puffy clouds scudding across the Channel skies. We assumed Applegate had poisoned the tea.

"Mac, Dr. Applegate was the one who poisoned you," I told him. "You, and our client Fitzhugh, and an entire family, a Scottish servant, and very nearly Barker and I. The man had gone mad. He lost his career after a botched surgery. Barker and I caught him and gave him over to Scotland Yard."

Mac wiped his lips with his hand. His eyes looked glazed, and I wondered how much medication he'd had and if he understood what I was telling him. I didn't want him to fall asleep and wake up later having forgotten my arrival and everything I had revealed. I reached forward and seized him by the wrists.

"Mac, this may be difficult for you to hear," I said. "Applegate came into the house. He was in there for hours while we were at the hospital with you."

"And?" he demanded.

"He poisoned all the food in the pantry. He killed Mr. Barker's fish. He set up traps to try to kill us."

"Traps?"

"Yes, and he went through our private things," I said. "He even took your keys and used them to get into our offices in order to poison Barker's brandy. It's a blessing the Guv gave a key to Miss Fletcher or he might have invaded her rooms, as well."

"My keys?" he asked in a strangled voice.

"Yes, and of course we couldn't know how many traps were set or where, so we had to have in a man to hunt for us."

"A man?" he said.

"Yes," I answered. "Stop repeating everything. We had a man in to find the traps before we could move back into the house."

Jacob clapped his hands over his ears.

"By the way," I added. "I had a piece of toast in the library while you were gone, and I'm afraid it fell jelly-side down on the carpet. Can you get red stains out of a tan rug?"

He cringed.

"What?" I asked, all innocence. "I picked it up. I even gave it a wipe 'round."

An orderly entered the room.

"My clothes!" Mac shouted. "I demand to be discharged!"

I choked back a laugh as Mac leapt from his bath chair. My work there was done.

ACKNOWLEDGMENTS

I f this Covid year has taught us anything it is how to be flexible and to adapt and learn new skills. Most of these involved the uses of the internet but often it resolved into communication between one person and another, or a group of others. We just couldn't communicate face-to-face. So, while I have been isolating, I have relied even more upon the friends, family, and associates that figuratively surround me.

I'd like to thank my agent, Maria Carvainis, who has been a steady advisor and friend throughout my writing career. I'd also like to thank my editor, Keith Kahla, and his assistant, Alice Pfeifer, for keeping me informed about shutdowns and changes, often from their own homes.

I've spent most of my adult life associated in one way or another with the Tulsa City-County Library and was impressed this year at the way it continued to offer customer service during an unprecedented time. In particular I'd like to thank its CEO

Kim Johnson, Ben Drake-Willcox, Jason Little, Jason Patteson, Lisette Rice, Mark Carlson, and Ann Gaebe, for their continued support and friendship.

Closer to home, I'd like to thank my daughter and I.T. person, Heather, who helped navigate me through Zoom meetings, symposiums, book talks, and interviews. I literally could not have done it without you.

Last, I relied upon my wife, Julia, as each of us wrote a new novel while facing down a deadly pandemic during a long and dangerous winter. You are and always have been a pillar of strength. I can't thank you enough, but I'll do my best to show you how much I appreciate you.